Pillars of Salt

PILLARS OF SALT

FADIA FAQIR

A NOVEL

INTERLINK BOOKS
An imprint of Interlink Publishing Group, Inc.
NEW YORK

First American edition published in 1997 by

INTERLINK BOOKS
An imprint of Interlink Publishing Group, Inc.
99 Seventh Avenue
Brooklyn, New York 11215

Library of Congress Cataloging-in-Publication Data

Faqir, Fadia. 1956–
    Pillars of salt : a novel / Fadia Faqir.—1st American ed.
      p.   cm.
    ISBN 1-56656-220-1.—ISBN 1-56656-253-8 (pbk.)
    1. Psychiatric hospital patients—Jordan—Fiction. 2. Women
patients—Jordan—Fiction.   I. Title.
PR9570.J653F356   1997
823—dc20   96-46044
                                                          CIP

Printed and bound in the United States of America
10 9 8 7 6 5 4 3 2 1

Acknowledgments

Being part of the first Ph.D. in Creative Writing in Britain, this novel needed (and received) the contribution of many. I am greatly indebted to Malcolm Bradbury for his invaluable support and advice; to Jon Cook who was there whenever I needed him and whose criticism and support helped me through every stage; and to Julian Hilton for his continuous and thorough assessment of the manuscript. Special thanks to the late Angela Carter, whose criticism and support will be greatly missed. My thanks also go to fellow graduate students at the School of English and American Studies, University of East Anglia, especially Anne Enright, Mark Ellis, Belinda Hamer, Louise Doughty, Kathy Page, Gerri Brightwell, Janet Hutcheon, and others, and to Rolf Hughes whose encouraging letters made it all seem worthwhile. Special thanks to Soul Hyman, whose friendship and assistance have kept me going, and to my friends Nawal and Roger Fenwick, Samira Kawar and Yakoub Dawany, and Karim al-Rawi whose encouragement made me persevere. I am also grateful to the Royal Jordanian and the Overseas Research Scheme whose financing of the Ph.D. program made this novel possible.

For Haytham, my son
And my tribe, the Ajarimah

Historical Chronology

1187   Saladin al-Ayyuby crossed the Transjordanian highlands to inflict a decisive defeat on the Franks at the battle of Hattin, near Lake Tiberias.

1878–1909   Immigration of Circassians to Transjordan from the Caucasus region where they had been persecuted by the Russians.

1916   Sharif Hussein proclaimed the Great Arab Revolt against the Ottomans in Mecca.

1917   The British Foreign Secretary, Arthur James Balfour, committed Britain to support the Zionist aspiration to a Jewish "national home" in Palestine.

1919   The Treaty of Versailles assigned Arab lands as mandates to Allied powers.

1920   When King Faisal was forced out of Syria, many of his political entourage — Syrian, Iraqi, and Lebanese — fled Damascus to seek refuge in Transjordan.

1920   The British mandatory authority undertook the administration of Transjordan as part of the Palestinian mandate.

1921   Emirate of Transjordan was created by Britain.

1923   The Emirate of Transjordan was recognized as a national state being prepared for independence.

1923   Sultan Ibn Adwan began his revolt against Emir Abdullah and the British. He pressed the emir to redress urgent fiscal grievances, mainly the collection of tax arrears dating back to 1918. Later that year Sultan advanced on Amman; government troops under the command of Peake defeated Adwan's forces after a fierce battle.

1925–7   Emir Abdullah gave refuge to Druzes fleeing the French in Syria after a local uprising.

1926   Villagers of Wadi Musa rebelled against the government and refused to pay tax arrears. Their rebellion was suppressed by government forces.

1928   Transjordan signed a treaty with Britain which gave her more independence.

1946   A new Anglo-Transjordanian treaty granted Jordan formal independence.

1952   Hussein succeeded his father, King Talal.

1953   Hussein was crowned King of Jordan.

1956   The British commander of the Arab Legion, Lieutenant-General Sir John Bagot Glubb, was dismissed. The complete independence of the Hashemite Kingdom of Jordan was achieved.

The Storyteller

I n the name of Allah the Beneficent, the Merciful: "Confound not truth with falsehood, nor knowingly conceal the truth."

Oh most illustrious masters, pray for our prophet Muhammad whose soul is like the moon, and his righteous companions. Tonight, the first night of Ramadan, the month of fasting and worship, I will recount to you an horrific story. During the month of Ramadan, Allah the Mighty King revealed the Qur'an, mankind's guidebook through the forest of right and wrong. But I, Sami al-Adjnabi, the best storyteller in Arabia and the oldest traveler in the Levant, will reveal to you the tale of Maha, unfold the multi-layered secrets of both past and present, and leave you shaking with terror and thirsty for more. Invoke Allah for mercy and forgiveness and plead for his pardon.

On second thoughts, it is my she-ass Aziza who should tell you this story. What do you think, Aziza? Will you speak to these people so that one of the jinn soldiers, one of the goblins with strange powers, whom it is said our master Solomon the Great did command, will

1

decode your braying and show us how you are misinterpreted by mortal ears: ears attuned only to jabbering? Ladies and gentlemen, as you can see, my companion Aziza is shaking her head, swishing her tail, and stamping her feet. How wise of you Aziza. You do not want to relate the accursed story. Let us then, most generous masters, try to persuade my everlasting love, my monkey Maymoon, to tell you the tale of the damned woman who turns whatever she treads on to basalt. Black rock! Allah, His angels, His trumpets, and His insatiable hell turn whatever Maha touches into waste. Maymoon is shaking his straw skirt and his golden earrings.

Slap the tambourine across your thigh.

> Maymoon, sweet Maymoon,
> Take us to the moon,
> Shake your body,
> We shall perish soon.

Men say Allah turned my friend the man, Maymoon, into a monkey when he wiped his ass with a piece of bread. And if he does it again? Will he be turned back into a deformed mortal like us? Ha Ha Ha. He. He. He. May Allah wipe away all our sins and grant us His forgiveness.

Maha was her name. A deer that had been roaming the deserts of Arabia since Eve, made out of our father Adam's crooked rib, was cast out of heaven. Maha. A charming woman who challenged and surrendered. Some say that Maha was as pious and pure as Rabia al-Adawiyya, the mother of Sufis and Allah's chosen songstress.

> The acquiescence, the light,
> And the young houri.
> It is time for the stranger's soul,
> To reach his dwelling.

I say that Maha was a shrew who used to chew the shredded flesh of mortals from sun birth to sun death. She was a sharp sword stuck in the sides of the Arabs' enemies: the Tartars, the Crusaders, and the Romans.

Maha's soul was a lamp kindled from the glowing oil of an olive tree, that was neither of the east nor of the west. Light upon fire, or so it goes. Her restless soul has been haunting the desert for years gone by and will for years to come. Those who are in the know will tell that Maha was born when the first female child was buried alive by the tribe of Bani-Quraish. When the tribe was told that they had a daughter instead of a son, their faces turned black. At the very minute when the tears of Adam cleansed the body of the baby girl he was burying alive under the ground, the two wings of Maha's soul fidgeted, fluttered, and glided over the gloomy horizon of Arabia. It is that first girl child, killed in sin, that set the blood-feud between men and women. Her cry echoes in female hearts calling for revenge. That's why no man can trust his wife, no Lord can trust his mistress.

Two years before the child Maha was conceived, her mother Maliha bewitched her father as he passed through the arid land. The mother, who had some gypsy blood in her veins, seduced Sheikh Nimer of the Bani-Qasim. He first saw Maliha dancing around the fire in one of the gypsy shanty towns.

One day, I took my she-ass Aziza and my monkey Maymoon and set off for the dwellings of the tribe of Bani-Qasim. They chose the land of the People of Lot to settle in. Ill-starred tribe in an accursed valley which once in our glorious history an Ishmaeli king, inspired by spirits, called Jordan. Beyond a steep ridge of broken basalt — Aziza kept sliding instead of walking — stretched a valley of confused sand, which tried to be red, but remained yellow and hopeless. While trotting down to the village, I noticed that the plateaux were swarming with young English soldiers. They first arrived in the valley in the Year of the Lord 1921. My friend the English traveler, who turned over every pebble on their plains and mountains, measured the land and then took notes, called it the "Mandate." Their cars and tanks exhaled black smoke into the clear blue sky. I waved to the peeling red faces of the Mandate and continued walking. Mandate, or no Mandate, I did not care. I was half-Arab with an endless hunger for stories. My destination was the village of Maha, she whose eyelashes were as sharp as arrows.

There it was, the village of Hamia. Green and dull brown patches spread at the end of the horizon. The citrus plantations formed a belt of vegetation around its waist. The houses were made of mud and straw, their doorways were patted into shape by hand, some square and others circular. Cattle dung was as common as fleece in the narrow lanes of the village. Naked children played in the stable-like lanes, indifferent to the stink and dirt. Young men tried to show how active and courageous they were, especially if they found a spectator. They went to extremes to entertain foreigners before they even asked them their names. My Aziza brayed loudly and stamped her feet, objecting to the glorious but naïve exhibitions of power. The Arabs of Hamia, who had no dignity themselves, were born in that salty land, caught between the Dead Sea and the Jordan River. They lived there, counting winged cockroaches, then died there and were thus consigned to oblivion. And who am I? Sami al-Adjnabi. Who am I?

I am the storyteller.
My box is full of tales.
Yes, the yarn-spinner.
I spin and spin for days.

Most honorable masters, I saw her. Yes, I saw Maha. Kneeling on the soil of her farm, she was like a perfect moon, she was tall and firm, she was like the first woman, she was . . . Her eyes flashing, like those of the first girl-child Adam buried before Eve gave birth to Cain and Abel.

People pointed at her. They could not decide whether that shadow well-hidden behind the orange groves was Maha or Maliha her mother, so alike was she to her mother. Whispering leaves. Listen, listen, Maha was telling her story to the stones of the Jordan Valley. I was not sure whether she was ploughing or weeding, whether she was dark or fair; nevertheless, I was sure that she was as beautiful as the fresh dawn in Wadi Rum. When the misty light creeps into Rum, all the apparitions of my mind, my she-ass's mind, and even Maymoon's limited mind, sway in front of us on the sand dunes. The lovely sea of sand, light, shadows, and mirages. Mirages, light, and shadows. Listen, listen, I can still hear her words carried by the breeze . . .

Um Saad

I, Maha, daughter of Maliha, daughter of Sabha, tossed my head on the white pillow, examined the empty hospital room, then sighed. Allah created people and created parting. They brought me, Maha, the Indian fig — "strong," the people of Hamia used to say, "but bitter like colocynth" — to this hazy hospital besieged by lulling voices and fog because I would not even hear of the word "parting." Allah created separation. Allah was counting the days; was replacing them with years. I am sure in Allah's everlasting records I do not exist, my name is not even scribbled in the well-kept book of fortune. Maha became an open land where every shepherd could graze his sheep, where every nurse could stick her needles. They poison your running blood, push you into sand dunes and say, "We belong to Allah and to Him we shall return." The breeze in my favorite spot under the blossoming orange groves touched every part of my body. The scent enveloped the valley and carried me to another world. The cloud of perfume put out the fire in both my head and my heart. I became like

5

my friend Nasra and so my sheep would lead me to the meadows. Nasra's dangling earrings always clicked.

> My mother, I saw the moon at night.
> In the sky, its position was high.
> Forgive me, Allah, I have sinned.
> The fluid of passion has transformed me.

The noise of a woman shouting abuse had woken me up. My head cleared instantly when I saw the thin gray figure and her white bundle of clothes. "My name is Um Saad," she shouted at Salam the nurse and Kukash the porter. She pushed him and said in a voice so smooth that it could have lifted you up to heaven, "Curse your parents, bringing me to the madhouse. I'll kill you." She kicked Kukash and rolled herself on the tiled floor like a hedgehog. She screamed and screamed. Suddenly, her small eyes met mine. "What? A filthy bedouin woman. Cannot you smell the stink of dung. You sleep with your sheep."

I did not open my mouth, didn't utter a single word. I knew Um Saad's heart was being scalded with the flaring fire of parting. No matter what she said about bedouins, I would not get cross with her. Instead of shouting back at her, I covered my bare gums with my hands and smiled.

"I am an urban woman from Amman. I refuse to share the room with a grinning bedouin," she said. Her pink scarf slipped off her head revealing straight gray hair. She began stamping on the scarf and cursing the nurse's father, grandfather, and great-great-grandfather. Swearing, Kukash sucked the cigarette butt, scratched his disheveled hair, and rubbed his sleepy eyes. His patience was running out. He flung Um Saad's old body on to the bed and tied her legs and hands to the iron bedposts. Salam smiled angelically and stuck her needle into one of Um Saad's veins. She winced, shuddered, then sank into deep, dark sleep.

Salam covered Um Saad with a white sheet and Kukash spat on the floor and then left the room. Salam looked at me and said, "Maha, you have stopped having nightmares. You must be improving." I nodded my head in agreement. Whatever Salam says is true. The angelic future rolled out of the room like a white cloud. The clink of keys. Silence.

The sparrows outside the barred windows stopped twittering and the air grew warmer. It was noontime.

I thought the reapers must be busy cutting wheat with their scythes. My orchard, the jewel hanging on the forehead of the Jordan Valley, is under the mercy of Daffash. He must have sold it by now to Samir Pasha or to his masters the English.

The English had killed Harb, the twin of my soul. His gentle hand stroked my braidless head. "Don't cry, twin of my soul. Don't cry. By your grandmother Sabha's life you will be happy with me." Must lock out the memories. Hakim, the wise man, might have a special herb to heal the anguish welling up inside me. He buries the dead and has nothing to do with the living. A wanderer.

Are you heading towards the depths of the desert, oh gazelle?
Where are you going? Your departure brings sorrow.

"Where are you going?" A wanderer, following my heart. Look where my heart has brought me. To the end of the journey. The end that was never in my sight. To Fuhais Mental Hospital.

Hours later, when the sun was returning back to her world, Um Saad fidgeted in her bed then started moaning. I could hear faint sounds coming through the frothing lips, as if her heart inside her ribs was weeping.

I used to see the oranges dangling from boughs under the light breath of dawn and now I see them sitting silently on a plate under an electric bulb. I peeled an orange and squeezed the slices into Um Saad's dry mouth. After the needle, you feel thirsty, dry, your insides start cracking up. My heart too ached. My heart cried for Mubarak, my son.

She finally opened her eyes, looked at my face, and started sobbing again. With a voice as smooth and rich as thick velvet, she said, "Forgive me, sister."

I rubbed my forehead and said, "Forgive you for what? You've done nothing." She tossed her head from one side to the other and continued crying. I dipped a piece of bandage in the glass of cold water and wiped her face, her hands, her legs. Nasra used to wipe away my pain. Where is she, my friend and companion?

7

Through suppressed sobs, Um Saad asked, "Can you see the flames?"
"Yes."

Her face was past its springtime, with wrinkles around the mouth and eyes. Her small gray eyes must once have been big and black. Her nose was thin and pointed, above a generous wide mouth. Her skin, although limp, was smooth and clean. I squeezed her hand, tied to the bed-frame.

"What is your name, sister?" she asked.

"Maha."

"Maha?"

"Yes, Um Saad."

If I had had spans and spans of bandage I could not have dried the tears of Um Saad that night, her first night in the madhouse. I kept rubbing and drying until the glow of dawn crept into the pale room and she went to sleep. My bed was damp and cold. I covered myself from head to toe with the sheets to draw some warmth to my freezing limbs. I craved Harb's hand, his soft chest and his warm breath.

Maha

It was always Harb, the twin of my soul. What a lovely high forehead. Dignity. He used to say, "What I most love are those sparkling brown eyes." His were hazel. The hazy light of dawn fingered the round ceilings of the mud houses. Imam Rajab's powerful voice was calling for morning prayers. "Allah-u-Akbar." My father, Sheikh Nimer, was still asleep, was still dreaming of my mother Maliha.

"Maha, my Eyesight," my mother used to say, "drink some milk."

When I pulled the teats of Halabeh, our cow, the milk flowed over my hands. Harb was standing right behind me. The scent of musk got mingled with the smell of rich milk. Without raising my head, or stopping milking the cow, I said, "What are you doing here? If Daffash, my brother, sees you, he will kill us both."

"Good morning, my beautiful mare."

His eyes were teasing me, were challenging me. I smiled.

I had once emptied Daffash's pistol and rifle and hidden the bullets under my mattress. Daffash had just challenged Zaid, Sheikh Talib's son, to fight. I remember how he studied the barrel of the black pistol, and how I threw myself on the carpet I was trying to weave and cracked up with laughter. My brother ran towards me like a wounded mule.

"Why are you laughing?" He barked and pointed the pistol at my forehead.

I could not help it, I shrieked with laughter. "The pistol is empty."

Daffash looked at the pistol, looked at me, then roared with laughter. When I told Harb the story, he raised his eyebrow and smiled.

The sun crawled up the sky. Shivering leaves and flickering light. Harb stopped smiling and said, "I wish I could give you a hundred camels, a box of jewelry, and ten meters of pure Indian silk." He lowered his head, wrapped my shoulders in a bright purple shawl, placed his hand on the sheath of his dagger. "Maha, I want to see you tonight."

"Are you mad? For a girl to be out at night is a crime of honor. They will shoot me between the eyes."

"I will protect you, deer-eyes."

"No."

"I want to marry you." I pulled the shawl tightly around my breasts and shook my head. The women who loved my brother Daffash, who sneaked out stealthily in the middle of the night to meet him, were fools. Stupid idiots who risked honor for love. Did Harb think that Maha, too, the daughter of Maliha, was a fool?

Alone, dangling my feet in the canal, I was thinking of seeing Harb that evening. What if I did go? What if I did give in? I remembered Nasra my friend. Dark green eyes and a face framed with auburn hair. Big brown beads around her neck. Her shabby black dress in contrast with her bright green trousers. Her big mouth always hidden behind the reed-pipe telling her sheep the story of her sadness.

While I was thinking about her, Nasra came running at full speed as if she had been stung by a black viper. She threw herself on the ground near the canal and started slapping her face and swaying.

"Maha, oh, Maha. Maha, hey, Maha," she gasped.

"Sister, what disaster has struck you?" I held her shoulders firmly.

"Don't touch me." Nasra howled like a wounded she-wolf and wrenched away her body. She shook and swayed as if pain were gripping her stomach.

"What is the matter?" Her body was shaking, tears were running down her face, her dress was ripped open as far as her navel. My hands started trembling when I realized that it was too late. It was too late. All I could do was clench my fists and punch the air.

Nasra sipped some water. "Hurt me, him," she said in her shrill voice, then started weeping silently.

I wanted to cover my ears with my hands. "Please don't cry, sister."

"Uh! Allah," she gasped.

Our sisters think that when you place your hands on top of your head and press hard, you stop miseries flowing in. Well, eat dung. It didn't work that afternoon. "You unfortunate one. Who did it? Who did it?"

She looked down.

"Nasra, who did it? Please tell me."

She continued weeping silently.

"Who did it? Tell me, Nasra. Who did it?"

"Your brother, Daffash," Nasra whispered as she wiped her tears with her trembling fingers.

The bird of bad omen flew in the air and landed on my chest. Tears ran down my cheeks. Hit your chest, hit your chest and burst it open, let go. The pressure was building up inside me. "Nasra, sister, I cannot breathe," I whispered and rocked my body. My friend had lost her virginity, her honor, her life. She was nothing now. No longer a virgin, absolutely nothing. A piece of flesh. A cheap whore. Nasra mumbled away to herself and sobbed. Daggers in my heart.

"Daffash, son of Maliha, I will drink your blood." I tucked the end of my dress into my trousers and marched to our house holding Nasra's wrist firmly. The cool air captured between houses patted my face and begged me to slow down. No. Never. I would kill that mule and save the women of Hamia.

Nasra sat on the floor hugging her knees and sobbing. I pulled the English rifle off the wall, unhooked the safety-catch, and pointed it at my brother who pretended to be asleep. Sheikh Nimer, my father — Allah protect his right arm — taught me how to shoot years ago. We used to go hunting together, while Daffash stayed at home, either pretending to be asleep or hiding behind my mother. Unloading the cartridge, my father would say, "The daughter of the tiger of the desert must be a tigress."

I dug the metal barrel between his ribs and shouted, "Wake up, you dog, and see with your own eyes how I am going to kill you."

He opened his eyes slowly and saw Nasra. When he realized that I was serious, he shielded his head with his hands. "Don't shoot. I am your brother, the son of your mother and father."

"You ruined her life." I placed my cold finger on the trigger.

"By Allah, listen to me before you kill me."

"I will not listen to a shameless rapist."

"She asked for it. Whenever she set her greedy eyes on me . . . she tempted me."

"Tempted you?!"

"She was always playing tunes on her pipe. It called me to touch her."

"Called you? You . . ."

"The pipe is responsible."

"You are responsible."

"No, by Allah."

"Did she say yes? Did she?"

Nasra shook her head and said, "I went to the cave to find Nawmeh my goat."

"Did he force you?"

"Under my breast, his dagger, I swear."

Pointing his finger at Nasra he said, "You stopped struggling and lay back. You enjoyed it."

"Shut up. She's lost her virginity. You know what that means." I pointed the rifle at him ready to shoot. That heap of dung, that barrel of air deserved death. I was about to press the trigger when the room went upside down. Two hands grabbed my ankles and I fell down. Nasra!! Nasra? Nasra saved Daffash? Oh, why?

Daffash flung away the blanket, jumped to his feet, and picked up the rifle swiftly. "I will kill both of you, crazy whores," he barked.

I knew he was serious so I shut my eyes and hugged Nasra who started weeping again. "Don't cry. Your tears are gems. Hold your forehead high. Let him shoot us. Better than living without honor."

My father pushed the wooden door open and yelled at Daffash, "What do you think you're doing? Put that rifle down." With his long stick he hit the barrel.

"I wanted to put some sense into those crazy women's heads." He tapped on his belly and burst out laughing.

My father looked at Nasra: her tear-stained face, her torn dress. He looked at Daffash, then gave his right hand to Nasra. "Get up, my daughter. May Allah damn the devil."

He said to Daffash, "If you ever come near this woman again."

Daffash said, "I am sorry, father."

My father rubbed Nasra's back and said, "And you should not have tempted him."

I realized how high were the mud walls imprisoning us. I sat on the floor, pressed my temples with my palms, and started crying.

It was a long night. The hot and humid wind, carrying the salt of the Dead Sea, surrounded the mud walls of our house, laying siege to the village. I was able to see the rounded face of the moon through the small window. The moon kept asking me questions. Would I venture out at that odd hour to meet Harb? Would Harb look down on me if I did meet him? Was he like the other men in our tribe? What if Daffash found out? He would certainly kill me as he would a tiny rabbit. Nashmi, our dog, barked frenziedly. Nasra had lost her virginity. Harb was waiting at the edge of the farm. The moonlight transformed him into a tall, whitish ghost. The beat of my heart seemed so loud that it could be heard by all the men of Hamia. It penetrated the thick mud walls and sneaked through doughy ears. Don't listen to them. An ear made out of mud, another made out of paste. The cry of Raai, the watchman of the village, filled the narrow alleyways as he made his rounds. Turn your head slowly on the pillow, shut your eyes firmly and forget Harb. I stretched my trembling hands, held my thighs, and sighed deeply. Some words in my head. Repetition. Echo. I was a virgin — white as a dove — as pure as dew drops — a virgin — honey in its jars.

At last, sunbeams sneaked through the small, rounded window finding slight aches in the pit of the stomach. I pulled the black dress over my head, rubbed my eyes, and leaned against the mud wall. Tears were rushing down my face. The water of a new spring which had been imprisoned by the rocks for hundreds of years. I must have lost the love of Harb. Why should he love a coward rabbit? My mother was responsible. She had told me not to give in to men. Men, she had

13

said, believe that women are angels who descend from the seventh sky. I was a bedouin woman, free like a swallow and as courageous as my grandmother Sabha. I should have listened to the call of my heart.

My skin seemed to have shrunk, exposing sharp bones, my legs looked thinner in the pale light of the dawn and my hands grew shorter. I wanted to roll myself up and forget about what lay behind the wooden door. What I yearned for was Harb's arms. With his gentle fingers he could push open the petals of my flower. I wiped the tears with the end of my sleeve and folded the quilt and the mattress, then placed them on top of other mattresses piled on the long wooden trunk. I threw the red and black carpet over the pile of mattresses, quilts, and pillows, making sure that everything was well covered. Our house used to be bustling with guests when my mother was alive. Pillows and mattresses scattered around on the floor. My mother's dresses were rotting now in the trunk. Moths were eating feverishly. I, too, would grow old, decay, perish.

I filled a tin can with grain and another can with water. The hens clucked peacefully in their wire cages. I wished I was a tiny chicken eating grain with my bill. The grain when sprinkled flew out, off course, and landed on the head of sleeping chickens. "My luck is like flour scattered on a plain." Our cow, Halabeh, was chewing grass patiently. I threw a bundle of barley for Halabeh and Mujahid, the horse. He stretched his beautiful mane and neighed. I rubbed his muzzle. The camels were tied to the trunk of the palm tree at the corner of our courtyard. They chewed at the barley, chewed like an everlasting desert pestle. I grabbed Halabeh's tender teats and pulled and pulled. Milk flowed on my hand and dripped into the tin can. The soothing taste of warm milk stayed on my tongue.

Weaving was an urge to transform the dirty fleece. I found some yarn spun from twisted roves and a rust-brown spinning-wheel in my mother's big trunk. Nasra brought me a sack full of wool tufts. She had cut them off the sheep of Sheikh Talib, who had only one woman in his house and that woman was too weak-sighted to spin. I held the roves in my left hand and fed the small hook, then turned the wheel with my right hand. My mother had said that the key to good spinning was steady balance between the right and the left hands. Neither coarse and heavy threads, nor thin and weak ones.

14

Fine threads in my lap, threads across the horizon, a net which landed on top of the Jordan Valley, the Dead Sea, and the mineral springs. The threads spread far out, reached Mukawir, where the English hang their prisoners, where Hakim and his black goat lived, and asked him, "Is there a remedy for burdened hearts?" Hakim hugged his goat and said, "No."

Spinning helped me forget all about last night, the broken promises and the cowardly rabbit inside me. My father shuffled out of the house and, with the help of his stick, managed to keep a straight back.

The tunes of Nasra's reed-pipe had changed. They lacked the edge they used to have. Poor woman, she thought that by changing the tune she would protect herself from Daffash. Poor soul, she believed him.

"You should be in the field," my father said.

"My hands were itching for the spinning-wheel, so I thought why not make a thread or two."

"Your radishes and henna will be thirsty."

I put the wheel on the ground next to the master interrupter of my weaving. The carpet would never be finished.

To get down to the orange groves, I had to cross the old canal and walk on mud. It was always the same, the same serenity which filtered into my soul as I set to work. I touched every tree, cleared the bed of weeds, and pushed the sluice open, letting the canal water in. The soil that morning responded to my pick and fork as if it knew how sad I was. I dug the ground, and dug to find the roots of my pain and uproot it with my hands. The air was so bitter and salty that morning. Harb would despise me and already I despised myself.

My father's voice flew through the trees. "Maha, Maha my daughter. Come here."

It must be urgent. The old man never interrupted me while I was working in the field. Interruptions were saved for spinning. I plunged my hands into the cold water and tried to wash away the mud. The sediment under my fingernails resisted the rubbing.

We walked back to the house. My father sat on the half-finished carpet. My mother hadn't been able to finish weaving it. A cream and brown rug, ten handspans long. It should be at least fifteen. "Your grandmother Sabha spun the first thread. Please complete what your grandmother and I have started."

"Yes, father," I said.

He rocked his body, poked the soil with his stick, and said, "Sit down, daughter." He patted me on the back and continued, "Harb was here." Hot blood rushed to my face. I lowered my eyes. For Allah's sake, what did he tell my father? I pressed my hands on my tense belly, sighed and waited.

"He asked for your hand. Tonight Sheikh Talib and the dignitaries of the tribe will come to propose."

I could not grasp what my father was saying. Sounds hung in the air for a while then took the shape of a voice. Voices circled each other and formed words. Harb wanted to marry me?! But I hadn't ventured out of the house last night. My mother, Allah bless her soul, told me that men were birds of prey; they chased the quarry as long as it was alive and struggling, but when they had killed it and filled their stomachs, they look around for another. I shuddered and said, "May Allah protect all women from misery, birds of prey, and shame."

My father asked, "Will you accept Harb?"

Just like any other man in our tribe, he proposed to me because I said no. Like Daffash and Raai, he loved hunting. A bedouin and a son of a bedouin. My mother was right. The muscles of my belly tensed up when I admitted to myself how much I loved him. Despite my mother's wisdom, I fell in love with an eagle. Yes, I loved him like the love of henna for water. As long as camels chew the barley and groves yield oranges, I would love him. My eyes were full of tears when I nodded my head.

16

Um Saad

"Maha, where are you?" called Um Saad.

The pale light of dusk filled the hospital room. I shut my nostrils with my fingers to block out the smell of drugs, urine, sweat. The dark sky was raining orange blossoms. I smiled and said, "Sleeping on this bed, Um Saad."

"Maha, forgive me."

"I told you that there is nothing to forgive."

"My sister, when they drove me out of Amman towards Salt, I remembered the picnics we used to have when I was really young. I said to myself, 'Haniyyeh, you will see a happy day with your own eyes. They are taking you to the springs of Salt.' And then, sister, I saw the vine trellis of Fuhais and the winding narrow road coiled around the mountain like a snake. A rush of blood gushed down my legs. Cold panic, it was. They brought me to Fuhais where Christians live and where mad people go. Haniyyeh, I said to myself, they will put you in a prison built on a profane land. They put me in a straightjacket

17

and pushed me through the thick, high door. I looked behind me and saw the haze of the hot Jordanian sun turning everything yellow. The grapes at the end will wither into sultanas. If I cross the threshold of the big buildings, I said to myself, I will never be able to get out again. I am not a character from the *One Thousand and One Nights*. I will never be able to call al-Shater Hasan and wear his Vanishing Cap, I will never be able to roll into another identity, another body, travel to better times and greener places. This big man hit me on the back and I stumbled into his room."

"Kukash."

"What? Disheveled hair?"

"Yes, Kukash."

"The name suits him. His hair is like a sweeping broom."

We laughed. A strange broken sound of a *rebab*. We looked at each other, then stopped. Um Saad, still tied to the bedposts, turned her head to the left to examine the room.

"Don't strain yourself. This hospital room is empty except for the two beds and the side table."

"May Allah forgive me, when I saw you sleeping in that bed in your black robe and headband I could not help it. To stay with a city woman in the same room is one thing but to share a room with a filthy bedouin is another. But Maha, you are not filthy at all. Your hands when you were rubbing my body with cold water smelt of gardens, and meadows of ripe fruit. You transported me to my small garden at the top of Castle Mountain. By your life, you were not just rubbing my limbs with your fingers, but my heart too. I was four years old, wearing my bright orange dress and green boots and running breathlessly to the swings. I pressed the piaster my father gave me that morning until my knuckles were white. I was afraid to lose the piaster and lose with it a turn on the swings and a stick of candy-floss. They used to set up the swings near the small river splitting Amman in two. I never managed to go to sleep the night before the great feast. I would sit on the cushions waiting for the twenty-one shots declaring the beginning of the festivities. Tomorrow would be full of delights; full of candy-floss and swings. Tomorrow promised new clothes and some freedom. My mother, Allah bless her soul, made

18

me a dress out of the material leftovers that were kept in the wardrobe. There was turquoise chiffon studded with little white plaster hearts. I was sure I saw the hearts beating, sometimes. Tum-ti-tum-titi-tum. The swing would fly high up, up in the sky and all the children on the swings near the river would chirrup together:

'Today is my feast, Ya-la-la.
I wear new clothes, Ya-la-la.
A dress with frills, Ya-la-la.
With embroidered front, Ya-la-la.'

"My mother would never forget to give me a rubber band. I fixed the band around my skirt to stop it being blown off. I would stand on the swing. Land, sky. Land, sky. The Immigrants' Quarter where we used to live, followed by blue limitless sky. The houses were decorated with bright colored ribbons and paper flowers. Under the trees by the riverside, the candy-floss peddler had finished arranging pink hazy clouds on his barrow and started calling, 'Girls-curls, candy-floss, delicious and tasty.' The Box of Wonders played a bouncy happy tune. Land, sky. Land, sky. I tightened my grip on the ropes of the swing and flew, soared high, higher than the other kids, higher than the houses of the Quarter. Ya-la-la. When the man stopped the ropes from swaying, I was dizzy, my forehead was damp with sweat and my hands were shaking. Then, I swear, I saw the little hearts on my dress throbbing.

"With the remaining half-piaster, I would buy a huge, pink candy-floss and start biting it. The girls-curls would melt away in my mouth leaving nothing behind. I would suck some more to catch that tingling sweet taste. Maha, sister, my life is like candy-floss; fluffy and full from the outside, empty like this damned hospital room from the inside. And they called the candy-floss 'girls-curls.' It was like my life. A girl's life. A fluffy lie for half a piaster. Ya-la-la."

Maha

My father shuffled his feet across the damp ground and came towards me. "Welcome, my father." His half-shaven head reminded me of an old, gray mole. His white headdress was wrapped around his neck, and his striped shirt had stained hems. "Please, father, let me wash it for you." He would not let me because only Maliha knew how to wash his shirts. He must not go round like that with kohl running down his cheeks. He must have been crying over my mother again. He rubbed his flaky fingers together and asked, "Still working, Maha?"

Since I had become a woman, he did not want me to work in the field because it was exhausting and shameful. A woman's place was in a well-closed room. Yet he did not want me to stop working in the field either, because I was the only one who took care of the young groves. I could read all that in his question.

"Have you seen Daffash today? He must put the barley into store." What lay behind my father's misery was just one person, one word, Daffash. He wanted a good son. A peasant capable of digging his hands into the

20

soil and transforming that piece of land into a green orchard. Allah gave him a womanizer and a city-worshipper. He wanted to modernize the farm. He would hit with one hand and apply medication with the other.

"No, I haven't seen him. Maybe he went to the city."

He sat down, straightened his position, leaning on his stick.

I plunged the tin cup into the cold water. "Drink, father, with happiness and good health."

He started rocking his body while gazing at the setting sun. "My son is lured by the city lights. He navigates by false stars. Look at Sheikh Talib's sons. How they have kept their plough in the soil from sunrise to sunset!"

Daffash used to go to the city every Thursday morning and come back on Sunday evening. I knew the routine very well. Monday morning was the hardest of times. He dug out quarrels from under his fingernails. Where was his dagger, his breakfast, dog. Where were his sandals? He yanked my hair. Filthy rat, ugliest woman on earth. Do what I tell you. All that would check the flow of insults and slaps was my father's long wooden stick. Then Daffash would apologize and give me a packet of foreign chocolates.

"By my mother's soul, I will compensate you, father," I said.

He ran his flaky fingers over my plaits and said, "May you never see a bad day, Maha."

My father wove my long strands of hair into two plaits. The stroking eased my pain. He said that I reminded him of my mother, Maliha, Allah bless her soul. The same big brown eyes and quivering chin. My mother used to ask Allah to protect her from the evil eye and to give her a tolerable life. She died soon after the crops were gathered. The people of Hamia didn't know the cause of her illness. Half her body was paralyzed and her left eye stopped blinking. The sore eye gazed at the stalks of barley. They carried my mother out in the middle of the night and laid her down in the yard of Abu Aubayydah's shrine. They placed the coffin in front of the saint's grave, which was well shrouded with thick green carpets and red velvet cushions. You place your elbows on the cushions and ask Abu Aubayydah to recommend you to the prophet Muhammad. The night I lost my mother, the damp air covered us all like a sheet of wet black velvet. In the distance from the glowing minarets of Jerusalem came the frenzied cries, "Allah-u-

Akbar, Allah is great, Allah-u-Akbar." My mother gave up her soul, lying there on the flat concrete covered with rounded chicken dung. She expired wide-eyed because she could not blink. Oh, her sore eye. "Maha my Eyesight, drink some milk please."

Daffash, with the help of the young men of the tribe of Qasim, erected three tents for my betrothal. The dust cloud these men managed to raise blinded me. I could not see who was tying the ropes or who was pushing the poles. Hamda my neighbor rushed into the women's quarters flushed and gasping. "My sister, I wanted to come earlier. I was held up, forgive me. Flayyeh came back from the field and asked for a morsel to eat."

"Take your time. The men are roasting the coffee beans."

"May Allah grant you happiness for the good deeds of your mother Maliha, Amen," she gasped and tightened the black scarf around her head covering her wide forehead. "People of Hamia say that he is in love with you."

I shrugged my shoulders and looked through the slot between the curtains to see how many men had come, on behalf of Harb, to ask for my hand. Sheikh Talib looked solemn and dignified in his mud-brown cloak. The men wore cloaks with golden hems and anointed their gleaming beards with musk taken from the glands of a wild gazelle. The sheikh's sons sat in a crescent around him. Imam Rajab, the caretaker of the shrine; Jarbwa, the best shepherd of the tribe; Raai, the watchman; and Hajjeh Hulala, the midwife, completed the crescent, to make it a half circle. My father sat next to Sheikh Talib and glowed like a pearl among fake beads. "Allah bless our guests. Welcome to this dwelling," he repeated.

When Harb entered the tent with Daffash, my heart started to dance to the music Jarbwa was playing with the pestle and mortar. Dring-drang-dring-drang. His thick moustache and trimmed beard gleamed in the faint light of the gasoline lamp. The outline of the only palm tree extended into the pale horizon and stretched to the hazy sky. The sun was setting slowly and carefully. I placed my hand on my beating heart and tried to breathe evenly. Must not let the women of the tribe see how excited I was.

I sat down next to Hamda and took a deep breath. In the final glow before the sun went down, I was able to make out the orange groves, the radish and henna, the horses tied to the palm tree, the lonely house with round windows. Why had I agreed to marry Harb who was no different from any other man in the tribe; who proposed to me because I had said no? My father and mother used to sit under the palm tree chatting. She would lean on him and he would laugh. When Harb proposed it was like a big spade had struck me on the head, and I said yes. Yes, I would sleep next to Harb every night of my life, yes, I would wash his cloak, cotton shirts, and drawers. I would prepare a meal for him and see his sparkling golden tooth every day for the rest of my life. The vision of the hazy orange groves extended in front of my eyes. I nodded my head, thus tying my destiny to Harb's. My eyes made out a running gazelle and my ears heard the echo of Nasra's tunes and the jingle of her sheep's bells as they headed back home. I loved the smell of burning sandalwood enveloped by the scent of musk. Harb was in love with me.

The clink of the brass coffee pot and the small cups drew me back to the tent again. Sheikh Talib refused to accept the cup of coffee offered to him. He cleared his throat and said, "I will not drink your coffee, Sheikh Nimer, until you give me what I ask for. You have not answered us."

"Ay, by Allah, you would be delighted."

"We want your daughter Maha for our son Harb."

"By Allah, drink your coffee, Sheikh," my father answered in a shaky voice.

To marry me off must have been hard on him. I was his companion, his housekeeper, and the worker in his field. A warm tear ran down my cheek when Sheikh Talib sipped the coffee and said, "Your coffee is drinkable and your daughter is worthy of being engaged."

All the men raised their cups and said, "Congratulations. With prosperity and sons."

I hurriedly wiped my tears when I saw Harb's face. The first thread of light after a long night, a crop of lemons after three years of waiting — no, the radiant face of a new-born baby.

"Jarbwa, bring your *rebab*. Play some good music for us."

The hoarse sound of the sad *rebab* reminded me of my mother, Allah bless her soul. Oh, how I wished she were alive to attend the wedding and take the weight off my shoulders. Hamda must have noticed the sad cloud which overshadowed my face, so she started ululating. The long drawn and trilling sound told the men that the women were happy too. The ululating invited the rest of the people of Hamia to the gathering. Young children kept nudging and asking their mothers where the bride was. They were not convinced that the woman with the stained dress and dirty face was the glittering bride.

Nasra, Halimeh, Hamda, and their daughters formed a circle around me and started beating the drum and singing.

> "We are the woman of Qasim. Haya, haya.
> Tall like palm trees. Haya, haya.
> Perfumed like sweet basil. Haya, haya."

My ears were attuned to the sad *rebab*. Jarbwa was recounting the story of Umayma. The listening air carried his words to the ears of women. He listed the outstanding traits of Umayma. She was virtuous and pure, yielding and beautiful, generous and brave. When I looked at the rough faces of the women in the ill-lit tent, I realized that the Umayma the men were praising only existed in their own heads.

> "She charmed me, veiled her face from sight,
> For pure and holy is Umayma's name.
> Slender and full in turn, of perfect height,
> A very fairy she, if beauty might
> Transform a child of earth into a fairy sprite."

My palms started itching for the spinning-wheel, but Harb's mother, Aunt Tamam, was watching me. She had been watching me all evening, sitting quietly with the long pipe that she would not be parted from. I felt her tiny sparkling eyes follow me as I left the tent. I pulled some wool tufts, the wheel, and a few threads out of my mother's trunk and walked stealthily across the courtyard. I bumped into Harb, who was looking for coffee beans to prepare another brew. He grabbed my wrist and whispered in the darkness, "I miss those brown eyes. Our wedding will be next Friday. Prepare yourself, my bride!" I shook my head, snatched my hand out of his, and walked back to the tent to sit with the women of the tribe who were still praising themselves, while the men were dreaming of Umayma.

I was not allowed to spin one thread that night. Hajjeh Hulala and Aunt Tamam insisted that spinning on the night of your engagement was a bad omen. I was not allowed to spin one thread that night.

The Storyteller

I n the name of Allah the Beneficent, the Merciful, sayeth the Lord, "Verily did We create man of potter's clay, of dark mud altered. And the jinn did We create aforetime of essential fire."

Oh, most illustrious masters, say a prayer for our prophet Muhammad and his righteous companions. Tonight is the third night of Ramadan, the month of charity and blessings. Throw away your sins, repent and return to Allah who created us all from dirt, then from a drop of seed, then from a clot, then from a little lump of flesh, shapely and shapeless. Maymoon, my sweet monkey, where was I? Do you remember? My mind is becoming like an Ottoman inspection center. More and more people can easily get in than can get out. The treacherous years are vanishing in front of my eyes and all I can do is tell stories. I build magical kingdoms and give life to the dead. Glory to Him who will revive the bones after they have rotted away. Alas, His kingdoms remain and mine dissolve in the sea of forgetfulness.

Uooooof, Uooooof, Yaaaabbba.
My master, the imam of the mosque,
ordered me to repent and forget her.
I said, by Allah, repent I will not.
For I will always love her.

My masters, forgive me, the Queen of Sadness reigns over my mortal body. The cursed land of Qasim leaves you with nothing but bitterness: arid, pale, and sickly. The other light in the sea of darkness is Maha's shadow.

Maha's mother, Maliha, taught her how to hold the axe, cook the best *mansaf*, and how to spin the wheel. The soul of a fiery jinnee escaping from the depth of the sea must have possessed her. When she was ten years old she managed single-handedly to plough her father's field, to cook and feed twenty tribesmen, and to spin some threads for her mother.

Maliha was not a mortal, like us. Her beauty exceeded the beauty of our master the prophet Joseph and her wisdom was as famous as the wisdom of our master Lord Luqman. The lights of her house attracted visitors — travelers — who like moths marched blindly to their death. She managed with the help of her daughter to feed every living creature in the house, field, and sky, even migrating birds and honey bees. We are talking here of twenty camels, an orchard of oranges, hens, cows, horses, guests, and a hive of bees. The birds of happiness hovered over their heads. With my own eyes, which will be eaten by the ants one of these days, I saw peace and harmony rule over that land. A garden fell from heaven and landed there. I held my she-ass, placed my face on her neck, and started crying over my youth wasted in cold distant lands which never saw the warmth of the bedouin sun.

My she-ass Aziza has blue eyes. Have a look at her big eyes while staring at the sky, Allah's throne. Azure blue like the color of our mother earth when seen from the second heaven. Muhammad, while riding the winged horse al-Buraq, saw the earth; saw a blue ball floating in the darkness and fell prostrate. Praise Him who created the night and the day, the sun, the moon, and the earth, each floating in an orbit. Blue are Aziza's eyes.

Damn the devil! When she saw me wiping the hot tears of jealousy, she gazed with her big blue eyes at Sheikh Nimer's house and — boom — the evil eye hit them. Big blue eyes, a piercing chin, and a destroyed house. A destroyed house, big blue eyes, and pierced chin. All that was good now became evil. I seek refuge in the Lord from the evil of the envier when he envies.

My brothers, soon after Maliha died, Sheikh Nimer collapsed and Maha turned into a she-demon. People say that Maliha was taught witchcraft by Harut and Marut, the accursed angels and masters of black magic. She used to spin and recite spells all night long. Harut and Marut were falsely related to King Solomon who was a true believer. They teach mankind the magic which was revealed to them at Babel. If they but knew, surely evil is the price for which they sell their souls. Yes. Even Raai, the watchman of the village and one of its best men, swore to me that he overheard Maliha and Maha whispering to each other, "The blood of men . . . flesh of prey . . . eagle's kidneys . . . quiver in his blood." The good man hugged his rifle and started invoking Allah. He went weak in the knees when he heard them. They must have been talking about him. He knew they didn't like him because he kept an eye on them and prevented them from gathering poisonous weeds. Raai lost his fertility then and there. Fear, my masters, strikes the spines of men and makes them sterile with not a single living seed left inside them. Although watchmen are courageous, they don't tread firmly on the ground: this is in order not to step on some kind of crawling horror. Continuous observation in the dark makes their eyes grow bigger and bigger until they become as wide as owl's eyes. They die prematurely because they cannot see properly in the daylight. After death they seek eternal darkness. The Arabs did not lie when they said, "He who watches Allah's worshippers, dies prematurely of distress." Praise be to Allah, Owner of the Day of Judgment.

A sharp cry tore off the silence besieging the village and woke every soul and spirit up. Aziza stamped her feet and Maymoon squeaked. Maha, they say, bayed out, "My mother, where are you going? Why are you leaving me here?" The deep bark had an otherwordliness about it that made hair stand up and knees turn to moss. I hugged my monkey and started reading verses of the Qur'an over his head to calm him down and stop him from shivering. Maha's cry was as ear-piercing as the disobedient angel Iblis's shriek when he was cast down to earth. May Allah grant us His pardon. What I saw next was a procession moving slowly towards Abu Aubayydah's shrine. Every man, woman, child, and breastfed baby participated in the funeral. Azrael, the fierce angel of death, roved over the cursed land of Qasim with his bloodshot eyes and pitch-black cloak. Nasra the shepherdess cried at the top of her voice, "Goodbye to your necks. Here, Azrael."

When they laid Maliha's open coffin on the courtyard of the shrine, I managed to see her face. Her wide-open eyes stared at me accusingly. She must have been touched by a demon, judging from the twisted muscles of her face. Playing with the soldier jinn of our master Solomon is bound to be dangerous. Shammar, the evil jinnee, stuck his fingers in her eyes and she passed away immediately. A ghostly figure wrapped in a black cloak stood near the coffin like a scarecrow. Allah, save my neck from Azrael's stained hands. "Maha, her daughter," an old hag muttered and vanished in the darkness. Two big horrifying eyes bulging out of a small, rounded skull. I muttered, "I seek refuge in the Lord of Daybreak from the evil of the darkness when it is intense."

The men of the tribe looked shaggy and startled. They crowded around the coffin and bowed down to pray. I remembered then that I was a foreigner to their land and that I studied the Qur'an when I was young, but never prayed to Allah. I tried to imitate the Muslims when they bent their backs and bowed down. The people of Qasim had a funny way of praying and I struggled hard to suppress my laughter. They first straighten their backs and place their open hands behind their ears then suddenly fold them around their bellies. They whisper for a while then bend their knees, bow down, and fall prostrate. At the end of this exhausting ritual — repeated several times — they turn their heads first towards the right shoulder, then to the left, saying, "Peace and the blessings of Allah be upon you." They actually believe — I later on discovered — that the Angel of Good Deeds is sitting on their right shoulder and the Angel of Bad Deeds is sitting on their left shoulder busily recording sins and virtues. At the end of the funeral they repeated together, "O Allah! change my fear in my grave into love! Make me know that of which I have become ignorant! Amen!"

The village sighed with relief when Maliha died, but her offspring roamed the alleyways promising more evil and destruction. Maha, my honorable masters, with the help of Nasra the shepherdess planned to kill her poor brother Daffash in order to inherit the farm. Daffash is a thin, bright man, full of ideas and keen to modernize his backward village. He used to go to the city, talk to the learned English, and design together with their engineers plans to develop the valley. He used to carry the compasses of travelers, feed the horses of engineers and relate to them what people say about them and translate what is written on the stones from colloquial into standard Arabic. The travelers and engineers spoke standard Arabic and were able to read the Qur'an perfectly well, but nobody spoke the language of the holy book in Arabia. So, Daffash used to listen to them spelling the words (he could neither read nor write), composed out of these sounds a set of phrases, then deliver them in his broad bedouin accent. For example, "Down with the Balfour Declaration" when subjected to the complicated process of Qasimi translation, became "Somebody up there must fall down." The sounds are very similar. Ha Ha Ha. He He. Damn the devil. Daffash was rewarded generously by these foreign travelers. And now we will reward our ears with a song. Beat, beat, beat the drum.

> I am the storyteller.
> My box is full of declarations.
> I am the yarn-spinner.
> I spin and spin Balfourations.

Ladies and gentlemen, Balfour, my friend the Englishman told me, was an English lord who lived in a faraway land called Britain. The English lord after hunting foxes with his pack of hounds for days on end was still bored. He felt like playing a game called "Lands." According to the Englishman, Lord Balfour gave the piece of land extending west of the Jordan River to a tribe without dwellings of their own. A land without people for a people without a land, he thought. He gave the land we are sitting on to a Saudi tribe, then shook off the dust of his boredom. Flocks of English army officers and their families invaded the valley. Rose, the daughter of the head of the English tribe, attended the Qasimi wedding. But before the wedding, I must tell you about the two vultures, the two birds of prey.

Daffash was asleep when Maha and Nasra burst into the room, pulled the rifle off the wall, loaded it, and pointed it at him. The previous night they had sat beside the canal and planned to kill him. They agreed to shoot him, then bury his corpse in the courtyard. The best time to carry out the plan was late afternoon when the sun was about to sink behind the mountains and the night was approaching. His father usually went to the mosque to prepare himself for the sunset prayer. The house would be empty and the man defenseless. But Allah is always wide awake and will always protect His weak worshippers. When I saw Maha in the mosque she looked evil, haunted, and capable of slaying a man and taking part in his funeral procession the next day. Both of them spat on Daffash's face and said, "We will throw your corpse to the hungry eagles." Allah may blacken these women's faces. They have less brain and less faith in Allah. At the very moment they burst into the house Sheikh Nimer came back unexpectedly because he had forgotten to put on his sandals. He knocked the rifle from Maha's hand and started reprimanding her. Raai heard them arguing loudly. Nasra pushed the door open and bolted towards the misty mountains as far away as possible from the bewitched house. Maha howled like a hungry ghoul deprived of her prey at the very last minute. Although I am a stranger in their land, I managed to learn their shameful news. Praise God for we shall all die soon.

Maha

The five camels Harb gave to my father as part of the dowry hobbled in the shimmer of dawn. My father's thin figure and the huge camels looked unreal that morning. The sky descended with its hazy glow over our heads. I washed my face and handed a cup of milk to my father. His flaky fingers were getting more ragged and darker. I pitied the old man because he was getting weaker while I was getting stronger. I used to be afraid of him. But after my mother died his eyes lost their fierceness.

"Good morning, father. Drink, with happiness and good health."

"I will miss these hands when you leave."

"Harb is a horseman and all the plains and deserts are his home."

"What do you mean?"

"When he is out, I will come and visit you."

"Your place is by your husband."

"You are my beloved father."

"My daughter, Daffash went to the city to bring his friends."

"May Allah help us. How can I be the bride and serve those guests at the same time?" My mother died open-eyed on the floor of Abu Aubayydah's shrine. The only thing she wanted me to do was to finish the short carpet. That carpet will remain unfinished, mother.

Jarbwa and Raai came to slaughter the sheep. "Greetings to the men," I said, while masking my face with the end of my veil.

"Where are the sheep?" asked Jarbwa, sharpening his two daggers.

I led them to the back yard and pointed at the five sheep which were patiently waiting to be slain. They forced the sheep to lie on their backs, tied their hind legs together, and cried, "In the name of Allah." I wiped my forehead with the back of my sleeve. The sheep struggled and kicked continuously. Their throats were slit and their bodies writhed as they delivered their souls to their maker. Raai's white robe was stained with blood and his daggers were dripping. When the sheep stopped jerking their heads they tied them to hooks attached to the back of the house, then began flaying them with their daggers. The sun was setting. A cool breeze fingered my hidden face. The goat would not feel the pain if flayed after being slaughtered.

"Hey, women, the slaughtered animals are yours," cried the watchman and the shepherd.

With the help of Nasra and Hamda, I managed to drag the corpses to the front yard and cut them into pieces. We put the meat in big pots and lit the kindling beneath them. Hamda's daughters went to the plains to collect more kindling for the two big containers of rice. Hamda kept an eye on the rice, so I decided to bake the bread. Halimeh sang while stirring the boiling mutton. Her voice was sad:

> "Hey, you, leaning on your sword,
> Your sword has wounded me.
> Among the creatures and the people,
> Your love has disgraced me."

I poured half a sack of flour into a basin, added some water, and started kneading until my fingers felt as if they were worn to bare bones. When Tamam saw me, she smacked her lips and said, "A bride and baking. This is the end of time." I smiled, then lit a fire under the baking tin and stirred it up. I threw a handful of dough from one hand to the other until it became as thin as the gypsy peddler's scarves. I wished the gypsy would pass by in the afternoon so I could buy some spirit of jasmine and a transparent brocade scarf for my face. I thought I saw in the roaring fire under the baking tin the hands of my mother flinging the dough. Sweat mingled with tears. Her gentle touch on my plaits used to wipe out the pain of Daffash's slaps. "What do you expect? He is a boy. Allah placed him a step higher. We must accept Allah's verdict," she used to say.

Through the bluish smoke I made out a Land Rover approaching our field. It stopped in the bed planted with radishes and henna. Struck with anger, I ran towards the vehicle waving my fists. Daffash, two painted women, and an immaculately dressed man were in it. "Move your Land Rover," I cried at the top of my voice. "Oh! my radishes and henna." The driver smiled and started the engine. I could not see the damage it had caused because of the cloud of dust it raised. Damn Daffash and his city friends!

He pointed his finger at me and said, "My sister, the shrew bride."

The women burst into laughter and said in their urban dialect, "Impossible!"

The strangers' faces showed surprise and contempt. The soot, blood, and tears must have looked revolting to them.

They were women and I was a woman too, but they were so different. One of them was wearing a tight dress with a wide, shamefully short skirt. Pulling my dress to the front, I lowered my eyes. Every part of the woman's body was revealed by the light material. The slender cigarette-holder the woman was sucking was similar to Tamam's long pipe, but Tamam's pipe was made of rough olive wood and hers was slim and made of a sparkling black stone with a golden rim. I didn't know why they had their plaits cut off and why they tied ribbons with some feathers around their almost bald heards. One was dark and the other was blonde, a foreigner to our land. Crimson lips, fair hair, and thread-thin eyebrows. I felt like heating some water and washing the colors off their faces. Maybe I could give them long black Qasimi robes and headdresses. The shame of it! By the gray hairs of my father, these women were not shy of showing their bodies to the gazing men.

Daffash twisted his thin moustache with his thumb and forefinger, stretched out his arms, spreading out his wide cloak, and said, "Welcome, pasha. Welcome, our guests. You are members of the family and our land will be green under your feet."

I hurried back to prepare the house for the guests. I carried the mattresses and placed them next to each other on the thick rugs. When they entered the house they stood in front of the painting of Sittna Badryya. "Mmmm," they murmured. I explained breathlessly that Sittna Badryya was a famous bedouin beauty.

"Strange," said the man Daffash called pasha, "she is not dark." My shyness overcame my wish to tell him that not all bedouins have dark skin, that "dark" has limitless variety. I bit my lip and brought two towels for the city women to cover their bare wide-open legs. The blonde fiddled with it, folded it, then placed it around her neck. I suppressed a giggle.

"Hey, girl. Bring the coffee," Daffash barked and gave me one of his fierce looks. He then said, "It's your wedding day. Let us not spoil it."

When I went out of the house I started laughing at city women who had no sense of shame. I bumped into Hamda and told her the story of the towel.

"They are used to it, my sister. By Allah, the men get bored with them very quickly. They show them everything, but we hide our treasures. When Flayyeh sleeps with me he feels as if he had conquered the cities of Andalusia," Hamda said. "City women. No shame or shyness."

She patted me on the shoulder and said, "I will make some coffee for the guests. You'd better have a bath."

"The house is occupied."

"In the storeroom."

"Will you give the coffee to Daffash?"

Hamda waved her hand ordering me to go. I filled the barrel with water, added some lemon leaves, and let it boil on the fire. The smell of lemon leaves reminded me of abundant seasons. Nasra helped me carry the barrel to the storeroom. Our horses and camels were grazing near the Dead Sea. May Allah lengthen Jarbwa's life. I placed two sacks of hay behind the closed door and started taking off my dirty clothes. The soles of my feet were rough and dry, my toenails and fingernails were ingrained with mud and soot, and my skin was dark. I was not like the painted smooth women sitting open-legged on our mattress. Harb loved me, though. People said that I had my mother's almond-shaped eyes. I scrubbed my skin with a loofah and Kanan soap, made in the town of Nablus. The scent of olive oil and thyme filled the dim room. The dog Nashmi barked. How can I part with him? How can I sleep next to a strange man? My father would be helpless without me. May Allah punish Daffash for his shameful deeds.

I called Hamda at the top of my voice. "Please bring me my mother's clothes. They're in the wooden trunk." I was shivering when Hamda finally threw the bundle through the small window near the ceiling. I grabbed every garment as if shaking hands with my mother. I sniffed the shimmering red trousers, the bright pink petticoat, the long velvet dress embroidered with golden beads. Thin golden threads ran down the black veil like sparkling tears. The glittering figure of my mother crossed the storeroom leaving glowing beads behind. I started crying again. My mother was the only person who could guide me, help me and take my hand. Where was she? What should I do when Harb's arms reached for me? If I had gone to the Dead Sea that night when he asked to see me he would not have proposed. My mother was right. Could we spend our wedding night near the Dead Sea, under the solitary stars and yearning moon?

Um Saad

"Maha, sister," called Um Saad.

I looked at the barred window and at the misty moon. A remote white lie. A hospital. Drugs and clouds. I turned my head and said, "Yes, Um Saad."

"All the eyes of human beings are asleep including Kukash's and Salam's, all except our eyes."

"Yes, Um Saad."

"Allah and His creatures are against us. Since I opened my eyes, I have not seen anything except misery and pain. I search my head, looking for one pleasant memory and find none. My father used to come back to our house in Hamidiyyeh in Damascus covered with soot and mud. His face was tired and stained. A rifle dangling from his shoulder. My father was a rebel against the French in Syria. He must have frightened the French because he used to frighten me. He would keep shouting and pacing the small room until I swam in a pond of fear under the blanket. He would keep talking about killing and blood,

36

about explosives and corpses until my blood would freeze in my veins. He used to wear black baggy trousers, cross his chest with leather ammunition belts, and cover his head with a turban. I would shut my eyes firmly to ward off the seeping red liquid and the decaying corpses.

"One morning, my mother woke me up and said, 'Prepare yourself, Haniyyeh. We will travel to Transjordan. We will leave Syria.' I loved the name of the country we were about to go to. Transjordan was music to my ears. I loved the sound of that country. I packed my dresses, pants, undershirts, shoes, and my cloth doll Habibeh in a bundle and walked behind my mother. A cart tied to two mules was waiting for us in front of the house. My father placed the big tin trunk in the back and asked us to hop in. Slowly, the Hamidiyyeh market began to disappear, the greenery began to dissolve. I did not realize then that this was to be the last glimpse of my birthplace. From the back of the cart, while holding the rail tightly and singing in my head, 'Trans-trans-trans-Jordan,' I watched the land turn whiter, drier, and harsher. My father would stop fighting the French, and he might then leave me and my mother alone. I did not like my father, but I really hated the French who made him restless and dirty.

"The rhythmic trot of the mules lulled me to sleep. I slept for a long time and when I woke up the cart was surrounded by horsemen and wagons. With other fighters and families, we formed a winding caravan crawling slowly towards a place called Amman. After four days of traveling, dust, and the noise of horses, Habibeh my doll stopped sleeping. At night, the stars sparkled and I wanted to pick them and make a necklace for Habibeh, my stained doll. Then, a startling shout. 'A — M — M — A — N.' I held the rail of the cart with both hands and looked at the green dot. Maha, sister, it was love at first sight. As we approached I could see the trees and the water, I could see these gallant people, these Caucasians, ploughing the land and singing, I could see the carts of maize and the tops of mountains. Damascus was boring and flat: Amman was exciting and hilly. Tra-la-la. Trans — trans — trans — Jordan, where the mountains were high, the plains green, and the houses white, full of honey and cream."

Suddenly, Dr. Edwards and nurse Salam unlocked the door and entered. "You are still awake," he said, holding his stethoscope. We shut our eyes firmly.

Even through my closed eyelids, I could see Salam smiling mechanically as she said, "I think our kids will go to sleep now." They left the room and locked the door. I heard a distant clicking of keys and the dwindling sound of footsteps.

"Who is he?"

"He is a doctor from a land called England."

"What is he doing here?"

I shrugged my shoulders. "Please continue, Um Saad."

"Maha, lady of the people, they sent me to school. My mother made me wear a long black skirt, a black cape, covered my head and my face with a black veil. Hot, masked, and unable to breathe, I walked to the *kutab*, the religious school run by the mosque. I could barely see the sidewalk, could not distinguish the faces of passers-by. People around me were like hazy figures made of trails of smoke. The *kutab* was not far from our house. The teacher was an old Circassian woman called Rahimeh. She wore a white veil and a long dress, but she did not cover her face which shone like a circular moon. She welcomed me and asked me if I had brought a sandwich for the break.

"I stood up and said, 'Yes, teacher, white cheese and cucumber.' Everybody laughed at me and I felt hot and clumsy under my cape.

"'Sit down. Did you bring your Holy Qur'an with you?'

"'Yes, teacher.' I stepped on the end of my skirt and fell down in a heap of cloth.

"'Right. I will teach you the first verse and how to write some Arabic.'

"'Yes, teacher.' We sat down forming a half-circle and repeated after Miss Rahimeh the verses of the Qur'an. In the name of Allah the Compassionate, the Merciful.

"'You must not make mistakes while reading the words of Allah. Take off your mask, Haniyyeh, you cannot see with that thing on.'

"With trembling fingers, I lifted the veil and saw the faces of my classmates. The faces of Transjordanian girls beamed with happiness. I smiled back and sighed. The air grew cooler and the room bigger. I felt so excited because I was learning something new, the verse of al-Fatiha. My favorite *surah* was the Blood Clot. 'Read: In the name of thy Lord who created. Created man from a blood clot . . . Who taught by the pen. Taught man that which he knew not.' And I, like a dry sponge, sister, I absorbed things which I knew not. School provided me with an excuse to leave our house and escape my father's wrath. But the wind always blows against the ship's wishes. One year later, when we reached *surah* Ya-Sin, the midpoint of the Qur'an, and I had learnt to write my name, my father ordered me to stay at home with my mother. 'You are growing up.' But I hated growing up, I wanted to push my body back to its former younger shape.

"I missed Miss Rahimeh and Dalal my friend, I missed the walk to the *kutab* every morning and the sandwiches of soggy flat bread, white cheese, and cucumber. 'Yes, father,' I said and heard my classmates repeating, grammar-lesson style, 'Haniyyeh, two years later mother of Saad, said yes to her father.'"

Maha

I sneaked slowly into the room in order not to be noticed by the
wedding guests. The man from the city saw me and said, "Charming
bedouin eyes!" I felt hot in the heavy velvet dress and prayed to Allah
that Daffash would not ask me to do something. My father shuffled
into the room and looked disapprovingly at the uncovered legs of the
city women. His eyes did not meet mine when he said, "May Allah
protect you, my sweet child." My heart flew out of my breast and
hugged the old man. He was sad. "Daffash, prepare the *mansaf.*"

I sighed, "The rice is ready, the mutton well cooked in yogurt, and
the bread is wrapped with a sack." May Allah bless my neighbors who
had done most of the work. Without the hands of Hamda and Nasra,
I could not have finished the cooking.

The end of one of the mattresses looked so comfortable and welcoming that I fell on it, folded my legs, and tucked them under my
long dress. The city people were talking about English clubs, captains,
and churches. I had never set my eyes on any of these. The blonde

woman said in timid Arabic, which had no guttural sounds in it, "Entrance for the English only."

The dark woman asked in her watered down Arabic, "What about officer's friends?"

Daffash twisted his thin moustache and said, staring at the blonde, "What about me? I've spent a long time translating old Arabic inscriptions for travelers."

The blonde patted him on the shoulder and said, "You are an open-minded Arab. Not many of them around."

He twisted his thin moustache with his thumb and forefinger and whispered, "We just want your approval and acceptance!"

Although they all started laughing noisily, I felt uncomfortable among them. Daffash was stupid. The beat of drums, the singing and ululation of the women of the tribe seeped through the room and saved me from listening to more timid Arabic.

"Sheikh Nimer, Allah increase your wealth.
You are the best father-in-law.
Bless the house of Nimer."

Harb's family were coming to take me to my marriage nest. I was suddenly struck with fear. My heart hovered in the room fingering every item: the old mattresses sewed by my mother, the wooden trunk, the oiled spinning-wheel, my father's English rifle, the old clay jar, the half-finished woolen carpet, and the rounded mirror. My old father might see my quivering chin, so I pulled down the brocaded veil covering my tear-stained face.

The tall, cloaked figure of Harb's uncle seemed to fill the room. His mother stood so near to me that I could smell her tobacco-laden breath. When Tamam had finished her inspection of her son's bride, she decided to sit down. Then I was able to see the young girls of the tribe dancing in the middle of the small room. I felt a bit dizzy. No air in the stuffed space. The drum, the jumping girls with colorful scarves, and Harb's aging mother were all part of a heavy dream. My father's wrinkled face sprang out of nowhere. I couldn't meet his eyes, so I lowered mine and fixed them on my toes. He took my hand with his own flaky one and squeezed it. His shaky voice flew to my ears,

41

"They have come to take you, bride." I stood up while gazing firmly at the tip of my toes which were barely covered by the hem of my mother's long velvet dress. My father approached and kissed my forehead.

I whispered, "Father, don't forget to eat."

"Take good care of her," he said to Harb's uncle.

"We will hold her in our eyes."

Harb's uncle stretched out his long arm, took my free hand and said, "Come with us, my daughter."

The warm night breeze fondled my veil. Gasoline lamps were held over my head. The scent of orange blossoms settled heavily on my heart and reminded me that I was parting with my farm, my henna and radish beds, the camels and hens, our dog Nashmi, our Arab horse Mujahid, and our amber cow Halabeh. Harb's house lay calmly on the outskirts of the village. The procession moved forward to the well-lit tents in Sheikh Nimer's courtyard. The gypsy dancers were already there swinging and swaying in translucent costumes amidst the men of the tribe. Shame on them, like city women, almost naked! The gypsy drumbeat was more persistent and sharper than the Arab beat.

> "Our bride is green, green.
> Her cheeks like apples.
> Sprinkle jasmine flowers.
> Light candles, burn incense."

I was neither green nor apple-like. I was nineteen years old. My back muscles ached with exhaustion. I entered the tent, sat on the thick carpet, and stretched my stiff legs.

The wedding procession moved again, but this time to Harb's house. The men were riding their horses and the women were walking on the ground. Some of the cloaked riders held flickering lamps. The women listed the good traits of the bride. Her ancestors were generous, her mother was a pious housewife, and she was chaste and pure. The fickle light kept covering, then uncovering smiling faces. My feet felt sore and tired despite the cool soil. I saw the Land Rover whizzing by the procession. My brother Daffash left with the two women and his master for the city. My father, I hoped, would not find out. He did not stay in his village, even on his sister's wedding night.

Nasra squeezed herself between the women and walked next to me silently like a shadow. "Give you success, sister, Allah," she whispered. "Cannot get married, me. Want a child, me."

I held her hand and said, "It's all right. Maybe it's better for you. Allah chooses what's best." I lowered my head. The only earring Nasra was wearing swayed in the dim light of distant lamps and reminded me of the humiliating deed of my brother who followed that foreign woman like a loyal dog.

It was a long walk through the sleepy alleyways between the mud houses with tiny shimmering windows. Abu Aubaydah's shrine stood high and clean on the left side of the village. I imagined that my mother's hands were holding the spinning-wheel in the dark, trying hard to collect some serene moments and to catch a stitch or two. In the dim light, she sat gazing at the patterns of her half-finished carpet. Cream background and brown shapes. The sleepy alleyways extended under my feet like a never-ending river. The Jordan River ran deep in the valley, sprinkling green thyme and basil on the banks. It streamed to the Dead Sea, the lake I was in love with. Every now and then, my tongue yearned for the taste of salt.

Harb's well-lit house looked unfamiliar in the darkness. Some tents for the guests were erected in the courtyard. Our own roof was dome-shaped and low, Harb's was flat and high. When my father built our house he patted the doors into arch-shapes. Harb's house had straight lines which met to form sharp angles. The lines in our house were circular and stooping. My body would not fit through the rectangular door. It was my new home. I must loosen up. I repeated that several times, until the minaret of the shrine caught the echo and repeated, "Loosen up. Turn into a rectangle. Allah-u-Akbar."

When I squeezed myself through the unfamiliar door, I was welcomed by Harb's shining face, his thick moustache, the golden tooth, and his tall, lean body. His firm thighs told the story of endless days of riding strong Arab horses. I forgave him for being like any other man of the tribe and embraced my love for him. He held my hand and his fingers made me feel thin, soft and fine. When he helped me to sit down, my lungs seemed to tighten. My ribs grew wings and soared high when Harb pushed up the brocaded veil, uncovering my face. He looked at my tear-stained lashes with praying, submissive

43

eyes. My heart flew out of my chest and hovered over my husband's head.

When Hamda approached and kissed my forehead, I could not cry. Harb was the only presence every nerve of my body was aware of. She looked at Harb and said, "She is very precious to us. Take good care of her."

"By Allah, don't worry. She is as fine as a thoroughbred mare, as dear to me as my eyesight." When Hamda went out of the room everybody else left with her. The drummer girl, the dancers, Tamam, and Hajjeh Hulala. My friends Halimeh and Nasra kissed me on the cheek and flicked out of the room like bats sensing darkness.

Harb stretched out his arms and hugged me tightly as if I was going to disappear like the riders of Karak. My mother had told me that the people of Karak were sometimes woken up by the neighing horses and clinking swords of the warriors of the prophet in the Battle of Mutah. When they looked out of their doors, the horsemen dissolved in the hazy light of the morning. My horseman cupped my face with his hands and ran his eyes slowly over my trembling lips and quivering chin. A demanding, tender touch. Through the beating of drums and ululations of women I was able to hear the wedding night song.

> "Hey bridegroom,
> We are as pure and
> As soft as rose petals."

All the members of the tribe would wait outside the door for proof of my virginity. Young girls, young boys, half-naked children, toothless old men, and horsemen were all thirsty for my blood. My heart started beating fiercely. What would he do to me? I was about to lose some blood. Was it like an ordinary period? The questions flew out of my head like pigeons when Harb massaged my legs. I was able to see his thick hair and the dark skin of his shoulder. I had never felt so smooth before.

I jumped away from Harb when I heard Tamam's knock on the door.

"My son," she said, "let me hold my head high for the rest of my life. Show the whole tribe that you are the pride of Qasim."

Harb put his head in his hands. He had lost interest in my body. "I won't be able to do it if they keep knocking on the door."

I held him tight. I kissed his damp forehead, his eyes, his nose, his mouth. I could hear the galloping of horses and the shooting in the air. The young men of the tribe were getting restless. Harb lay on the floor, closed his eyes, and stretched his legs. I felt that I had to do something to help him. I didn't know what exactly. I lay next to him and held his head between my breasts. He began to breath evenly and reached out for my legs again. His face was covered with sweat, and his arms were shaking.

"It is all right," I said, "it's all right."

"Yes," he said then kissed my parted lips.

A fierce knock on the door stopped Harb dead in his tracks. He stood up and kicked the wall with his foot.

"Come on, son," she hissed, "the whole tribe is waiting. Shame in my old age is also waiting."

Harb was in tears when he said, "Maha, I cannot do it."

I was thinking of my honor. I was a virgin: I had the blood in me, but Harb was the one to spill it. Harb was the one who was supposed to prove that I was a virgin. What if they were never given the sheet with blood on it? They will think I had no honor. The shame of it will kill my father. "They will not leave us alone until we hand them a piece of white cloth dripping with blood. If we don't get that piece they will think I am not a virgin. My family's name will be tarnished forever."

Harb's face was pale when he said with difficulty, "Maha, I cannot do it."

I suddenly smiled and said, "We can fool them."

"That's impossible!" he sighed.

"Prick my little finger with the end of your dagger . . ."

"No, I will not."

"It is my blood they are after."

"I just cannot hurt you on our wedding night."

I snatched the dagger and nicked the tip of my finger in order not to bleed too much. While wiping the blood I saw tears captured in my husband's eyes. He kissed my hand and said that he didn't want me to suffer, that he loved every part of me, even my little finger.

45

"Give them the proof of my chastity. Quickly."

With a shaking hand he held the cloth then thrust it out of the door. He was supposed to be naked. I giggled.

The whole tribe went mad when they saw my virgin blood. They would stick the cloth to a rifle barrel, ride their horses, and shoot some bullets in the air. Another woman of their tribe had proven to be sealed, and had now been opened. The honey in its jar was safe; I was pure.

Um Saad

"Maha, sister," sighed Um Saad. I felt tired tonight as if my limbs were made of moss. I had no energy, no will to stay alive and see the morning light. I recovered my voice and whispered, "Yes, Um Saad."

"My heart tonight is yearning for something, something beyond my reach. Allah created us like that. Yearning, wanting, wishing, desiring. I remember the first and the last time I went to the cinema."

"What is the cinema?" I asked, to keep Um Saad talking, happy.

"You go to a vast hall, sit on a straw chair, and watch the wall. Suddenly a beam of light comes out and you start seeing people and hearing what they say. Fantastic."

"Why go there to see and hear people?" Why go anywhere to see or hear people. No place is good. It is a small world, a narrow hospital room with no air at all.

"It is different. You see people you cannot see in real life and visit places you can never visit in real life. The film I saw was acted in

47

Cairo. I loved the Egyptian accent and the bustling noise of the big city. I was playing catch-the-stone with Dalal on the steps when my mother called my name. She said that Omar, Um Abdu's son, would take us to the cinema the second day of the feast. Before the sun of the second day rose, I already had my bath, put on my new clothes, and combed my hair. I waited for Omar and Dalal silently in order not to draw my father's attention to our outing. By your life, it was the longest wait I ever experienced.

"When Dalal and Omar knocked on the door, I caught my breath. They entered, shook hands with my father, and said, 'Happy feast, Uncle.'

"'Haniyyeh, bring the sweets.' Trembling, I offered them some chocolates and gave them a secret sign to keep quiet. Dalal understood, but Omar revealed the secret.

"'Uncle, I want your permission to take Haniyyeh to the cinema.'

"I covered my head with my hands to protect myself from the debris of the explosion which was bound to happen. I waited, eyes closed, for metal buckles, splintered glass, and piercing words. Nothing. I opened one eye and looked around me. They were all still seated and smiling.

"'I will send them with you, Omar, because I trust you. You are a man and can protect them. Bring them back early, though.'

"I was almost in tears when I put on my Turkish *mulaya*. I fixed the cape, mask, and veil and descended the narrow steps of our house.

"'Girls, this way,' shouted Omar.

"Bedouin men and women filled the streets of the Sugar Market."

Beduoin women? Like me. They do exist. My village Hamia does exist. "By Allah, like me."

"Yes, like you, Maha."

"I have never been to the city. Just to Fuhais."

"And I wish you had never left your village at all. I wish I had never gone to the cinema. Maha, I wish many things, I did not know then what I know now. I just held Dalal's hand and filled my eyes with the sight of the glittering clear water of the stream. The old houses built of white stones shone in the sunlight and the lace curtains wavered in the breeze. Then and there, I caught a disease called 'longing.' I yearned to see, hear, touch what takes place behind closed doors and quivering curtains. The life of the city and the people of the city started streaming in my veins. We walked by the offal market where they sell entrails of sheep, the Catholic church where nuns go to pray, the Bukhariyyeh market where Persians sell beads and spangles, and the Roman ruins, until we reached open green fields. The smell of wet radishes and lettuce filled the place. The stream running through the fields made the air cooler. 'Come on, girls,' shouted Omar, who was always a few steps ahead of us. Red letters on a white sheet said, 'Al-Amir Cinema.' Omar asked us to stay outside and went to buy the tickets. We were surrounded by boys and men. Not one single girl. I held Dalal's hand tightly until we entered a big, almost empty hall and sat on low straw chairs.

"Repeated clicks followed by absolute silence. Sister, if you threw a needle, you could hear it hitting the floor. The sound and the picture started flickering on the wall. Advertisements for Lifebuoy soap, Marie biscuits, and Kiwi shoe polish. All made in England. It lasted longer than our rubbish. Excellent quality and high standards. Then, the film started. Farid al-Attrash appeared on the screen and a funny feeling hit me as if I had lost the lower part of my body. He sang to Samiyya Jamal, who because of her poverty worked as a belly-dancer in a night club. But she was a moral and straight artist. Loud-mouthed women looking through small windows kept gossiping about her and accusing her of immoral things. Samiyya Jamal was innocent. She continued dancing to Farid's tunes. She would sway and swing her firm hips and shake her breasts and Farid would sing about the sorrows of love. One night, he drove her back home and kissed her gently on the lips. The lower part of my body fell down to the floor. I felt like stretching my hands to hold my thighs and hips. I couldn't. Could not budge or blink.

> 'With you, with you, always.
> Hearing your footsteps, always.
> Adoring your beauty, always.'"

"I hear the footsteps of my son, always. The tender sound echoes in my head, Um Saad." She ignored me and continued talking about the film.

49

"I cried when they did not allow him to see his beloved. I cried when they accused her of being loose. I cried when they kissed and cried and cried when they got married at the end. Dalal asked me why I was crying. 'I cannot stand happiness,' I said. I cannot bear happiness. I cannot smell happiness. My sister, happiness splits my heart open. Allah created human beings with a hole in the chest. They cry when they remember the sad moments; weep when they remember the happy moments; wail when they realize they have neither happy nor sad moments to ponder upon. Curse this living.

"That night, Maha, I discovered the shutter and the star-shaped holes. I sat on the cushions and peeped through the holes at the dark city. Amman was sleeping like a baby. Oblivious to broken hearts and to sad empty streets. I felt like falling to my knees; I, Haniyyeh Um Saad, felt like calling someone's name; I felt like . . . I felt like stroking something; I felt like reaching out to touch, to fondle. I wanted to rub my nose on somebody's chin. All I managed to do in that long, sweaty night was to caress myself and embrace the darkness."

Maha

It was nearly dawn. The cries of men had subsided and I realized that I was in Harb's arms. We lay down next to each other on the mattress, quietly. He ran his fingers through my hair, slowly unbinding my plaits. I pushed his headdress off and held his neck. Collusion against the tribe had brought us closer to each other. When my hair was set free it danced across my shoulders. His thin fingers ran over my eyes, nose, cheeks, ears and landed on my lips. Ease, pleasure, and an irresistible hunger attacked my body from every direction. I was a virgin and virgins must not respond to their men. He might think I was a loose woman.

He kissed the left side of my mouth, the right side, then the center of my trembling lips. Nothing like it, not even kissing the henna, the horse, or the oranges. Allah damn old hags and old rules. I moved closer and put my arms around him.

"My heart starts stamping and jumping in the air when I see you," he said.

"Horsemen of tribes must not like women."

"Just you, Maha, the companion of my soul."

Every word he said, every move he made, brought more freedom and joy. My body grew lighter and lighter until I turned into an ostrich feather. "Harb, I have a wish."

"Your wishes are orders to me."

"Can we go to the Dead Sea?"

"Yes."

"Now?"

He pushed his hair off his face and said, "It's too late."

"It is not far," I said in a pleading voice.

The warm and humid breeze brushed my face and my loose hair. Harb held my hand. All the village was sleeping heavily except one or two lit windows. Restless breastfed babies. I sniffed the scent of orange blossoms, filled my lungs with the perfume of my happiness. We strolled along the bank of the Jordan which was covered completely with citrus trees. I left my slippers in Harb's house and trod on the cool soil barefoot. The cooing of doves was washed away by the persistent sound of running water. Was I really there with Harb? I shuddered. He opened his cloak, pulled me closer to him and wrapped it around my shoulders. His warm body next to mine made me feel safe and at peace with the whole world, even with my brother Daffash.

I remembered my uncertainty when Harb proposed to me after I had chosen not to meet him. I thought then that Harb was like Daffash.

"Are you like my brother Daffash?" Harb laughed as if he was able to see the doubt inside my head.

He tightened his grip around my waist and said, "No."

"But you proposed to me although I had not come to see you."

"Yes and no." He stopped talking and his body stiffened. I followed his eyes to see some lights crawling on the west bank of the Jordan.

"Who are they?" I asked.

"The English."

"What are they doing in our land?"

"Digging out the bones of Salahudin."

"Salahudin?"

"Salahudin al-Ayyubi, the medieval Muslim leader who defeated the Crusaders."

"Why do they want to dig his bones out?"

He looked at the west bank and shook his head like an angry horse: "No, I am not like your brother Daffash."

He stopped in front of me and cupped my face with his hands. In the cold glow of the moonlight I was able to make out the expression on his face. I had seen it before on my father's face when he said goodbye to my mother's corpse. Sheikh Nimer, my father, went on weeping for three days over the grave of my mother. Harb pulled me closer to his warm body, stroked my hair, and fingered my face. My hand rebelled against old advice and held Harb's waist. He pushed his hair back and quickened his pace, eager to reach the sea.

A massive dark plain opened up in front of us where the fresh water of the river merged with the salty water of the sea. The cold breeze blunted the edge of the heat. The moonlight transformed the sea into a huge mirror, like the one my grandmother had given to my mother. Just a piece of melting silver lying on its back. There were a few palm trees and a handful of camels which looked ridiculously small in the vast plain. All was cool, calm, and calling. My inner soul reached out to touch the sky and bowed down to kiss the sea. I felt content with the gift of life and forgave time for all the miseries it had inflicted upon me. Daffash used to be in a rage when he beat me up. Surely, he hadn't meant to hurt me. My mother was in constant pain and had to depart. Carrying water, comforting my father, and running the house were not draining. Not at all. I opened my arms and swore never to cry again, to wear a smile and love my husband till the end of my life.

I burst out laughing and ran towards the silver water to fill my nostrils with its saline air, to breath in the stinging smell of acids and minerals. The water cures all ailments of the skin. I ran my hands over my hair. Harb was unbuckling his belt which carried the dagger and the sword's sheath and threw it on the ground. I sat down on a flat black rock and watched my husband. His cloak slipped down to the ground. He unbuttoned his robe then took it off revealing a dark chest. I lowered my eyes, and focused my gaze on the salt-covered pebbles. Blood rushed to my face when I realized that my eyes wanted to see more of him, my ears wished to listen to his breath, and my nose reached out to smell his musk-anointed body.

My body shivered as he undressed me. Off went the veil, my mother's velvet robe, the petticoat, and the trousers. He hugged me tightly. Hand in hand we immersed our bodies in the warm water which had been heated by the blazing sun all day. Hands holding, questioning, resisting then surrendering. He kissed my forehead. The water was still, the palm trees were not swaying, the sky held its breath. I swam closer to my husband, stood up, then kissed his forehead. I would not listen to old advice. My body burst with heat and life. No, I would not follow my mother's advice. Forgive me, mother. The look in his eyes was one of respect and delight. So, he didn't look down on me because I kissed his forehead. Women of Hamia, you were living in a heap of dung. I leapt towards him to receive every drop of the sea's water.

"You are my woman," Harb gasped, holding me firmly.

"I am your woman," I repeated. My fingers were dug deep into his back.

"You belong to me," he insisted.

"I am yours," I whispered. My whole body shivered as I received him. I called my mother's name, arched my body, then let go. The stars winked and the horizon grew wider, becoming limitless.

The Hamia Mountains, black rocks, mineral spring, and, beyond them, high Jerusalem, witnessed the birth of our love. Exhausted and contented, the moon retired to its world. I loved that man who was wiping his wet body with his cotton shirt. I would protect him, accept his protection, and be his woman till the soul seeps back to its creator. "I am sitting on a stone, and you are sitting on another. Will you accept me as your companion?" Harb asked.

"I will." We laughed. The sea turned into a cloud of light gleaming in the hazy fog, eager to ascend to the mountains of Jerusalem. Fiery gold, sparkling silver, deep brown, and a cheerful white light. Harb cupped my face with his hands and said that I was the Arab mare who would accompany him wherever he went, the herb which would ease his pain. I laughed while trying to avoid his eyes. The grains of salt clinging to the hair on his chest sparkled in the creeping light. My hands were stained with acids and minerals. Swimming in the sea, making love in the sea, crying in the sea, surrendering in the sea. The basalt, the patient camels, and the river of Jordan which poured its sweet waters into the Dead Sea sang to the tunes of my love.

I shielded my eyes and inspected the surroundings. Latroun Mountain stood erect, the Hamia Mountains stooped protectively, and the sea lay playfully on its back looking at the sky. That morning the mountains had a certain sheen around their edges. It must have been the bright dawn which had started breaking. My whole body became stiff when I made out the crooked shadow of Hakim climbing up the mountain. "Hakim," I cried at the top of my voice and pointed at the mountain. "Hakim exists," I said to Harb.

"Do you believe Hajjeh Hulala? She is an old hag."

Dew and light, the sisters of the bedouins, gave me a hand and helped me see Hakim with his crooked back, black goat, and long stick. My father had assured me that Hakim, the embodiment of Arabs' anger and resistance, never stopped breathing, would never die, and would always roam the deserts and mountains of Arabia. Many sought his blood, but he managed to survive.

There was a strange expression on Harb's face when he said, "Hakim died forty years ago. This land was ruins then."

My body shrank because my husband refused to believe me. "I saw him."

"It is better for him to stay underground. He must not be seen." Jarbwa once told me that Harb was fighting the English. On horseback and with other men he raided army bases. He told me that Harb was fighting against the Mandate. I was upset because Harb wouldn't share all that with me. He chose to keep it to himself. He wanted Hakim and his resistance to remain underground.

I avoided the short cut and walked through a banana plantation. Hakim climbed up the Mountain of Hamia and disappeared in the hazy cloud enveloping the top. Harb must have been following me closely because I was able to hear the rustling of thick leaves behind. We reached a huge water valley with a thin stream running in the middle. I washed the salt off my hands and face and Harb started washing his hair. I cupped my hands and filled them with water. When I poured the water over his head he twisted his mouth with amusement. Fresh water filled his eye-sockets and trickled down his thick moustache. Every tree in the valley, every blind worm under the soil, every snake curled under the rocks, and every drop of water danced to the song of my recently-found happiness.

"Girl, do you have a protector with a sword and shield?
No, I don't have one, but to you I will yield."

The tunes of Nasra's melodic pipe drifted to my ears. They sounded more nostalgic, more yielding than ever. I sighed and said, "Poor Nasra."

"Your brother is responsible," Harb said in a condemning voice.

"So the tribe knows."

"Everybody. Young men harass her."

It was not enough for Nasra to be flayed to the bone; they wanted to chew the rest. I imagined her following her sheep to the meadows. A solitary dark figure in the distance. In the morning light, my hands looked like two captive birds. Harb hugged me. Holding my husband's hand, I continued walking towards the mud village.

The Storyteller

In the name of Allah the Beneficent, the Merciful, "As for poets, the erring follow them. Hast thou not seen how they stray in every valley. And how they say that which they do not."

Oh most illustrious masters, say a prayer for the soul of the full moon, our prophet Muhammad, and his righteous companions. Tonight, the sixth night of Ramadan, the month of forgiving and mercy, I will add one more spot of color to my story which is as precious and as varied as a Persian carpet. Although I traveled in Persia, I cannot remember anything except the magician kneeling down in front of a blazing fire. The sparrow brains worshipped the silent fire which a cup of cold water can put out. Let me add one more shadow to the mirages in the desert of the mind. The erring follow storytellers to the abyss of their inner souls. To put the pieces together and give you a perfect moon, I went astray in every valley.

The most staggering landscape is to the south of this windy tent. Petra. The majesty, the pain, the sculpture! Never saw anything like it in any other valley, even the forsaken valley of my mind. Rose-colored rock, caves, and temples. Two thousand years ago, when the earth was just a flat empty desert, the Nabataeans found a jungle of rose-colored rock and started carving and carving. I urged Aziza to climb up to the court, slide down to the treasury, and walk to the royal tombs where six monuments of six kings were sculpted. After fingering every wall, touching all the ceilings, and eyeing every pinnacle, I realized that the place will never be demystified, regardless of my efforts. Like eagles, people used to live in the caves dug in the mountainside. Maymoon squeaked, reminding me of the insignificance of humans who engrave, dig, carve, then die, who are always outlived by dumb stones and blue sky. The rose-colored rocks reminded me of the flushed face of Maha. Even if you lie with your she-ass and monkey on top of her chest, Petra will remain mysterious, unconquerable. Like Petra, like Jordan. Both are a locked box of jewelry lined with velvet and full of gold, turquoise, and pearls that you can imagine but can never touch with your trembling, eager fingers.

Maha — "bitter Indian fig" the people of Hamia used to call her — started working with a newly acquired enthusiasm on the farm. She would spend most of her time watering, weeding, ploughing, and even rubbing the oranges until they glowed in the sun. Why do you think? Can any of you tell me why? No, not because she was a hardworking peasant woman. The reason behind what she did was graver than that. The land. Yes, my masters, THE LAND. The source of all greed and every conflict.

She started farming vigorously as if the orchard belonged to her, not to her poor brother Daffash. Woman's cunning is great. A treasure, she thought, which she would inherit one of those days. If you divided the greed inside her it would have been enough for all our hearts. Allah's cunning devours the worshippers' cunning.

The first step to digest that piece of land was marriage. She had a glimpse of Harb one cold afternoon, while she was rubbing the oranges with the end of her sleeve. Right, she thought. That tall horseman must be fertile, healthy, and strong. A protector for my greed. What more did she need? What more does any woman need? She spread her mother's carpet and started spinning and casting spells, spinning and weaving until the horseman stopped and dismounted

from his horse. She sang, calling Gog and Magog, the masters of evil
and witchcraft.

> "Gog and Magog, bring him to me.
> Gog and Magog, tie him to me.
> Make him mine. Give him to me."

She looked at him with her wide eyes and the green boy fell in
love. People of the village swore that he used to spend his days without food and his nights standing opposite her window just to have a
whiff of her. He fell down and nobody said, "In the name of Allah."
Alas, the best horseman was bewitched and the wolves of darkness
kept howling in agreement. He used to go back to his house so pale
and sick with love that Tamam his mother used to cry and say that
the daughter of Maliha had licked away his brain.

After endless days of suffering and long sleepless nights, Harb became as thin and as fragile as a basil bough. His mother realized how
madly in love her son was and how strong was the spell cast over
him. Two weeks later, the drums of the wedding were beaten and the
procession started. I put Maymoon on my lap and sat under the palm
tree to watch the winding file of bedouins. Riders held lamps, offering
my dwindling sight some light. The shepherdess walked behind the
bride like a vigilant guard and didn't let any other woman get close to
her. A bright light hooded the face of the bride shrouded in a black
veil. At that sin-fringed moment, my monkey leapt to my shoulder.
He wanted to see her face, to memorize her features, and to imagine
the delights she reserved for her husband. Maymoon's face was soak-
ing with love, passion, merciless adoration. He too was bewitched.
His tears were bathing his hairy face. My friend, my love Maymoon,
don't cry over the past. Be wise, be happy, bang the tambourine across
your thigh, shake shake shake,

> Maymoon, sweet Maymoon.
> Go to the moon.
> Throw your body.
> You will die soon.
> Hihi-Haha-Hoon.

May Allah forgive me and accept my repentance. When the sound of drums subsided and the ululation of women ceased, the cold wind of faraway lands approached. The scent of honeysuckle wafted to my nose. I straightened my back and sat down on a rock overlooking the tents. The tent fires and lamps looked like stars calling in the darkness. The skyline glowed with the ashes of the burnt-out sun. The cold night wind stirred the dust of the hopeless ground into a hazy cloud. The horizon extended generously, promising more saffron covered plains. I placed my hot belly on the cold rock, watching the hazy dust-cloud which seemed like a halo around the tents' heads. At that sin-fringed moment, something really strange happened to me. Total exhaustion overtook my body and part of me became detached and watched me from above. I realized how futile my efforts were and how useless it was conversing with the self in the dark.

The wild cheers, galloping, and curvettings of men and horses snatched me from my misery. Maha was a virgin. The horsemen fired shots, shouted, and whirled round and round near the tent mouths. The croaked voices of men singing, "Hee-dehhyya, hee-dehhyya," penetrated my tired ears. Maymoon, who was gazing all the time at the closed door of the bride's room, started jumping when he saw the men waving the ends of their cloaks. The flag of her chastity fluttered in the pitch-dark night of the valley. If Daffash were there he would have grown a few inches taller. But Samir Pasha had convinced him to forget about the empty rituals of weddings and to go with him to see the new farm he had bought in the upper Hamia. A small house made of local stones was all he intended to build. Raai told me that Samir Pasha wanted to hire Daffash as a watchman and manager of the plantation. The dark-headed woman was an Egyptian dancer and the blonde one was Rose, the daughter of the head of the English army tribe.

Rose was like a white candle, was like porcelain. Whenever Daffash got close to her, she would turn her head to the other side. Ha Ha Ha, He He He. To move towards the white man and his bundles of money, Daffash wanted to get married to Rose Bell. According to the watchman, the English girl gave the bedouin horseman a shoulder as cold as her homeland. As far as Maha and all the women of the tribe were concerned, I, Sami al-Adjnabi, the lion of the desert, did not exist. I, my monkey, my she-ass, and tales were invisible even to Nasra, the idiot of the village.

While sitting on the rock thinking of the silk cushions, dangling curtains, bejeweled women, and belly-dancers, I made out two figures sneaking out of the house. The cold darkness wrapped everything and every creature. I could not believe my eyes. The bride and the bridegroom. I quickly tied my Aziza and my Maymoon to a big stone, threw my bundle behind the rock, and stealthily followed the two dim figures. They headed towards the Jordan. When they stood on the bank to look at the lights on the other side, I tightened my belt around my waist. Prepare yourselves for some fun. Harb kissed her and pulled her closer to him. Under the pale moonlight they strolled to the Dead Sea. I found some low shrubs and threw myself on the ground behind them. If they had seen me, Harb would have shot me. Ha Ha Ha.

He took off his clothes and started undressing her. I was able to make out a shining white figure with rounded breasts. When naked, she had nothing bedouin about her. White and glossy like porcelain, like candles, like Rose. Or was she? Hand in hand they immersed their bodies into the water. All the jinn and demons were flying freely in that devil-accursed land. She started pushing him down as if trying to drown him, or baptize him like the infidel Christians do, but he kept floating. A fierce struggle took place between them. Hands and legs were entangled several times. He was resisting her spell by pushing his head out of the water. She trying to capture his soul by immersing him in that sea of demons. A piercing shriek penetrated my bones when finally she managed to possess his body. The man was crying. Every part of my body was uncomfortably wet. I raised my head towards the sky and invoked Allah.

When the sun came over the shrub-covered plain, they started their long walk back home. My feet and my back ached when I straightened them. She talked about somebody called Hakim. She pointed at the misty mountains. Nothing! I made a note to ask Raai about him when I saw him. The minarets of Jerusalem echoed the call for prayer. I stopped following the couple and turned back towards the mineral springs on the seashore to wash my sin-stained body with fresh water. While I was rubbing myself clean, a verse from the Qur'an popped into my head. "The likeness of those who choose other patrons than Allah is as the likeness of the spider when she taketh unto herself a house, and lo! the frailest of all houses is the spider's house, if they but know." He is the Mighty and the Wise. My most honorable masters, what I have woven for you so far is as frail as the spider's house. A puff of air, tiny drops of rain can wash the spider out and destroy his thready shelter. We shall perish soon.

Maha

Aunt Tamam, Harb's mother, looked puzzled when that morning she saw me uprooting weeds from the small piece of land behind the two-roomed house. I wanted to clear the land and plant some henna, radishes, and one or two orange trees. The soil around the house was salty and needed to be washed with streams of water. I looked at Harb's house and its small windows. It was full of corners and ours had none. My mother did not like triangular shapes. The doors were patiently patted into arches, the mirror was circular, and even the unfinished carpet had rounded edges. I must get used to sharp angles for the sake of my newly born love. I must make the soil less salty and more welcoming.

Every morning, I would carry the water jar on my head and walk to the Long Well. When I threw the rubber bucket through the narrow opening of the well, I heard the cool sound of splashing. The plaintive tunes of Nasra's reed-pipe and the bleating of sheep echoed in my head. The bright morning light wiped away the heavy longing-filled night. I used to walk back through sleeping alleyways carrying my clay jar on my head. Jarbwa's husky voice traveled to my ears.

> "Hey, you carrying the jar,
> Hey, you carrying the secrets,
> Give me some water, O girl."

I would sprinkle the water around the house and wake every sleeping soul. Tamam rubbed her eyes and puffed some smoke. She eyed me suspiciously and said that since Harb had gone to the mountains, I had been doing useless chores.

Five days after our wedding, a strong hand knocked on the door. I was combing Harb's hair after we had finished our pilgrimage to pleasure. Allah protect us. Harb wrapped himself with his cloak and ordered me to stay where I was. He opened the door and went out. I heard Jadaan's voice talking breathlessly to my husband. Harb dashed into the room, put on his cotton robe and his sheepskin jacket, buckled on his ammunition belt, and checked his dagger. He was going for a raid. He fixed his headdress, slipped his feet into his sandals, and snatched the rifle off the wall. He asked me, "Did you feed my horse?"

I put on my robe, covered my head, and followed my husband to the yard. While filling his saddle with ground grain and dates, I noticed that he was waving his right arm in the air as he talked to Jadaan. I overheard him asking, "More taxes?"

"The English . . . in full force," Jadaan said.

"And tax arrears?" Harb asked.

"Yes . . . without consultation with chiefs of tribes."

My husband looked angry. Holding Jadaan's arm he continued asking questions. I felt that Harb might be away for a long time. I wrapped more butter in a piece of sash and tied it to the fringe of his saddle. His eyes met mine as he mounted his horse. "I entrust my mother to you, twin of my soul," he whispered and galloped into the kohl-dark night. The sound of the horse's hooves dwindled and was replaced gradually by the barking of dogs. I shuddered.

Harb spent most of the early days of our marriage in the mountains and I spent most of my time waiting for familiar sounds of galloping hooves. The radishes survived in the backyard, transforming it into a carpet of verdure and dew. When she saw the green leaves and the red roots of the first radishes, Tamam bit her lower lip, puffed some smoke, and said, "Allah is great." Tamam stuffed her old pipe with fresh tobacco brought from Damascus by the gypsy peddler Uqla. The small bells hanging around his donkey's neck jingled their warning to husbands' ears. Uqla introduced the young women of the village to colorful scarves, mother-of-pearl bracelets, Indian silk, and golden teeth. When the women of Hamia heard the tinkle of his bells, they started piling grains, oranges, eggs, and rugs to trade them in. Like ants, the women of Qasim gathered around Uqla and his donkey. Tamam watched the selling and buying from a safe distance, puffing her smoke every now and then. One day, Tamam said that she would like to cover one of her teeth with gold. My aunt still carried a green heart between her ribs. I turned my head towards the high mountains. No jewelry or scarves for me. Half of my heart was in the mountains and the other half was at the other side of the village with my father.

Jarbwa, the best shepherd of our tribe, used to visit my father regularly and carry back messages from the old man to me. Allah lengthen Jarbwa's life, he used to put out the fire in my heart whenever he came to visit me. Once, my father sent him with the carpet roves and spinning-wheel and asked him to tell me that he still loved Maliha. I loved my father. The latest news from our farm told the story of my father's illness. Daffash, my brother, carried the pick and dug the soil for two weeks only, before shouting at the old man and leaving the orchard to ants and weeds. Daffash was a city dweller and spent most of his time with Samir Pasha and the English. I decided to visit my father. Tamam eyed me and said, "You are a young bride. You must not visit your father. People will say that Maha couldn't stay put in her husband's house." I did not care about old pipes. If Harb was there he would have let me go.

The next morning, while watering the basil bed and thinking about visiting my father, I saw Nasra running towards me. She stood gasping for breath. That woman was followed by disasters wherever she went. "Save your brother," she panted.

"What?"

"Took Salih's wife to the cave, your brother. Looking for her with blood in his eyes, her husband."

I threw the ewer on the ground, ran to the house, knocked down the pile of mattresses, and snatched Harb's rifle. I hid the rifle in the folds of my wide trousers. "Aunt Tamam, I am going with Nasra."

"At this hour?" she asked, and puffed some smoke.

"I will not be long."

When Tamam could not see us any longer, we dashed up the mountain. The soles of my feet were blazing hot. Daffash's greedy fingers had even reached Salih's wife. The wife was an idiot. We went up the footpath leading to the cave of bad omens. Nasra pointed at a hazy blackish spot crawling in the valley and cried, "Oh, ill-fated, her husband."

Rifle in hand, finger on the trigger, I entered the cave quietly. Daffash's headdress was flung on a stone. When my eyes got used to the darkness I made out two figures on top of each other. "Enough," I cried at the top of my voice.

Daffash turned his head then barked, "You daughter-of-the-dog. What are you doing here?" He spat and the saliva landed on the terrified face of Salih's wife.

Nasra took her hand and said, "Put on your clothes. Quickly." Salih's wife started fumbling with the front of her robe. Her face was as white as a piece of cheese. "Looking for you, your husband."

Salih's wife started slapping her face with both hands and crying, "My face is blackened. It is covered with soot."

Nasra held her wrists and said, "Pull that robe over your head. Undressed, slaughter you like a chicken, your husband." I pointed the barrel at Daffash and ordered him to get dressed.

"You face-of-catastrophes," he snarled. "One of these days I will chew on your kidney and drink your blood from your skull."

"If you do not put on that shirt, your blood will be drunk instead."

Holding hands, Nasra, Salih's wife, and I staggered out of the cave and stood shivering in the sunshine. I stuck the rifle under my trousers and held it with my right arm to prevent it from sliding down. Salih was not far from us. "Wipe your tears and keep your mouth shut."

"Peace be upon you," Salih said as he approached and added, looking at his wife, "Curse your parents. What are you doing here? The cries of your baby filled the valley."

I stood in front of him to prevent him beating his wife. "My brother,

I dragged her out with me to help me look for bugloss. My brother, my back is killing me and Aunt Tamam said that boiled bugloss is the answer."

"She did not ask for my permission."

"Allah will forgive us all."

"Let's go, woman," Salih said and hit his wife on the back. She fell down, sprang up, lowered her head, and trudged down the mountain behind her husband.

"May Allah punish my brother Daffash for his shameful deeds, Amen."

When I heard Daffash's careless laughter I turned my head and spat on the clean stones.

"Thank you, little sister."

"What can I say? Nothing can describe your ruthlessness. Go and help your dying father instead of raping women."

"It was not rape. She was begging me for it and my manhood did not allow me to let her go without giving her what she asked for."

"Shame on you!"

He looked at the disappearing figures of Salih and his wife. "I am truly sorry," he said. He held my arms and kissed me on the forehead.

Nasra suddenly called Nawmeh, her goat, with a sharp voice. She was in love with Daffash, who raped her, made her life miserable, and slept with other women. By the life of Sabha my grandmother, I did not understand. For the second time Nasra had saved his neck. She picked up her pipe and strolled down the mountain. When she blew into the pipe and touched it with her trembling fingers it shed sad tunes. The reed-pipe had responded to the hot air coming from Nasra's lips, responded to the eager tongue. Wood had responded!

My body did not respond to the hot water of Harb. Flesh did not respond. Oh, how I hated the sight of my menstrual blood sticking out its tongue to me every twenty-eight days. Aunt Tamam used to puff some smoke filling the room with suffocating trails and ask, "Is the barrel still empty?" Yes, Tamam, the barrel was empty. Yes, Maha's belly was as small as ever, her breasts were as limp as ever, and her period visited her regularly. When I didn't answer, Tamam sucked her lip making a clicking sound. Just five months without pregnancy and the people of Hamia started adding, "May Allah give you a son," after every greeting.

My body was just a few muscles, bones, veins, and blood like the sheep Jarbwa had slaughtered for our wedding. I spent my days eating, drinking, and sleeping. My body preferred to have its own way and give me a sign of my barrenness every month, letting loose the merciless tongues. Our lazy village stuck to the mountainside like a leech. I saw myself in every dry tree trunk, in sacks of dry hay, in stretches of arid sand dunes which extended across the horizon. The Dead Sea was too salty and too stinging to give any chance for life to develop. The Jordan River tried hard with its fresh water to sweeten the stubborn sea, to make it less thick and more inviting, to shake it back to life to no avail. The Dead Sea died years and years ago.

The sea was my only friend. I sympathized with the water that smelt of sulphur. People committed all sorts of sins in that area, men were doing it to men, so Allah turned the land upside down, poured loads of salt, and flooded the area with water. The whole region was completely childless and arid. In the faint light of the morning, whenever I looked at the rounded sparkling oranges I saw rounded babies. I rubbed my breasts when I saw a camel breastfeeding its calf. I was besieged by fertility; ripe fruit and children playing in the yard all day long. Aunt Tamam saw them as a reminder; I did not need such a reminder. I spun and spun like a silkworm. The number of threads I managed to produce were enough to cover our hazy valley; enough to reach Harb wherever he was and even enough to reach my mother. I wanted to hug her and cry on her shoulder. Aunt Tamam looked at me suspiciously, smacked her lips, and said, "Darkness has landed. Are you still carrying that spinning-wheel?"

After sunset, I heard the familiar sounds of galloping hooves. Harb's appearance was as refreshing as the smell of cardamom, the scent of orange blossoms, even as the perfume of paradise. "Welcome, companion of my soul." He pulled me smilingly indoors and kissed me harshly on the lips. He smelt of long dusty nights and fatigue. I smelt of basil and wool tufts. I thought I would never see him again with my own eyes.

"Are you still spinning. It is not good for your beautiful eyes."

"It is better than listening to old women."

"Are they still talking about you?"

"It is just six months," I cried and pulled Harb down to the floor.

I sat on top of him and threw his headdress away, unbuckled his ammunition belt, and unbuttoned his cotton robe. I started kissing and nibbling at his naked chest like a ghoul that hungered for the flesh of a living creature. When I ran my tongue over his eyelashes, he shuddered. I must have hurt him with my sucking and biting because he tried to push me away. I dug my knees into the sides of his waist and gasped, "I am not barren. Do you hear me?"

"You are a strong mare. My mare." Then, gasping for breath, my husband said, "Don't listen to old women."

I placed my head on his thigh and started crying. Tears chasing tears, chasing anger and humiliation. Harb kept stroking my hair and kissing the hot tears, until I stopped crying and said, "Aunt Tamam wants me to go with her to Hajjeh Hulala."

"Allah knows that I want hundreds of sons. Your sons."

I wiped my tears and said, "Then, I will go."

"Count on Allah," he said, and ran his fingers over my empty belly. The touch of his rough fingers made me realize how worn and exhausted my husband was. "Have you been raiding other tribes again?"

"No, not other tribes. Do you have a morsel for me to eat?"

I unwrapped the bread and placed some loaves on the straw tray. When I left the room the air was cool and inviting. I heard the dogs barking and a shot in the distance. The cries of Raai, the watchman, added a familiar edge to the sounds of the night. I lit some kindling and boiled tea and fried two eggs in the baking tin. Harb would not leave me if I fed him properly and took good care of him. I was childless and must be a perfect housewife and mistress. I carried the loaded tray with difficulty and slid it through the half-opened door. My poor husband was in his seventh sleep. I covered him with his cloak and one of the sheepskin rugs. Where did he go when he left our dwelling? What did he do to make him that lean and tired?

Harb mounted his horse and galloped back to the mountains. I told Aunt Tamam that I would go with her to see Hajjeh Hulala. She puffed some smoke and said that it was time for me to be sensible. That was it. By agreeing to go to Hajjeh Hulala I stamped myself with the word "barren." Every living creature would know about my visit and start weaving stories and finding reasons for my barrenness. It must be fear because when she was young she saw the body of her mother flung on the floor of the shrine. She had to take care of her father at a very young age. She carried two sacks of barley and that broke her back and finished her chances. When she failed to pray for the soul of the prophet, an evil eye hit her. Men say that she spent her wedding night in the sea, the minerals and salts gushed to her womb and destroyed it. I could hear the hissing sounds of leaves when hit by a light breeze. The hissing sound which covered the whole valley and ascended to Latroun Mountain and tapped on the painted windows of the monastery; the hissing sounds which climbed up to Mukaber Mountain in Jerusalem and visited the Aqsa mosque which cried five times a day; the sounds even reached the mountains of Salt where my husband and his brothers lived and told them the story of my scandal. Harb's companions laughed and said to him, "If you bought an English rifle and found out that it did not shoot, what would you do? You would throw it away and buy another."

Um Saad

I was still holding my pillow and thinking of English rifles when Um Saad, my companion in the hazy hospital, called my name. "Maha, sister."

It was a moonless night. The cold breeze failed to blow away the smell of medicated soap and water. I lifted myself up, placed the pillow behind my back and answered, "Yes, Um Saad."

"Even the moon went to sleep. I used to watch it through the star-shaped holes in the wooden shutter. Eh, years had passed and I was still peeping at life striding by. The Father of Light was singing in Circassian as he lit kerosene street lamps. They reminded me of gallows, those wooden arms. Amman was like a spacious Ottoman prison. He used to hold the spark up and light the lamp. Gradually, the narrow streets were flooded with flickering light. My favorite time of the day. Sparkles and glitters and the sad voice of the Father of Light. He must have been mourning the loss of the vast meadows and the frozen springs of the Caucasus. My father used to call me Haniyyeh the dreamer.

71

The star-shaped holes in the wooden shutter used to let in a mild breeze to that crowded room. Full of cushions . . ."

"We use mattresses and pillows. Daffash sold most of them to Samir Pasha. He wanted to buy armchairs instead."

"Who is Daffash you keep talking about?"

"My brother, the son of my father. He was like winter sun. Now you know him and now you don't. Ruthlessness and kindness kneaded together."

"Daffash? What a name! Is he good-looking?"

"May Allah reward you, we are too old for that." I smiled and placed my hand over my mouth to hide the missing teeth.

"You are not. I am. Oh, yes, I am. Days have come and days have gone. I was even in love. Then my heart used to roll like the wheels of the carts carrying maize. Muhammad. Tall, strong, and blonde. He was Circassian. Whenever I passed by his store, I used to wrap the *mulaya* tightly around my chest. I wanted to hide my breast. My father used to say, 'You are not a child any more. Your breasts are as big as melons.' I was really shy of my melons. I used to bend my back to hide them, bury them in my chest. That is why I am hunchbacked now.

"Oh! The love and longing. For love I wanted to be taller, whiter, and more rounded. Funny. When it is too late, you learn to live with your looks. I believed that Abu Shawmer the chemist with his herbs and chemicals would give me a prescription that would make my nose smaller, my lips fuller, my ribs less protruding, and my toes shorter. It is too late now. Allah gave and Allah took, but the Father of Light outlived us all. The crooked streetlamps are no more. They slid under the carpets of the Grand Mosque. Amman has electricity now. The gallows were pushed under the carpets of the mosque."

"Electricity? My village has none."

"Darkness is merciful. Light is cruel."

"What are you talking about, my sister?"

"Nothing, the streetlamps, star-shaped holes, and the Father of Light. When I shut my eyes, when the eyelids slide over the pupils, I see floating stars. That was my world . . ."

Maha

I shut my ears with the palms of my hands and walked silently behind Aunt Tamam who dragged her old feet across the bare land. I stared at the tips of my toes and saw the smiling face of my mother and the gleaming eyes of my father. Dring-drang-dring-drang went the pestle and mortar inside me. Hajjeh Hulala took shelter in one of the old dolmens on the outskirts of Hamia.

Just two stone slabs covered with a larger third one. The decaying dolmen was surrounded with bitter zaqqum trees to ward off the young devils. When I entered the spacious room I realized how cold it was inside. Part of the roof must have fallen down and Hulala had covered it with a thick rug.

"Hajjeh Hulala," cried Aunt Tamam.

"Welcome, guests of the Merciful," she said, and stuck her head out of a small opening in the wall. She came through the trees and said in a husky voice, "So you managed to convince the young bride." I recognized the damp smell of gazelles' blood in the room. "Um

73

Harb, you have brought the patient. You can go now."

"No. Aunt, don't leave."

"Do whatever Hajjeh Hulala tells you. Peace be upon you," she said. A puff of smoke from her pipe, then she disappeared.

Hulala held my hand, squeezed it, then asked me to sit down. The scent of incense and smoldering ashes filled that space. Tears rushed to my eyes. It was a cloud of smoke suspended between the zaqqum trees. The blurred view of the brazier and ashes swayed to the left, to the right, then stopped in the middle. With her bony fingers, Hulala held my shoulders and pushed me gently to the mattress. Pieces of gray muslin, grains, dry herbs, metal sticks, and the evil eye were hanging from the wall. A heap of rubbish. "Lie down, my daughter," she said, and drew a circle in the air with her fingers.

The small black pot placed over the ashes added steam to the already stuffy room. The stinging smell of herbs filled my nostrils. The hissing sound of leaves was soothing. "Take off your clothes, Maha," she whispered.

"No."

"Just do what I tell you. We want to get rid of the evil spirit inside your belly." Unhooking a piece of muslin which was hanging on the wall she cried, "O Allah!" Hajjeh Hulala looked at me in a strange way and threw two stalks of dry herbs in the boiling water. With hesitant fingers I took off my robe. The bony finger pointed at my trousers and petticoat. I shook my head. "You must." Stretched stark naked on that soiled mattress, enveloped with suffocating smoke and steam, I felt that I was dead and was about to be fried in hell.

Hulala ran her fingers gently on every part of my body then started stroking my breasts. I stiffened. "Relax. You must relax for this remedy to work." I shut my eyes and tried to imagine that the bony fingers were Harb's hairy ones. He was stroking my hair, rubbing my nipples and my belly. Light circular movements all over my body. When she stopped massaging me, I opened my eyes and saw her draining the herbs and tying them in the muslin. She dipped the bundle again in the boiling water, placed her warm hands over my belly and started rubbing. Her fingers went lower and lower.

"Hajjeh!" I objected.

"Your body will suck the juices of the herbs. Relax." I soared higher

74

and higher like an imprisoned pigeon that was suddenly set free. When Hulala stuck the small bundle inside me, I exploded. The juice rushed, stinging its way up like ground red pepper. I started weeping.

"Don't weep. It should be hot. You keep it in there for three days and when your man comes back you let him mount you."

The juices ran up to my brain and scalded it. I had to keep that thing in for three days. While limping back to my house, I felt that the sun was playing games with me. It landed on my head then left me. My body was covered in sweat and my legs were too weak to carry me. When the puffing pipe saw me staggering back home, she held my hand. I lay on the cold floor and placed my cheeks on the cool surface. No use. I buried my head under the pillows and tried to think of our cool farm. No use. Roaring flames dashed up to my head which caught fire like dry palm leaves. The fire was too much to put up with, so I begged Tamam to cover the window with a sack. Voices. Just voices. "What has she done to you?" Uhhh. Blurred quizzical faces followed by absolute darkness.

They must eat dung. All of them. They wanted children from the milking cow. Eat dog's shit. They dragged me to the bed and tucked me under the blanket. I threw the blanket off with all the strength I had and spat on the floor. I must pull the sachet out. The more it hurts the better. I stuck my fingers into my trousers but two thin hands stopped me from pulling the herbs out and throwing them in their faces. "Patience, my daughter." It was only three days. Uhhhhh. I did not want children. I was barren. Barren. Do you hear me? "Tamam, get your son another wife," I cried at the top of my voice and started swaying. Recall Allah, recall Allah. "Oh my sisters. A fire that does not know Allah caught my belly."

Nasra dashed into the room and instantly the air became lighter. She dipped a piece of cloth in the can of water she was carrying and wiped my face. "From the Long Well," she whispered. Her earring was trembling. Very cold. Nasra rubbed my chest, hands, and feet. "Better, my sister."

I held the end of Nasra's sleeve and said, "Ask them to leave."

She clapped her hands and said, "Neighbors, wants to have some sleep, Maha."

Allah lengthen Nasra's life. Aunt Tamam was there because her smoke was filling the room. "I want Tamam to leave me alone."

"Go out, Tamam. The smoke." I heard the click of the withered lips and smiled.

Wiping my forehead, Nasra asked me earnestly, "Want children, Maha?"

I nodded.

"May never have children, me," she said.

Nasra's green eyes looked brighter than usual. I held her hand.

"Your brother, Maha."

I tightened my grip on her hand.

She smiled and said, "If you want children, only medicine, red pepper."

"It's only been six months."

"No mercy in the valley." She scratched her head and promised to visit me regularly and play me the pipe. When she played her reed-pipe the room was filled with serene tunes, tunes that lull you to ease and oblivion. That night, I dreamt of green meadows, grazing sheep, and a spakrling blue sky with bright beams of light. Nasra's cold cloth and tunes helped me to stay alive for those three days. I pulled the sachet out and sighed. Tamam said that I would be one of the selected people who would go to paradise because of the beautiful dream I had. Harb's arms were my paradise. I smiled and turned my head towards the window and followed the sunbeam which landed on the unfinished carpet.

When I saw Harb that morning my heart fluttered in my chest like a small sparrow. When he hugged me I started weeping like a baby. The twin of my soul was leaner than ever. I sat next to him and told him about the remedies they stuck into me to give him a son. "Do you want me to get married to another woman?" The old puffing pipe must have told him about my fit. May Allah break the pipe of Tamam.

"No," I said.

"I don't want any other woman. Maha, the mare which has noble origin will let nobody humiliate her."

I held him tight. Soon, he would ride his stallion, gallop up the mountain, and disappear in a cloud of dust. I held him tight. He was thin, tired, and about to depart again.

It was still very early in the morning and the sunlight did not yet

76

give color to the creatures of Allah. The mud houses and the court-
yards crowded with sleeping animals were swathed in silence. The cooing
and twittering of doves and sparrows swam in the river, soared high,
then became clear and harsh. I would never part with the sound of
running water. Summer's golden feet had turned the few pieces of cul-
tivated land to seas of Ottoman gold. I could hear the songs of grain
reapers rising from the threshing floors. Nasra was already in the
mountains and the breeze carried the plaintive tunes of her pipe. The
cries of Raai no longer urged people to get up. The cocks started
crowing when Raai stopped calling. I put on my mother's velvet robe
and my plastic slippers and told the old pipe that I was going to visit
my father. I must consult him before they cauterize me.

Walking back to our orchard, I realized that I was returning empty-
handed. Nothing in my hands, nothing in my belly. I was still without a child. No remedy left except cauterizing, except burning my
skin and scarring me for life. When I entered our courtyard Nashmi
ran towards me and started licking my feet. I hugged him and realized how much I had missed the old farm. While stroking his neck I
noticed that Nashmi's eyes were full of tears like the eyes of his master Sheikh Nimer. My father must have heard my voice because he
went out of the house still fumbling with the buttons of his striped
shirt. I kissed the back of his flaky hand and hugged him. He smelt of
manure and dry yogurt. "Maha, my daughter," he said in his gritty
voice. I used to fear him when I was young, now my heart reached
out to hold him. Nashmi and my father were growing old and could
hardly feed themselves. He could not wash that shirt which time stepped
on whenever it passed through our valley. I kissed his hand again and
asked him why he was so thin. He tried to laugh, exposing toothless
gums. "Welcome, daughter of Maliha. Come in."

The room was almost empty except for a mattress which was flung
on the floor and a sheepskin rug. The pile of mattresses had disappeared and the walls were almost bare. My grandmother's circular mirror
was standing in the corner. My father saw the surprised expression on
my face and said, "Daffash lent the mattresses to Samir Pasha. He's
having a party." Say goodbye to the pure wool mattresses sewed by
my mother. Our cow Halabeh, our horse Mujahid, the two camels,
and two young ones were missing too.

"Where is our herd?"

"Daffash sold them. He wants to buy a Land Rover."

There was nothing left of the henna and radishes.

"He talks about modernizing the farm. He wants to build a villa and import Indians to work in the field," he said.

"Jarbwa told me that he is neglecting the farm," I said.

My father poked the floor with his stick and said, "He is trying to raise money for the farm."

I walked out of the house. The only living creatures in our yard were a few hens which, instead of living in their cage, strolled in and out of the empty storage room.

The farm looked abandoned. The orange and lemon trees were all crying, "Water, water." I sat near the old canal and shed tears, adding to the water of the Jordan and to the saltiness of the Dead Sea. If my mother Maliha came back to life and saw her once prosperous house turned to ruins she would choose death again. My father, like the farm, was weak, dirty, and decaying.

He stroked my hair with his flaky fingers and asked me to stop crying. "I am happy the way I am." He hit the ground with his stick and continued, "The people of the village want me to get married. I do not want another woman to sleep next to me."

"I am afraid that one of these days you will die alone."

"I am waiting for that day to meet Maliha," he said, and limped back to the house leaning heavily on his stick.

Um Saad

"Maha, my sister."

I was fingering the sheath of Harb's dagger. The silver had lost its brilliance and turned dull gray, but the turquoise resisted the dampness of days. "Yes, Um Saad. All the creatures of Allah have gone to sleep. You can now pour out the sorrow of your heart."

"I don't know what to say, where to start. They just beat me without a reason. I will never forget the moustache of my father and his wide black trousers. Two eagles could sit on his bushy moustache. The soothing songs and cries of the night.

> 'Dark-haired beauty.
> Oh dark-haired beauty.
> You are the glass,
> And your lips are wine.'

"The neighborhood singer was chanting in his clear voice. The cries of babies being bathed or demanding the breasts of their mothers filled the pine-covered riverbed. When I heard the breathless tunes of a Circassian accordion, I sighed. There was a wedding in the Immigrants' Quarter. I looked through the star-shaped holes and wished that my soul could extend and sneak out through the holes and touch the shoulder of Muhammad. 'Why did you lift up the shutter, girl?' my father shouted at me, and started beating me with his leather belt. The buckle was cold and sharp. When I stopped whining and whimpering, I slept under the window on the cushions. That night, I dreamt of the Vanishing Cap. I wanted to be invisible like ether. I wanted to slip into another identity. Can you cast off your identity like dirty underwear? Can you?"

"Identity? What is identity. I think I have none."

"Maha, poor Maha."

"Please continue, Um Saad."

"I put on the *mulaya* after covering my face with white powder. My mother allowed me to use her make-up for the first time that morning. I did not want Muhammad to see the bruised chin. I entered his store and stuck my shaking fingers into the grains of rice. He looked at me. I started crying like a fool. He snatched my right arm scattering some rice grains on the cold concrete. 'Follow me,' he said. I followed him. In the small cave behind the store, he lifted the black veil and kissed my powdered chin. 'No, you must not. Do not touch me.'

"'I want to marry you,' he said.

"I panicked and dashed out of the store to the hot street. If my father had seen me, he would have beaten me to death.

"My mother would kill me if I didn't buy the dry roses. I pulled up the black cape and walked to Abu Shawmer's shop. Dry roses for the throat, dry jasmine for the voice, Bride's Cream for a clear complexion, Cow's Bead Jam for fuller breasts. Oh, I wanted all of these. I wished I had round hips like Hind Roustom."

"Who is she?"

"A beautiful Egyptian actress. Her voice is husky and she wiggles her hips. I had no hips, nothing. When I heard the clicking of the liquorice juice peddler's cymbals and the cries of candy-floss sellers, I realized that I was happy. The gold market's roof was a café then.

Um Kulthoum was singing to hookah smokers and card players,

'To whom shall I turn?
You are my wound.
You are my happiness.'

"Be happy my heart. Your turn would come. Amman was lovely, was green, was great. By your life, I, Haniyyeh, later on Um Saad, believed then that my turn would come. Happiness was just a few steps away."

Um Saad is happy. I have to eat Sura's food which is like mud. Tasteless. Um Saad talks about happiness. I am cold and tired. I have forgotten the taste of happiness. My life is like scattered flour in a thornfield. O my people, Um Saad never stops talking about happiness. The sheath is without the dagger, without the horseman.

Maha

My father was carrying a heavy load to which I could not add the weight of my barrenness. I dragged my feet across the soil of that forgotten village which stuck to the mountainside like a leech. I shielded my eyes and saw a cloud of dust going down the eastern mountain. The horsemen of the tribe were back. Slowly they approached. I heard the familiar sound of galloping hooves. I knew our horsemen had been out raiding because they had tied both ends of their headdresses together. The war cries filled the lazy alleyways of the village. Allah protect us, our men were fighting. About twenty horsemen drew the reins and dismounted together. Both horses and men looked dirty and sweaty and were panting. One of them was heading towards me and holding his shoulder. "Haaarb," I cried and ran to meet the twin of my soul. He slid down from his horse. I took his hand and led him to the house. His face was covered with sweat and soot. "What have they done to you, my love?"

Hulala boiled some herbs and dressed the gaping wound on Harb's shoulder. I rubbed his face with rose water and was shocked to feel his protruding cheekbones. Poles of tents, which were made of goats' hair. I made Harb drink a cup of boiled milk mixed with honey and raw eggs. He threw up most of it on to my robe. My eyesight was as hot as a smoldering cinder. "You must tell me who did this to you. By my grandmother's soul, I will drink his blood."

He shook his head and then placed it on the pillow. "Maha," he pleaded, then went to sleep. I spent the night watching the moon through our small window. It seemed to toss its head, now here, now there. His intermittent moans and mumblings filled the valley. The "aah" flew from his lips and then landed over every tight chest in Hamia. I should have added some camomile to the milk to ease his pain.

After a short sleep Harb woke up and looked at me prostrating beside him, as if I were praying. "Is that you, Maha?"

"Yes," I held his hand. His face looked darker and his eyes brighter in the moonlight. Our men must have been fighting for days.

He looked me in the eye and said, "It was a big battle."

I wiped the sweat off his forehead and, not expecting an answer, I asked, "Against whom?"

"The Turks and the English. They both want more money."

"Taxes?"

"Yes, in arrears. One foreign rule was replaced by another. First the Turks and now the English."

"We are free bedouins. We never accepted foreign masters," I said.

"We attacked one of their bases at dawn. They attacked us with what looked like metal eagles. We lost many men," he said with tears caught in his eyes. I lent down and kissed him. He buried his face in my chest and said, "We had to withdraw. We had to withdraw."

I pressed his head to my chest. I felt helpless. The village wouldn't allow me to join Harb on the battleground. Harb needed my support. How could I fight the English? I must do anything to get pregnant.

Two rays of light flew out of his lips in the morning when he called my name, "Maha."

"Harb, I am your supporter."

"Lie beside me, deer-eyes." He held my waist tightly with his left arm. I touched his tired eyes with my lips then licked the exhaustion out of his lashes. He kissed my neck and I felt that he needed me, he yearned for rest, for peace. I helped him take off his clothes and stripped myself and made love to him gently, lightly like a feather flowing and landing on a velvet pillow, a feather carried by the lazy breeze of hot summer nights. I curled around him to keep him warm, protect him and save him from the gushing wind which shifts the shape of sand dunes.

"My love for you is frightening, Maha. Like Antar Ibn Shadad, I gallop towards metal eagles because I see a glimpse of your face there, our children's faces and the high foreheads of the Arabs."

My bottled tears rushed up to my eyes and slid down my face recklessly. "By the soul of my grandmother Sabha, I will give you a son."

"Don't cry. I fight in order not to see you crying. Arab mares never cry."

I told him about my father. He said I could go there every afternoon.

Suddenly he said, "If I die, will you take care of my mother?"

My soaring heart sank in the Jordan. "Why do you speak of death?"

"I don't know," he said, and started putting on his raiding gear.

"You cannot fight with that shoulder."

"Just give me your blessings, deer-eyes."

I cried at the top of my voice that morning, "Go. May the eye of Allah guard you. Go. May Allah break the spears of your enemies." I undid my plaits and continued, "Go. My eyes will never know the taste of sleep until you come back." Hands outstretched towards the forgetful sky, I ran behind Harb's galloping stallion, invoking Allah, His angels, His books, and His prophets to protect my man, bring him back safe and wealthy and lengthen his life to see his children crawling around him. I hoped that the ears of the sky would not be deaf and the gushing wind would listen to us instead of listening to its own howl. The sun turned its back on us at sunset and I braided my hair into two plaits.

The Storyteller

In the name of Allah the Benificent, the Merciful, "Lo! ye come with lust unto men instead of women. Nay, but ye are wanton folk."

My most illustrious masters, pray on the soul of the Chosen One, our prophet Muhammad and his righteous companions. Tonight, the fifteenth night of Ramadan, the month of fasting and worshipping, I will tell you the most shameful part of our story. The part that shook Allah in His throne and made Him strike the earth with His cane causing the land to turn upside down. If you dive in the sea you find figures made of salt; pillars of salt, with absolute horror on their faces. Wide-open mouths, crying for help and forgiveness. Yes, the people of Lot in this most contaminated of lands, and the most evil of nations. The hand of the Almighty struck with all its might and fractured the face of the earth. The crack starts in Damascus and ends in darkest Africa. Bang the tambourine across your thigh and let us dance. Let us praise Allah, the King of Judgment Day.

Allah, Allah, is generous Allah,
Allah, is merciful Allah,
Allah, is powerful.

Maha, yes Maha, started howling and barking when she saw the
gaping shoulder of her man. People say that metal bodies crossed the
blue belt surrounding the earth and bombed the man and his band.
My masters, they were winged jinn who wounded her husband as a
warning. She kept playing games with the codes of the soldiers of our
master Solomon. Raai, the watchman, told me that she undid her
plaits, rent off her robe, then, in front of his own eyes, her feet began
twisting backward. A ghoul. A daughter of a ghoul. May Allah protect
us and surround us. She had a glimpse of Raai and opened her mouth
wide, exposing long sharp teeth. The wind she blew out of her mouth
whirled in the village for three days. The hot air slipped through slots
and clefts, making babies cry and bells jingle. Her skin turned into
fish scales; her eyes became rounded and lost the lashes and the lids.
Raai smiled nervously, "When I saw her, my brother, I did it in my
pants." Fear dried Raai's juices, and he has remained sterile until this
very day.

Every tiny mud window, every drop of water, every sleeping soul
heard the hyena crying at the top of her voice when her man left the
village and rode to the mountains. She invoked Gog and Magog and
Harot and Marut, the devils of witchcraft. She warned the evil spirits
that she would go through her initiation ritual in order to acquire
new powers of protection for her and her husband. She cried and the
blowing wind carried the long drawn shrieks to the hollow of the
Dead Sea, then to the mountains of Jerusalem.

"The daughter of Maliha, I am.
The daughter of Sabha, I am.
If you but come near my man,
I will burn you to mud."

The fearless woman kept threatening and reciting. Allah created the
jinn out of fire, and if they get burnt to mud they become human
beings like us. They lose their powers, grow old then die.

The two ravens of parting, Tamam and Nasra, walked to the dolmen for Maha's initiation party. She thought that by acquiring new powers and help from other magicians, Allah preserve us, no creature whether jinnee or human could come near her or her man. They advanced along the dung-covered alleyways and greeted no one. A knot on each forehead like a cross and a blood spot in each left eye. You can hear the hurried slamming of doors and urgent clicking of windows. The people of Hamia, who had no dignity whatsoever, tried to shut out evil. My Aziza shuddered and started braying. The scene of the three ravens of parting, the smell of burnt herbs and the sick yellow sun foretold that all the jinn of the earth were about to meet in the devil-accursed valley.

Most generous masters, the name of Allah shield us, I heard a distant whistling of huge objects then a horrible explosion. Drops of blood hovered over the mountaintop. The oozing blood covered the blue sky and trickled down to the valley. When I blinked the whole redness of the horizon disappeared. I slapped my face to see whether I was asleep or dragging my feet across the blazing sand of the bleak valley. I sat on a rock that was sticking out of the mountain ridge like a tooth and watched the three ravens shrink until they became three blurred cockroaches. I scratched my lard-covered head and descended the mountain to peep through the slot of the dolmen. When I was not far from the magicians' den, I saw Tamam and the mad shepherdess leaving hurriedly. My heart started beating because I knew that I would see something great, an unforgettable incident that would leave its mark on my heart, on Maymoon's heart, and in the tired heart of Aziza.

I tied my she-ass Aziza and my monkey Maymoon to a dry tree trunk and trod gently through the dry bushes. I held a bow of zaqqum and peeped through the slot between the stones which were built by heathens thousands of years ago. Infidels inhabiting the houses of infidels. Masters and mistresses, who am I? Your slave Sami al-Adjnabi. Who am I?

> I am the storyteller,
> My box is full of tales.
> I am the yarn-spinner,
> I spin and spin for days.

I peeped through the opening between the large flat stones and what did I see? I saw a naked white figure lying on the floor and — may Allah forgive us all — a black figure leaning over it. Black smoke, kissing, and oh's. Sighing and licking and black smoke. I started sweating like an overworked mule and mentioned Allah. If you sliced the two figures from each other with a sword, you would not tell whose blood you shed. The land of Sodom and Gomorrah shook with pleasure and disgust. The Dead Sea roared its approval and the ignorant village did not know what took place under its roof.

Hulala, the daughter of a well-known Moroccan sorcerer who came to Arabia to look for treasure, stuck her head between the lean thighs of the barren bride. The sound the bride uttered was like the purrs of a cat lying in the warm sunshine being rubbed upon its belly. Purrr. Defying and yielding sound. Purrr. I tightened my belt around my drooping stomach and prayed two prostrations asking for Allah's forgiveness. I was sitting under the zaqqum tree counting the beads of my rosary, when I saw her. Yes, I saw Maha. Limping out of the den, she was; gazing at the hot sun, she was; swimming in pleasure and sweat, she was. She fell down on the ground, stretched her hands and legs, then struggled to her feet and walked back to the village. I did not see her face, but I saw the red spot in the whiteness of the eye and the black clot in the heart.

At that moment, I asked myself what was I doing in that mad valley? Allah might strike the land again and bury us all alive underneath the earth. I held the halter of Aziza, carried Maymoon on my shoulder, and headed for the mountains. The fluid would not reach me there, but I might turn into a pillar of salt. The crimson sunset burned on the cliffs of the mountain, slanting ladders of hazy fire down the sharp rocks. The clear sharp landscape cleansed my mind and rendered my soul vacant from pressure and misery. I must leave the valley of bad omens. The sunlight grew pale, mellowing the hot wind. I shivered and sat down on the top of the mountain, facing the monastery of Siyagha. The monks of Madaba used to send messages to the monks of Latroun on the West Bank by waving their lamps at night. Just a shimmer of light escaped through the narrow painted windows. "Kyrie Eleison, Kyrie Eleison," they must be repeating now. Latroun Monastery glittered in the distance. The lights of the village sitting in the bottom of the valley were going off one after another.

I wrapped my shoulders with a sheepskin rug and scratched my skull. The blacksmith Salih must be beating his wife now. Nasra was still playing her stupid pipe and collecting her sheep. Sheikh Talib must be dreaming of Sittna Badryya who was sleeping on silk rugs. Sheikh Nimer was crying over his Maliha and feeding Nashmi his loyal dog. Raai had finished with his wife and was ready to go for his round. Imam Rajab was preparing for his Friday trip to the shrine of prophet Shuayb. Maha? Maha was till trying to drown the horseman in the sea of her magic. Daffash? Where was Daffash?

The lights of Samir Pasha's villa sparkled like the reflection of moonlight on calm water. I pulled Aziza's halter and trudged down to the north side of the village to keep out of Raai's path. The sound of heavy breathing and the smell of soap and water filled the deserted alleyways. Dirty dogs, all of them. They washed once a month and combed out the fur regularly. The wide road was bordered with willow trees. The shack of the guard was empty except for a Jeft rifle leaning on the wall. I sneaked in quickly and tied my Aziza to a lemon tree. I hugged Maymoon and ran to the villa as quickly as possible. Like wind, I sped down the narrow road leading to the thick garden. The smell of wine and roasted duck wafted out of half-opened doors. The sound of drum and brass made my heart sink between my knees. Full of nostalgia, it was. With the end of my sleeve, I wiped a circular hole in the thick layer of dust clinging to the window shield.

O what I saw! Flickering candles, semi-nude women, and men in black suits. There was only one long robe and a cloak. Who was it? Daffash? Yes, yes. Like her shadow, he followed the English girl who had attended the wedding of his sister Maha. Rose Bell, her name was. She pushed his hand away and danced with Samir Pasha. They started swinging and jumping like monkeys, then the English girl flew in the air and slid between the wide-open legs of Samir Pasha. Half-naked women sliding between the thighs of men? Allah protect us and forgive us. The Englishmen did not even raise an eyebrow. By Allah, we live and see.

The dark girl cracked with laughter at a joke whispered in her ear by a person wearing white gloves. The spacious room was crowded with blonde people smoking fat, brown cigarettes. The windows steamed with their breath. I could not see properly. Shadow drinking and laughing and persistent drums. Suddenly, Daffash shouted something and stood in the middle. He held the end of his cloak and started dancing the Dhiyya. They all pointed at him and shrieked with laughter. He drew a long breath and sang,

> "Welcome, welcome, hey boy.
> My friend, my ally, hey boy."

In a different tongue, a woman said something which sounded like "Aba-al-Jimaal" or "Ora-Jinal." Praise be to Allah who gave us the use of tongues and languages. Praise be to Him the One and Only. "Father-of-Camels"? What a funny lady. With her feathers and tight black dress, what does she know about camels? Ha Ha Ha.

Maha

I asked my aunt Tamam to take me to Hulala for cauterizing. She puffed some smoke and said she would ask Hamda and Nasra to go with us. We walked slowly on the almost bare ground. It was the funeral of my peace of mind. After that day, I never saw the face of deep sleep nor had a lick of happiness. The croaks of a frog echoed inside my head. Croak, croak, croak. I had promised that wounded man to do whatever I could to give him a child. The wind erased my footsteps and even Shamam, the best tracker of Arabia, would never find me.

When we entered the dusty room of Hulala, we found her bowing and kneeling, praying to the Allah of the universe. After she had greeted the two angels sitting on her shoulders, she greeted our group of women. She invited us to sit down. "Welcome, Tamam."

"To the one who welcomes us," said Tamam, and added, "This woman is still not pregnant. She depends on Allah first and on you second."

91

Hulala nodded her head, spread a sheepskin rug on the floor, and placed a number of big iron bars upon it. Some bars were long and sharp, some were short and heavy, others were thin and winding. I shuddered as if stung by a bee on the lobe of my ear. The ends were pointed and sharp. The big pestle inside me started grinding. If the bars were going to be stuck inside me I would not be able to bear it.

"Aunt, is it painful? Cauterizing?"
"Rely on the wise Allah."

Hulala chose a thin iron bar and threw it in the air. It landed in the smoldering ashes and started ticking. The bar resisted the melting influence of the fire. Nasra blew her pipe and it screamed, then uttered a long sigh. The smoke trails of Aunt Tamam's pipe gathered in the air and formed all sorts of shapes: a galloping mare, a flying dove, flocks emigrating from that forgotten village. A basalt quern ground all the grains of bravery, all my courage and left me sweating and shivering. Hamda turned her head away from the fire. Hulala sat on the floor and stared at the roaring flames. She suddenly began swaying and swinging like the flames. When the bar turned into a piece of smoldering iron, Hulala cried,

"Of fire, fire, fire,
Mother, mother, mother,
Scald and smolder,
Cure and linger."

"Ooooh fire, fire, fire," the women joined in.
"Lie down and take off your clothes," Hulala ordered me. My clothes? I had to take off my clothes this time too. My luck was like scattered flour. Hamda dug her knees into my shoulders and Tamam sat on my feet. "Ooooh fire, FIRE." The dolmen was full of the stinging smell of ashes and sweat. They were about to scald me and mark my skin for life. "No! No!" I cried. My friend Nasra dashed out of the stuffy den. A blazing iron bar passed over my head and landed on my belly digging its way down my skin. I kicked Tamam and sent her pipe flying in a cloud of smoke. Generous drops of water. Hamda was crying over my head. A

distant shot, a camel grumbling in the desert. I departed the world of light to the world of darkness where you cannot see and be sorry.

When I woke up I heard the tunes of Nasra complaining. I wanted my mother, Maliha. My flesh was tearing itself apart. A pack of wild dogs chewing at a shot fox. Harb must save me. The water slapped the tender parts of my body. Now inside, now outside. The mist prevented me from seeing the expression on Harb's face. My tired ears heard the sound of waves and the groans of Harb. The stuffy den was besieged by the cursed zaqqum trees. It floated in the forgotten village which clung to the mountainside like a leech. I bent my back to see the mark. Muslin soaked with dark blood lurked on my belly, like big-eyed owls sit on boughs of cedar trees.

"My sisters, I am under your protection. Please give me something to stop the pain." Hulala handed me a drink so bitter that it tasted as if aloe had been squeezed and boiled. I drank it quickly. My skin shrank, tightened, including my cauterized belly.

Nasra came back and started the usual cool wiping.

Hulala sat in the corner and hummed, "O fire, O mother."

Hamda took my hand and helped me to stand on my frail legs.

Tamam pulled the pipe out of her twisted mouth and said, "May Allah bless your hands." Hulala did not answer. She went on swaying and singing.

We left the zaqqum island and crossed to the boiling sea of sand. The soles of my feet dug the surface looking for a cooler layer. Nasra blew into her reed-pipe bringing it back to life. The plaintive tunes carried with them spring, marguerites, red anemones, green meadows, and contented sheep. I tried to see the greenery, the dew and bright morning, but all I managed to make out was the small mud houses with washed-out eyes. The sun was merciless that afternoon and scorched everything it touched: the old walls, the scattered palm trees, and my brain.

I swam in a pool of sweat. Hot. It was very hot. I tried to summon a cool memory, our citrus orchard, the misty canal, and the henna and radishes. My father sat on the doorstep of our house at the other end of Hamia where the soil was more lenient and giving. There, the sun wore a translucent veil like the costumes of the gypsy dancers. The old man was perishing silently under the thick roof of our storeroom. I should have asked him about cauterizing. But my poor father had enough devils of his own.

Um Saad

"Maha, my sister."

"Yes, Um Saad."

"What shall I tell you? What shall I recount to you about the days of crying and laughter in Amman. We used to have a reception once a month. My mother, Allah bless her soul, chose the first Monday of each month to be her guests' day. All the neighbors and relatives used to visit us on that day. These used to be the hardest days for me. We started sweeping at sunrise and finished at sunset. The house had to be clean and the floor spotless. By your life, I used to have great fun. Instead of sitting behind the wooden shutter, I sat behind the big black stove. I used to squeeze my thin body behind the stove and ended up smelling of kerosene.

"Mother looked at my fingers and said that I was not squeezing the almonds quickly enough."

"Squeezing almonds? City people!"

"Crushing the wet almonds against the rough surface of the clay bowl was so painful. I kept rubbing and pushing until my knuckles became red and swollen. After beating the mattresses and carpets with the straw duster, sweat dripped down my nose. My mother, Allah bless her soul, pushed her wet hair back from her round face and asked me to wear something decent. She had no time for me. Decent? The mauve mohair sweater and the checked skirt. What else? I had no other clothes. I combed my short spiky hair and squeezed my thin body between the walls and the giant stove. I had a good view of the main door.

"Long life for you, they are all dead now. Um Abdu with her co-quettish laugh, Um Sameh with her fat neck and protruding eyes — she had a problem with her thyroid — and Um Rida. As soon as she entered the room, Um Rida used to take off her veil, her black cape, and her thick black tights and throw them on the floor with disgust. She would stand half-naked in her brocaded see-through dress, and would start shaking her belly and wiggling her hips. I wanted to be like her. I wanted to show my melons."

"Your melons?" I asked. Melons? Um Saad's pale, yellowish face.

"My breasts. Um Rida's white skin was so smooth that I used to touch her arm whenever possible.

"When they sat down on the mattresses and armchairs, my mother used to bring the lute, the cymbals, and the drum then shout, 'Haniyyeh, where are you, broken-neck?' She said she had always wanted my neck to be broken because I, the first-born, was a girl and not the boy she had longed for. 'Bring the tray.' The ladies would start playing the lute and singing and I would offer shivering glasses of almond juice. Whenever I used to see a brownish flake floating in a glass, I used to think that it was my skin they were drinking. I was stupid. That's what I was, a stupid idiot. I actually believed that my turn would come.

"After I had offered the cold drinks and the date cakes, I used to sit behind the stove and listen carefully to the women singing,

> 'Hey Saideh, listen to your master.
> I am having a bath.
> Obey your master.
> I am cooking.
> Go to your master.
> I am . . .'

95

"The women would stop singing and start giggling. I would shut my eyes and fill the gap Um Abdu used to leave.

> 'I am looking through an open window.
> Listen to your father.
> I am in Muhammad's store.
> Obey your father.'"

Um Saad stopped singing, turned her head to face the barred window. I was tired. Tired of her stories of "crying and laughter in Amman." I was bored with stories about city life. I craved for a small village with blind mud houses and a river that sped down to the Dead Sea. I yearned for the orange blossoms' cloud of perfume. That night, my heart looked through my ribs and called, "Mubarak, my son. Mubarak. Mubarak."

Maha

Her body was not purged by fire, the mother of Hajjeh Hulala. That day, the sun emitted yellowish beams which made the wound ripe. I gave birth every morning to dark blood and pus. The red swelling discharged a yellow matter and agony became my daily companion. I used to gather brushwood, herbs, and strange-shaped pebbles and my wound used to gather dirt, flakes of skin, fluff, blood, and pus. Nasra came to visit me while I was lying on the floor like an empty sack. She said in her shrill voice, "Weave the carpet. Lying on the floor, idle cock."

"My sister, when I lean forward it hurts."

"Curse their religion," she cried, and dashed out of the room.

Whatever I heard in these days was only with one ear because the other was tuned to the sounds of the galloping hooves of Harb's stallion. The twin of my soul had not yet come back from the raid. Was he all right? Who took care of his wound? What if it were to swell and gather pus like mine. Could he lie down? A word, a sign, anything was better than this silence.

One morning, Nasra brought with her another shepherd called Murjan to see me. Tamam disapproved of her bringing an unescorted young man to the house so she went out. She plodded around the house like a cat on a wintery night.

"Maha, trust me. Knows the secrets of herbs, sheep, seasons, and grazing lands, Murjan. About to lose her leg, my goat. Cleaned and cured, Murjan," Nasra said.

I looked at Murjan's keen and dark face and his honest eyes and said, "Yes." The grinding mortar inside me started its funny tune. Was there anything worse than the state I was in? Harb had disappeared without a word, by body was getting weaker and weaker, and I swam in blood and pus every morning.

When Murjan smiled and said, "Allah is the healer, my mother," I started crying. He actually called me mother. The fifteen-year-old shepherd made me realize how sweet motherhood was. I felt that I would never see children of my own with my eyes.

"Shhh! Nasra, boil some water and add a big quantity of salt," he ordered. He pushed the robe and gasped. "My mother, how can you tolerate such a big swelling? You are like our prophet David." David? The worms ate his infected wounds. Whenever a worm fell off, he used to return it on his body again. I needed David's patience because Harb was away all the time. Murjan dipped his sharp dagger in a brownish liquid and said, "In the name of Allah." The dagger slashed open my wound and I howled. Nasra dashed into the room, splashing water over everything on her way. "When I give you a sign, you pour the water over the wound." Nasra twitched her neck. His hands pressed my belly and the pain they caused was like waves which hit then retreated, hit then retreated, leaving the pebbled shore gasping for breath.

The stinging water burnt its way down the wound. I pressed my chest to stop my heart bouncing out of my ribs. I heard Murjan's pleasant voice but could not understand what he was saying. "I will put some bandage on the wound to drink the pus and poison. You will be all right." For the first time in days, my belly did not feel damp, brackish.

Nasra placed a pillow behind my back and said, "Now, weave, you." Murjan insisted on my sitting down to keep the wound well pressed. He gave me a cup of steaming herbs and said, "This is a combination of rare herbs which I gathered from the mountains of Maan." He smiled, wrapped his cloak around his young figure, and said, "Peace be upon you."

Nasra placed the straw tray on the floor next to me. She must have milked one of her goats. I tried to eat some of the fried egg, but my mouth refused to swallow anything except a few dates and some milk. I leaned on the wall and looked at the rounded hems of the carpet. The glowing orange light which penetrated the small window told me that the sun was turning its back on us. The cries of children being gathered from alleyways and the sounds of horses were soothing sounds, but the ears and the heart were eager for that other sound of galloping hooves.

I stared at the carpet, then touched the uneven surface where my mother must have placed her fingers. Tears have a spirit of their own and they run down whenever the jinnee feels like coming out of its bulgy bottle. I began crying over my beloved husband who had not sent me a word since he left our dwelling. I cried over my mother and my unfinished carpet, over my dying father, and over my barren womb which saw terrible days of festering and fire. I cried over Hamia with its handful of mud houses and careless sun. The river passed by the western side of the village without ever throwing a greeting, and the sea at the southern end shook and swayed, captured in its low land.

Um Saad

"Maha, are you all right? Your face is as pale as a lemon."
"Yes, Um Saad, just keep talking. Your voice eases the pain in my heart."

"Once I was sitting on the cushions and peeping through the star-shaped holes at the Father of Light. His song that night was so sad, so nostalgic, about snow-covered lands and cavalry. Because of religion, they left their country. They came to the country of bare feet. That is what they call the Arabs. I sat there thinking of the Vanishing Cap, of al-Shater Hasan. Disappear, fly, then soar high. A big hairy hand landed on my face. A glimpse of my father's fiery eyes. Beating up, battering. Without uttering a word, without opening my mouth, I ate about a hundred lashes. My father's belt reduced me to a heap of flayed meat. He stood like an eagle above my head and shouted, 'Who is Muhammad?' A quiver started in my heart and spread to my treacherous limbs. Later, I thanked Allah, his prophets and angels because He made me lose consciousness. One of the bastard sons of Amman must have told my father about my visits to the store.

"I was floating in a cloud, when I heard Muhammad's voice in our house. Allah protect us. I jumped out of bed and peeped through the keyhole. There he was, sitting on our worn-out sofa, there he was tall and heart-stirring.

"'My uncle, I came here tonight to ask for the hand of your daughter Haniyyeh.'

"'You know her name as well,' said my father threateningly.

"'I don't want any trouble, I just want to propose.'

"Oh, Maha, my heart was pumping like the grinders of Abu Jamal's mill.

"'But you are a Circassian.'

"'I am a good Muslim.'

"'Our daughter was given to her cousin.'

"I placed my hand on my contracting stomach. My father was lying. I had no relatives in Amman.

"'Is she engaged?'

"'Yes, she is.'

"Muhammad stood up then sat down again. His face seemed flushed and circular. It must have been the keyhole. I rubbed my trembling hands together.

"'I am a strong man and will take care of your daughter. I promise that I will preserve her dignity.' It was important for Circassians. Dignity that is.

"'The answer is no.'

"Muhammad dried his forehead with a white handkerchief, then rushed out of the house. Before falling down to the floor, I heard his heavy footsteps going down the narrow staircase. I collapsed and started calling al-Shater Hasan at the top of my voice. Roll into oblivion. Roll into another identity. Depart this body. My mother poured some icy water over my shivering body. I could not stop the flooding tears; I could not move my arms or legs, I could not stop shouting, 'Hey, Shater Hasan. Bring him to me.'"

I rubbed my eyes. I began understanding what Um Saad meant when she spoke of "identity."

"By your life, my bedouin sister, one week later, they asked me to put on the best dress I had."

"The mohair sweater and checked skirt?" I asked.

"'You will wear one of my dresses,' my mother said in her dwindling voice.

"'But I am too thin.'

"My mother threw a white dress on the old bed and started lining her lips with a purple pencil. Gazing at the reflection of her bright mouth in the mirror, she said, 'We are invited to a wedding.'

"I started jumping up and down. 'Am I allowed to leave the house?'

"'Yes, you are. Your father, with his big heart, has forgiven you.'

"My mother's dress smelt of Ramaj, the cheap Korean perfume she used to wear. I slid it over my head and tied a silk fuchsia scarf around the wide waist of the dress. A needle wrapped in a handkerchief. She even allowed me to put some make-up on. I lined my eyes with kohl, drew a purple circle on each cheek, and painted my cracked lips crimson. Shushu the clown with his everlasting white tear sprang out of the mirror. My hair was longer because of my imprisonment in the house. Um Abdu used to cut my hair with her sharp scissors.

"When we stepped out of the house, a cold wind hit me in the face. I was happy to feel the cold stone steps which led to the street underneath my feet. I looked at the closed shutters and smiled. I did not realize then that I was saying goodbye to the star-shaped holes. While walking on the sidewalk opposite Muhammad's store, I heard his yellow canary singing. My heart shuddered in my tight chest. I fixed my gaze upon the filthy sidewalk.

"Drumbeats and singing flew through the ornamented window,

'We came, we came, we came.
We brought the bride and came.'

"I placed my hand on my chest and asked, 'Whose wedding is it?'

"My father looked me in the eye and said, 'Yours.'

"'Father, please?'

"'Yours.'

"My wedding? My wedding! My wedding. I laughed then started dancing on the doorstep of the big house. Tra-la-la, tra-la-la, be happy my heart."

Um Saad stopped talking and toyed with the pink scarf covering her gray hair. The blue moonlight shone on the metal bars across the window. She raised her eyes and saw me crying like my son Mubarak when he was four months old and teething. She tensed her back and asked in a suppressed voice, "Why are you crying?" I did not answer. I could not answer. Suddenly, her face collapsed and she started crying too. Together we had a fit of howling over her wedding, my wedding, her luck my luck, her life and my life.

Dr. Edwards, with his white coat and steel-blue eyes, dashed into our room and said in a tired voice, "It is very late. You are upsetting other patients." He was about to smile, then changed his mind. "Take this pill, please." We both swallowed the tiny pills and placed our heads on the pillows, waiting for peace to prevail.

I cannot control the evil jinnee when he decides to leave his bulgy bottle. My tears that night washed the sheets, the pillow-case, the hospital room, and even the mountains of Fuhais. With every breath I drew, with every sigh, I called, "Harb, Harb, Harb."

Maha

I welcomed the bright sun the next morning and had a look at the wound. It was clean except for some spots of blood scattered on the surface of the bandage tied around my waist. I felt dry and healthy. No yellow dampness or red swellings. I held the spinning-wheel and fingered the tired wool. My hands missed the roves, the oiled wood, and the rough carpet. I leaned forward and hit the fine wheel to produce thin threads. My threads spread over the valley to protect it from aggressive assaulters, from the forgetful sun and the raids of enemies. The warmth of Harb's hands seeped through my robe and the dressing of my wound and comforted my exhausted body.

Murjan came the same morning to check the dressing. He soaked a cloth in olive oil and some lemon juice to seal and purify the cut. The stinging of the juice made me wince. My belly was even drier and cleaner than before. Soon, I would see the salt of the Dead Sea creeping over it.

Murjan said, "You look much better today."

"I feel better," I smiled. "May Allah protect these hands of yours."
Tamam's old pipe puffed its disapproval, filling the room with suffocating smoke. Hamda's youngest daughter, Jawaher, who had come to
visit me, started coughing. My heart started coughing too when I saw
the glowing brown eyes of Jawaher. The twin of my soul had disappeared in a cloud of dust several weeks ago. I wanted a piece of him,
a child with the same bright eyes, a baby to prove that what took
place between us was not an imagined pool of fresh water at the end
of the horizon, nor a creation of my head which was cauterized by
Hulala's fire.

My father, carrying a sack of oranges, came to visit me. He shuffled
his feet across the clean floor, handed the oranges to Tamam, and sat
at the end of the mattress. "I wish I had become blind before seeing
my little flower this dry and thin. These Arabs, don't they feed you?"
In all these years of heat and pain, I had never seen my father lose his
temper.

"I am fine," I said, and hugged him. He smelt of chicken dung,
cardamom, and thyme. I could feel the sharp bones underneath the
wide cloak.

"Your man took longer this time and they cauterized you. When I
was young I wanted to leave this place. Your mother, Allah forgive
her, prevented me," he said in his gritty voice. The merciless years
passed over the plain of my father's face and shifted the shape of sand
dunes. In the tanned skin whitish lines were carved and looked as
permanent as the tattoo on my mother's chin. She had tried to erase
it using all sorts of acids. I wondered why time instead of tiptoeing
through the desert stamped its feet, weakening limbs and eyesight,
thinning hair and bending bones. The stick my father was leaning on
while squatting on the mattress was straight and firm. "Sheikh Nimer,
you don't eat properly," I reprimanded him.

"I do. We cannot consume our years and our children's years. May
Allah the Merciful bring a good ending." Before leaving the room he
pointed his stick at me and said, "If your husband does not come
back soon, you must move back to your father's house."

The only thing I was able to do while my man was away was to
weave. I stretched the loose woolen threads at the end of the carpet
between the two cross-pieces of wood. I passed wool back and forth

through the long threads supported by the horizontal bar. I hit the pattern into place with the loose shutter. Silence, click, then bang. Silence, click, then bang.

> "My luck is like flour
> Scattered in a thornfield.
> On a windy day, they asked
> Barefoot men to collect it."

My mother had not dyed the roves so I followed suit. Tamam wanted me to boil the wool with saffron, but I refused. I let the brown and cream threads find their own pattern. The rough texture had funny shapes on it like flying sand dunes. For me, all the bizarre drawings were Harb's horse galloping back home. If it was a brown projection, then it was the muzzle of his horse, a circle was the belly of his horse, and if it was just a brown thread then it was the tail of his horse. Days folded days and distances swallowed distances and Harb did not cross the distance between him and me.

Nasra's visits became more frequent. She would sit at the end of the mattress and ask me about my health. "Wants to know if your wound started itching, Murjan."

"Yes. It is drier than the coast of the Dead Sea."

She ululated and said, "Healing, your wound." She started blowing into her pipe and singing:

> "Waiting for the horsemen, we are.
> Slash the long night, he will.
> Bring the sun home, Amen."

I joined in and our voices roamed the valley, begging our men to return to our dwelling. My voice was like the croak of a black raven which brings parting and destruction. "Amen," I used to cry and toss the shuttle to form the dignified face of Harb on the rug. "Amen," silence, click, then bang.

Aunt Tamam entered the room one morning scratching her head. She looked me in the eye and said, "Your wound has healed. Shake your waist and start working."

"Aunt, I want to finish the carpet."

"Your mother's rags. Nonsense."

"This carpet is not the rags of my mother. Her life, her fingers, her skin were spun into this magnificent carpet."

She stuffed the pipe with fresh tobacco and smacked her lips. I folded the carpet, rolled the threads on the spinning-wheel, and placed the shuttle in a sack. When I tried to stand up for the first time in weeks, the floor started swaying beneath my feet. I leaned on the wall and the room went back to its previous position. I tied the scarf and fixed it with a black headband, then stuck my head out of the door.

Summer had landed in the valley and I was able to hear the reapers singing,

> "Our golden crop, ya ya ya
> Cut, put on top, ya ya ya."

My soul welcomed the smell of orange blossoms. Soon the crops would be sold and patient girls would get married. The shooting and horseracing would prevent us from going to sleep in the hot summer nights. I went round the house to say "Good morning" to my plants. In the small bed the radishes, henna, and basil were all yellow, limp, dead. A strange wind had blown in the valley and something evil had fallen upon our heads. Just for some stupid, limp stems. Must not be stupid. The brownish leaves which yielded to their maker spoke to me of death and bodies stretched in shrines. I was sure that what I smelt was the stink of decay and life deserting creatures.

Um Saad

"Maha, my sister."

"Yes, Um Saad."

"Are you better now? Did the fog wrapping you clear up?"

"Yes. The room is cloudless," I said, and looked through the barred window. I shook my head to get rid of the dimness caused by the English doctor's drugs. The steep valley surrounding the hospital was full of mist, fog that made fields invisible. You heard the songs of peasants, you smelt the tilled soil, you even felt the frost, but never saw it.

"Who wants to have a clear head? Who wants to remember how my father slapped my face there and then and pushed me inside the house? By your life, when I saw the gleaming faces of the women waiting to see the bride and inspect her, my legs started trembling and I looked at my father again who stood at the door, blocking the sight of the street. With a shaky voice, I whispered, 'My father, Allah protect your women, Allah lengthen your life. I will be your slave girl for the rest of my life.' He shook his turbaned head. I was pushed by the eager women to the dais and sat there with my hands folded in my lap. I felt like a glowing goat stuffed with rice and minced beef and decorated with parsley, ready to be served to the hissing heads."

Through the window, I made out a black figure in the distance. A black ant? A woman uprooting weeds from her land? I looked at my fingernails. Clean. White with no mud lining.

"When I saw the soggy cheeks of the bridegroom and his aging hands, I looked pleadingly at my father who was still standing in front of the door and holding the frame with his hand. Maha, strange, I cannot remember what happened to me that evening. Just two gold bracelets, a ring, and soggy cheeks. That is all. No, may Allah never help me to lie. An old imam asked me if I could write my name. I nodded. In a blank white square I wrote down my name, Haniyyeh Fuad Hajjo. I heard the voice of my *kutab* teacher reading the Qur'an and shouting, 'Repeat after me.'"

Looking at the frost-shrouded vine trees, I said, "I don't know how to read and write."

"It is better for you. You know what makes me really angry?"

I thought of how the peasants of Fuhais lost this year's crop. "What?" I responded to Um Saad's question not because I wanted to, but because she expected me to.

"Amman, the people of Amman. I used to love that city from the bottom of my heart. Now, I cannot stand hearing Amman's laughter. I stood behind the barred window of the bridegroom's house and heard the clicking of cart wheels and the tinkling cymbals of licorice-juice peddlers. It is an absent-minded city."

Talking to the frost, I said, "Our village is just forgotten."

"I will never forget one thing. At night, the man, my husband, who afterwards I discovered was called Abu Saad, chased me and ripped my dress apart. Then he asked me in a weak, thin voice that made the bulk of his body look like a mistake, 'Have you had your period?' I shook my head. 'All the same.'

"He looked at me assessingly, patted my hairless stomach with his cold fingers, forced my legs open, then penetrated my discarded body. O bride, candles around us, sang the women outside. A sticky yellow liquid ran down my thighs. O bride, you are a carnation. I hugged myself tightly and kept repeating the name of al-Shater Hasan. If I am really mad, then my brain must have crumbled down that night because I saw a flying cap in the room."

"Shhh, we are not mad."

Doctor Edwards and Salam, the angelic smile, entered our room. I could not hear their light footsteps. He said something in English, "Impossible," then said in broken Arabic, "You two never stop talking."

"Yes," we said together.

"I will increase the dose."

I looked at Um Saad's face and one of the muscles in her cheek was twitching. She was laughing. I placed my hand over my mouth to cover the bare gums and started giggling. Um Saad suddenly roared with laughter. The doctor loosened the tight collar at his neck and gazed at us, baffled.

Maha

When I turned my head, I saw Nasra and her sheep running down the mountain edge at full speed. The cloud of dust descended and stopped near my feet. I was able to see Nawmeh, the goat of disasters, and the joggling earring. "My sister," she gasped. Curse Nasra's religion, she was always gasping for breath. She held my hands and repeated, "My sister."

"You wrenched my heart. What is it, raven of parting?"

"The horsemen of our tribe," she panted. Her puzzled green eyes looked at me.

"By Allah, I am the daughter of Sabha. Say it."

She pulled the lobe of her ear and said, "Slaughtered like sheep." His body knocked down; blood, veins, and muscles. Destroyed. I pressed my hands on my eyes, blocking away the scene of falling men. I pushed my headband up.

"Hakim. Raided them with metal eagles, the English. Sparkling balls over their heads. Shreds of cloth and oozing flesh, our men."

111

I uncovered my head, undid my plaits, and shrieked, "Harb." I yanked my hair and threw myself on the ground shouting at the top of my voice, "Harb." I tore the front of my dress, filled my palms with soil, and threw it over my head. My outstretched hands and the dust-covered head begged to be buried. "Harb, the twin of my soul," I howled, and the echo of my wounded voice broke over ridges and the tops of mountains, then slid down to the deaf sea.

The Storyteller

I n the name of Allah the Beneficent, the Merciful, "When Earth is shaken with (final) earthquake, and Earth yieldeth up her burdens, and man saith: What aileth her? That day she will relate her chronicles."

Oh most illustrious masters, pray for the souls of the full moon, our prophet Muhammad, and his righteous companions. Tonight, the twenty-first night of Ramadan, the month of fasting and worship, I will recount to you a horrifying part of the tale of Maha of Qasim. Allah the Beneficent, the Merciful, created Maha out of a foul clot of blood. The earth shook when it delivered its burden, ridding itself of the evil spirit. Invoke Allah for mercy and forgiveness and plead for His pardon. The earth shook as if struck with an earthquake when Maha heard that her husband, Harb of Qasim, was slaughtered like a sheep. She started wailing and cursing, weeping and laughing until a hawk flying over her house stopped in mid-air and asked, "My sister, my sister, what aileth thee?"

And she replied, "Bird in the sky, a heavy burden in the heart."

And the hawk asked again, "My sister, my sister, what aileth thee?"

And she replied, "Bird in the sky, a fire tearing me apart."

When the sun was kneeling down, praying to the Allah of the universe, I with Aziza and Maymoon trotted to a low land, in the middle of which was a silent well. There, Maymoon jumped off Aziza's back and filled the plain with his squeaks. The well of sorrow was choked with human flesh, blood, and soot. Camels and horses lay on their backs, pointing their black limbs to the sky. The stink was foul, unbearable, as if the devil was blowing his bad breath upon the ground. I tied a piece of cloth around my face, breathed deeply, and started turning the heads of corpses. Maymoon sat on the edge of the well, dangling his feet, his hands over his head, whimpering. Aziza stamped her feet and brayed in a husky voice. Sssh, animals. Shush.

My trembling fingers were dripping with blood. Whenever I turned a head, an expression of horror was drawn on what was left of the face: an eye, a nose, or just gleaming teeth covered with blood. I recognized the face of Jadaan whose body was flung near the mouth of the well. His jaw was broken as if wrenched apart by giant hands. There was no corpse, just a few burnt shreds scattered around the head. The ground was swaying under my bare feet as if the jinn soldiers — in the name of Allah — had not completely got rid of their anger. The soles of my feet sank deep in the soil, wet with horsemen's blood. Total silence except the croaks of birds of prey eager to chew at the flesh of men. Blue flies buzzed over our heads, forming a dark cloud. In one of the pockets of a dead white soldier, I found a tiny silver box with a roaring lion engraved on the lid. When I opened it the smell of ground tobacco filled my nostrils. I held Maymoon in my arms, sat down near the wellmouth, preparing myself for a session of inhaling. I sniffed tobacco and sneezed; sniffed and sneezed until it spread in my head and made it lighter, clearer, able to see the battle between the English supported by the soldiers of Solomon, the jinn, and the Arabs backed by their vanity.

The truth is, after a light breakfast, the horsemen of Qasim decided to raid one of the white camps of the English. A young man passed their hiding place and asked them for a drink. He drank the milk and ran to his masters the English to describe to them the location of the men of Qasim.

The fighters of Qasim were cleaning their rifles and filling their waterskins when they heard the noise. A sharp noise of gunfire. Spurts of dust shot up, and in the blink of an eye the men jumped on horse-back as they fired back at the white men in their ornate uniforms. The lean men wrapped in their brown cloaks shot at the advancing English army. One would fill the rifle and the other would shoot. The foreign army swayed on camelback followed by three cars which looked like crawling giant insects.

The Qasimis fired at the cars, fired at the army clad in green uni-forms and at the camels, but could not stop the English from advancing. Suddenly, a huge bird of prey made of metal circled lower and lower and pushed its nose down, searching. The bird supported by the wings of jinn — in the name of Allah — roared over the well-bed and started climbing upward until it became as small as a grasshopper. It flew back and when very close to the heads of the horsemen, the huge bird of prey dropped a metal egg. The jinn eagles were laying eggs. Oh, my masters, what eggs? What eggs? When hatching, the eggs gave birth to a blazing fire and destruction. A huge explosion shook the area and threw the riders off their horses and scattered their rifles. The bombing split open the bodies of men, exposing their entrails. The bird kept banking and swooping for bodies, and banking and swooping for more bodies until the well-bed became like a volcano crater, lifeless and smoldering. Black smoke filled the air, the stink of burnt flesh and blood filled the air. The raid on the well left no sur-vivors, no chicks, no insect on the face of earth. The only thing which could be heard was the sizzle of dying fire and the beat of jinn drums and bagpipes celebrating their victory. A drumbeat and a fizzle, a hiss and a bang. A bang, a hiss, and roaring laughter. No bearer of news survived the battle except the everlasting Hakim and the English traveler.

After clearing my head with the snuff, I went down the steep ridge to meet Raai, the watchman of the village, and ask him about the news of Maha. Pray for the soul of the prophet. When the mad shep-herdess told her about the raid, she bolted to the mountains like a wounded deer. Life was seeping out of the remnants of the fighters when she reached the bed of the well. The Damascene sheath of Harb's dagger was flung on the wet ground next to his deformed head. The hyena, when seeing her husband's plucked-out eyes, collapsed on thorn shrubs and uttered one of her shrill laughing cries. She started digging the ground, pouring sand over her head, then yanking her hair crying,

115

"Black over your heads, darkness." Raai heard her cries and was afraid that Allah would not send the sun the next morning and give light and warmth to worshippers. She wept and cursed, howled and cursed until her voice disappeared. Raai swore to me that he saw fresh blood running down Maha's cheeks. She wept and wept until every piece of burnt flesh, every cut toe or finger, every lock of hair was flooded with fresh warm blood. The horizon was splashed with crimson light and the sea surface became coral-red.

People say that Maha of Qasim dug a small grave and placed her husband's head, his chest, his fingerless right hand, and one of his feet in the small hole. She kissed his lips then shrouded his body with soil until he was completely buried.The faint light of the dying sun made the corpses look bigger, darker, and more haunting. She dug more soil and scattered it on the bodies of the horsemen while reciting one of her spells and singing,

> "My luck is like scattered flour.
> Collect and count the dust."

She covered her face with soot, squatted, and began cursing Allah, His universe, His angels, His books, and His prophet Solomon. "Curse the white soldiers who killed my husband. Devastate their crops and plague their cattle." She kneeled down, plunged her face into the soil, and howled. Shrill cries filled the valley of misery and echoed in the coral-red sea. When the dawn blew its breath in the valley, Sheikh Talib found the black widow running aimlessly like a newly slain chicken. She rent the front of her garment so the top half of her body was revealed to the naked eye. Her breasts were like two soft sunbirds trying to escape the firm chest. Sheikh Talib saw the young, soft birds, fed on the nectar of flowers, and lost his peace of mind.

Men say that Maha lost consciousness for three days and three nights. She would not eat, drink, talk, or walk. She would cover her eyes with the palm of her hands in order not to see her guests. My masters, ladies and gentlemen, who were her guests? Her guests were sadness and grief. There they come, laying a carpet of despair. There goes the night to tell the story of her pain to the stars. There comes the morning to open the wounds of memory.

Maha

I scratched my head and tried to understand why I was sitting in that village, listening to the sound of running water and the cries of migrating birds. They gathered in the sky like a black cloud and dived to pluck out eyes from sockets. No. No. My aunt, my father, save me. The twin of my soul had departed this earth. No departures. I could not bear departures. If only people could spin some harmony in the threads of their life. If only, I started slapping my face and yanking my hair.

Nasra dashed into the room and shouted, "Stop, mad, you. Say, people."

I sprang up and ran outside shouting, "Yes. Mad. I am mad. Do you hear me?" Did Harb hear me?

Nasra dragged me inside and said, "Listen. Must listen. Thinks you are pregnant, Tamam. Wailing, instead."

The sunbeams sneaking into the room were glowing red. I shook my head, shut my eyes then opened them. Allah of the universe! Yes,

117

I had not seen my blood for thirty-five days. I sat on the floor, put my head between my hands, then started weeping silently.

"Damn your religion. More tears left, Maha?" I stood up and began wailing and jumping in the air. Harb was not dead, was not dead, was not dead. Oh skies, oh stars, my husband was not dead.

Nasra held my hand, "Mad, Maha? Lose the baby, you."

"The baby? Yes, yes," I said, and ran my hand over my belly. I laughed again and remembered the bright brown eyes of Harb. "I want a son, your son, my beautiful mare." I sat down, leaned on the wall, and wept silently. Harb should have been there. Harb had to be there. I placed my head on the pillow, wiped my face with my sleeve, then closed my eyes. The colorful rings of light floating under my eyelids were swallowed by darkness.

When I woke up the next morning, my muscles, bones, even veins ached. The old mirror showed a stained face, disheveled hair, and big eyes. My grandmother Sabha was shaking her finger at me. Grandmother, what could I do? The garment I was wearing was rent by days of sadness. It was soiled shreds and threads beyond repair. The soles of my feet were covered with flakes of dry skin and dirt. I flung the blanket on to the floor and went out of the house. The meek sun of autumn told me that the season of engagement was over. Girls who had got married were lucky and girls who had not would spend the year waiting for the summer. I wished Nasra could get married. Poor Nasra.

I boiled water in a small bowl, then carried it to the kitchen. I undressed and inspected my body. My breasts were bigger and my nipples were darker than usual. Two light trails of scalded skin ran on my stomach like snakes. Allah punish Hulala and her fire. I scrubbed my back with the loofah. My period had not visited me for about forty days. I must be pregnant. I rubbed my belly gently and whispered, "Welcome my son, the herb that will heal all my wounds." When I washed my hair I found I could hold it in one hand instead of two. I would use the henna, eggs, and olive oil to make my hair stronger and thicker. My son would arrive soon. I would welcome the twin of my soul with a bright smile and a healthy body. He must not suffer the pain of departure. I would tell him about his father's heroic deeds and noble nature.

I put on my mother's petticoat and robe, then weaved my oiled hair into two plaits. I flung the mattress and the blanket into the sun and swept the floor. Through the open window, the sound of twittering sparrows traveled to my ears. I knocked on the door of Tamam's room and whispered, "Good morning, aunt."

Tamam gasped then hit her chest, "Praise be to Allah that I see you walking and talking again." With her thin lips, she kissed my forehead. No smacking of lips that morning.

I looked at Tamam smilingly. "I am pregnant."

Tamam sat on the floor and started crying, swaying and mumbling, "My son Harb is still alive. He who gives birth is never dead. Praise be to Allah. Allah is Great and Merciful." I had never seen Tamam cry before. I remember her wide-open mouth and loose hair. My own chin started quivering but I stopped myself from crying. My son must fall on a rug of happiness and light. I must not cry because Harb's son would be born soon and I would fill my nostrils with his smell.

I had a look at the henna and radishes beds. Nothing. It was just an empty piece of land with no traces or footsteps, as if I had not lived in Harb's house for two years. I walked out of the arid yard. I breathed in the saline air. The narrow alleyways of the village seemed even narrower. The minaret of the shrine cried frenziedly, "Allah-u-Akbar." The blind village was still clinging to the mountainside like a leech. Stupid village! Salih's sweaty face glowed in the distance. From his high platform he waved the hand holding a blazing iron bar. I waved back. "Long life to you and your children," he said. I lowered my head and walked past the platform.

I walked towards the Jordan, leaving the village behind. The mountains hovered behind the village protecting it from enemies. People wearing the same clothes as ours and speaking the same tongue, but foreign. Home was the smell of basil and thyme which restores your soul. The cooing of doves and twittering of swallows carried me back to more pleasant times. Times when Harb used to wrap my shoulders with his cloak. I was cold. Part of my beloved was growing inside me like a blossoming flower. No spring flowers. The sound of running water and the smell of a dying fire made me feel lighter, thinner, and cleaner. I squatted, plunged my hands in the river, filled my cupped palms with water, then splashed my face. The cool drizzle seeped through

119

my skin to my tight lungs. I looked at the sky, then sighed.

Sitting on the mattress, I realized that the room was dark and damp. The afternoon sun failed to enter through the tiny window. With the bright purple shawl Harb had given me, I wrapped my shoulders. The angles of Tamam's house were sharper than ever. Tamam was puffing trails of smoke that looked like the cloud of sand raised by Harb's stallion. She had lost her son and I had lost the twin of my soul. When I saw the unfinished carpet lying in the corner, I realized how long I must have spent in oblivion, suspended between a bored sky and a cruel earth.

I stretched my body on the mattress and watched the fine grains of light floating through the tiny window at the top of the wall. I spent most of my days hoping to hear the familiar sounds of galloping hooves, but instead I heard cocks crowing and sparrows twittering. I ran my hand gently over my belly and felt the kick of a small limb. My mother, Maliha, had a grandson! Oh! My baby? It could not be. The window grew bigger suddenly and the grains of light were all smiling. I saw a flock of doves landing like a rain cloud on top of the orange trees in our orchard. I made up my mind. I would move back to my father's house. Yes, I would. Harb asked me to take good care of his mother. I needed the orchard. I must start working.

Um Saad

"Maha, my sister."

"Yes, Um Saad," I said, and turned my head on the pillow. The barred tiny window let in a faint light which made the bed, the tables, and Um Saad with her pink scarf look unreal.

"Salam has shut the doors and switched off the lights. I can start speaking, can't I?"

"Yes, Um Saad, you can."

"A big 'Aaah' drawn from the bottom of the heart first. When Abu Saad returned from work, I used to place his feet in a bowl and wash them with soap and water. He was a butcher in the offal market on the roof of the stream — they had covered the stream with concrete — in the middle of Amman. His long black rubber boots were always covered with the blood and dung of sheep and goats. By your life, I used to spend hours scrubbing and cleaning; I even used to add kerosene to the washing liquid to clean the cutlery and get rid of the clinging smell. A damp stink which reminded me of death and sewage.

121

He would call my name in his thin voice and ask me to lay the table. Our meals always had meat in them, kidneys, chickens' hearts, goats' limbs, and sheep's intestines. Once my stomach turned upside down and I threw up all over the low rounded wooden table. I don't know how on earth I got pregnant.

"My body took over and started swelling and swelling like the giant balloon the English flew over the Castle Mountain. That is where I lived most of my life, the Castle Mountain. I hated my body, my sticking-out navel and the baby which was sucking my insides. I used to spend hours rubbing the sheep stomachs with flour and lemon and never had time to look through the windows at the Roman amphitheater lying on its back in the valley. Abu Saad's house was three rooms and a veranda overlooking the city center. The theater then was invaded by foreigners from all over the world. My sister, they cross prairies and plains to inspect old, mossy stones. Strange people. The past? Who wants to remember the past? Whenever Abu Saad came back in the evening, he brought with him a rubber bucket full of stomachs and guts still full of dung and rotten food. And the cleaning process would start all over again. Just singing and scrubbing,

> The mailmen complained
> About my many letters.
> When my eyes cried,
> My lamps were lit.
> O moon, O moon, say
> Good evening to my beloved."

"You have a beautiful voice."

"It is rusty now. When I was young my singing used to attract birds from their heights. I think my husband stopped being rough with me because of my voice. He felt that Allah had compensated him for his thin, trembling vocal chords. What was the use? Whenever I sang, I used to think of Muhammad while looking at Abu Saad shaking his head in intoxication. Like the meat he used to sell, he was lumpy and soft. I used to close my eyes, shut my nose, and hand my body to Allah. If you are patient you go to paradise, my *kutab* teacher said. I wanted to go to paradise in order to sit behind a georgette curtain and look at the indistinct figures of people passing by. Abu Saad was a fat and ugly butcher in the offal market. A disgusting profession. Nobody would let him marry their daughter. My father had accepted his proposal one Friday morning when he went to buy humous for breakfast from the coffee shop next to Abu Saad's butchery. Because I am an immigrant's daughter, people think that I come out of a wall. No family tree or past. So, nobody would propose to immigrants. Abu Saad and me. The dropouts for the outcasts. The refuse for the junk."

Maha

When I opened my wooden trunk, the joints squeaked in complaint. I placed the carpet, the loom, the shuttle, and the spinning-wheel in the bottom of the trunk, then gently folded my tattered robe and the headband. The sheath of Harb's dagger and a lock of his hair were under my pillow. I tied them with the brocaded scarf and put them on top of the wool roves. I looked at the ceiling-high pile of mattresses and shook my head. They didn't need these in my father's house any more. The smell of tobacco told me that Tamam was in the room. I turned my head and met the tiny questioning eyes. "Forgive me, aunt, I must go back to my father's house." As I lowered my head I caught a glimpse of shining eyes. "I promise I will visit you once a week. You must visit me whenever your chest gets tight and your tongue craves to mention Harb."

"Allah is the Great Designer. Go to your sick father. He needs you. I will visit you." She puffed a cloud of smoke and smacked her thin lips. "Maybe I should stop smoking?" she murmured and inhaled more smoke. My aunt had never thought about smoking before. She must have been tired. I hugged her and kissed her tatooed forehead.

Nasra and I carried the wooden trunk and walked back to Sheikh Nimer's orchard. My back was pierced by eyes peeping through small windows. The hissing leaves and whispers. The young widow trudged back to her father's house with empty hands. No wealth, no son. Just an aging face and bent back. My husband was not the first or last horseman killed by the English. As if Allah created her and destroyed the mold. I shut my eyes then opened them. Where was Maliha, my mother?

I didn't know why I remembered my wedding procession, the bullets fired into the air and the curvetting horses. A bright promise was at the end of the path then. Looking at the stooping sun I realized that the village had changed. More concrete rooms replaced the goat-hair tents, the goldsmith had a thriving business, and the shrine was bigger. The alleyways were cleaner and the children wore loose pants instead of remaining naked. I wrapped the shawl more tightly around my neck to protect myself from the cold eastern wind and continued walking.

Nasra watched our footsteps on the dry soil and started counting. Her pronunciation was different when she said, "Going with you, coming with you, me."

"What happened to your teeth?"

She opened her mouth wide then said, "Morning. Running after Nawmeh, fell down, me."

"I wish you would get rid of this goat which only causes disasters."

She twitched her neck and said, "Baa, baa."

Our washed-off mud house, with its dome-shaped ceiling, tried to look healthy and dignified but was betrayed by the layers of sand covering it. The small clay pots in which I planted thyme, mint, and basil were missing from the yard. Sahi strutted in the yard followed by several meek hens. I placed the wooden trunk on the ground to greet Nashmi who limped towards me with difficulty. "Oh, what has happened to you, my old boy. Look at the tearful eyes and the sniffing nose." He must have recognized my smell because he started barking and rubbing his muzzle on my feet. While hugging Nashmi I heard the shuffling feet of my father. I raised my head, and there he was with his dirty striped shirt and kohled eyes. He hugged me with his trembling hands. I cried and cried on his shoulder.

He was crying too and mumbling, "There, there, Maliha. There, there, Maliha." He stroked my hair with his flaky fingers and said, "Shhhh, Maha my daughter is an Arab mare. Arab mares never cry."

With the end of my sleeve, I wiped my tears and said, "I've come back to stay."

"Your house and your orchard, my child."

When I entered the room I found two mattresses, a clay jar full of water, two sheepskin rugs, and a big brown wooden box with a white belly and two black knobs squatting in the corner. "What's that?"

"Your brother Daffash had brought it. He calls it *radion*."

"*Radion?*" Nasra danced around it.

"You give it two lumps of food, then you press this knob and turn it round and it starts singing and talking."

Nasra quickly pressed the knob and a strong loud voice said, "This is Radio Jordan from Jerusalem."

I started laughing at Nasra who jumped back shouting, "This box is possessed by the jinn soldiers and our Master Solomon."

Daffash entered the room suddenly, eyed us suspiciously, and said, "Whatever Allah intends! The whole tribe here is fiddling with my radio."

"My brother, how are you?"

"I see you brought your trunk with you. A long stay, it seems."

My father waved his wooden stick in the air and said, "Very long."

Daffash twisted his moustache with his thumb and forefinger and said, "This stupid idiot is afraid of the machine. They speak in Jerusalem and we hear them here, simple. An important friend of mine gave it to me." He turned the knob and got a language I could not understand. As if somebody was suffocated or were not allowed to draw a breath. At least I understood some of the Arabic but could not understand any of that other gibberish.

Daffash switched it off and said, "They are speaking English. Right. Go home now, the wedding is over."

"This is my home and I am staying."

"The face of miseries is back," he said, and slammed the door behind him.

126

Our belongings were reduced to a cock, some hens, a dying dog, and a few orange trees. My father was sitting on the floor and leaning his back against the wall. He looked old, tired, and distant. I placed my head on his lap and said, "My father, my soul, I am pregnant."

He turned his head and I heard his heavy breathing. "Praise be to Allah the Creator of worshippers and Healer of wounds. We will call him Mubarak. Blessed and son of the blessed."

I hugged his thin body and said, "I will work on this farm, clean the house, and prepare bright happy surroundings for the birth of my son. I will start with you, lovely old man. Tomorrow morning I will give you a bath together with your clothes."

"No, I am ill."

I laughed and said to him, "No, you're not."

The next morning I asked my father to undress in the store-room. He kept his pants on. I asked him to sit down and lean forward, then I rubbed his half-bald head with soap and washed it with warm water until his gray hair stood up like freshly washed wool tufts. I rubbed his thin trembling limbs and chest with a rich lather of soap and water. His ribs stood out as if to be counted. "You must wash the rest properly," I said, and left him to throw his dirty clothes in a basin. Why not use the washing powder Daffash brought from Samir Pasha's house? I covered the clothes with some grains and started rubbing. Like magic, the grease sticking to the hems dissolved. Full of pride, I looked at the bright washing. I made sure that every piece of cloth or garment found in Sheikh Nimer's house was hanging on the washing line.

Wrapping his body with his cloak, my father said in a gritty voice, "May Allah forgive you, Maha, I am cold."

"Sit in the sun. You will soon get warm."

I handed my father a hot cup of milk and went to inspect the orchard. I crossed the canal. Although still running, the water was murky. The bed where I used to plant henna and radishes was covered with light green shrubs. A lot of weeding needed to be done. The orange trees, lemon trees, and grapefruit were still there, but some of their leaves had bright yellow spots on them. They had an uneven surface like tents made of goat's hair. They were ill. I must tell my father. The smallpox of the leaves, they called it. One year, and the whole field would be bare and scarred. I went back to the house and told my father who was sitting in the sun and stroking Nashmi's back.

"Daffash might come up with something since he had been bringing all sorts of magic powders to the house."

Daffash shook his head when I told him and said angrily, "I want to get some sleep."

Um Saad

I want to get some sleep. I want to have some rest. A repetition in my head. I wish that Um Saad would leave me alone tonight. No. The "Maha, sister," flew to my tired ears. I gathered some voice and said, "Yes, Um Saad."

"The nurses have gone to sleep. Haven't they? I can talk now."

I looked at the crooked moon in the middle of the dark sky and sighed, "Yes, you can."

"I will start with a small 'Uh' because days have gone and days have come, and I was still scrubbing the insides of stomachs, stuffing them with rice and chick peas, then sewing them. With the help of Allah, I filled the house with sons. Eight sons: Saad, Mahmoud, Farid, Jamal, Wahid, Walid, Shaker, and Rawhi. Not one single daughter. I wanted Rawhi the last one to be a daughter. I dressed him in skirts and tied his long dark hair with colored ribbons. When the neighbors saw his bonnets, they laughed at me and said I should thank Allah that he was boy. Girls are a worry until you are in the grave.

"Between cooking, washing diapers, cleaning the house to get rid of the damn stink of Abu Saad's boots and overalls, twenty-five years of my life have passed. Like a blink of an eye. Just incubate and boil caraway."

"What is caraway?"

"It is a seed. We grind caraway, mix it with rice, then boil it until it becomes thick. It is offered with pistachios and almonds to visitors who come to bless the birth of a new baby. It helps the woman who has given birth to get rid of the foul blood. Incubate and drink caraway.

"I stopped looking out of the window. Abu Saad allowed me to wear a veil and sit on the veranda which was totally surrounded with vine trees and jasmine. It looks ugly and bare in the winter, but white and green in the summer. When you sit on the straw chairs in the evening, the scent of jasmine flowers envelops your soul. Heavenly. I peeped through the vine leaves at the busy streets of Amman. I used to be in love with that city. It is a cruel city. It suffers from an acute loss of memory."

"From what?"

"Dr. Edwards told me that I suffer from acute memory loss. Memory loss? Empty talk. I remember everything, even the things I don't want to remember. Forgetfulness is a blessing. Listen, Saad and Mahmoud joined their father's business and got married. I remember that Farid wanted to be an actor and ended up smoking and playing cards in the League café. Jamal ran away to Europe and I never heard from him. Wahid was a baker's boy in Raghadan. Walid went to school every morning and spent the night studying under streetlamps. Shaker joined the army and Rawhi fell in love with a men-only public bath and started working there. You see, my sister, I remember everything. I wish I didn't. Just cut the thread.

"I used to cut the vine leaves with scissors, boil them, then stuff them with mincemeat and rice."

"City people!"

"It is very tasty, and with the stuffed intestines you eat and eat. Feeding my sons, filling their stomachs with delicious food was my happiest time. Farid had a bad appetite. Smoking, that's why. The first thing he used to do was drink a cup of Turkish coffee in the morning. Can you imagine what the dregs do to the tissues of the stomach? My tongue grew tired of talking to him, 'My son, my love, please drink this glass of milk before the coffee.' No. He used to live in one of the two rooms we built on to the side of the house. He was once about to set fire to his quilt. A lost case he was."

"My son Mubarak is with his evil uncle Daffash. Allah only knows how he is going to bring him up."

"Remember, my sister, that we agreed not to cry."

"I wish the English doctor would wipe out all my memories with a piece of white cotton."

"Pray for the prophet's soul, woman."

"Um Saad, I cannot take the separation any longer. Allah should pity me and take me to my father and Harb."

"Maha, shall I tell you how to plant Iraqi jasmine?"

"I am a peasant and I know how to plant the damn jasmine."

"You dig the ground and make a hole one foot long..."

"Shut up, Um Saad."

"You cover all the roots of the shoot with..."

Maha

Despite the diseased trees, my daily routine fell into place again. I got up in the morning, tied a scarf around my head, fixed it with a black headband and stuck the end of my robe in my trousers. "Good morning, my child," I said, and gently rubbed my swelling belly. Sahi crowed loudly in the repaired wire cage, pleading to be set free to strut in the courtyard. I repaired the chicken wire by closing the holes with palm leaves. The cry of Raai followed and Nashmi with a feeble bark assured us that he was still alive. After sweeping the floor and folding the rugs and mattresses, I prepared a breakfast for my father and Daffash. Milk, eggs, honey, and butter. Mine was a glass of milk mixed with two raw eggs.

It took a while for me to clean the house, the store-room, and the yard. The two palm trees were still standing erect in the front of the yard. Their beds were full of stones, weeds, and dirt. I cleaned the beds and sprinkled the dry soil with water. I put my pick across my shoulder, said "Allah," and headed towards the field. To see the sick oranges, talk to them, even sing to them while digging the ground underneath, helped me forget everything. Forget the village which was captured between the sea, the river, and the mountains, and the aging house and the merciless tongues which never seem to tire of eating the raw flesh of people: "The young widow — Allah protect us — runs the house of Nimer and everybody in it."

One morning while sweeping the floor, I switched on the radio and heard a familiar accent. "My brother the peasant, good morning," the radio chanted. "This morning we will talk about a disease that affects citrus trees. If you notice that the leaves of your trees are uneven," I threw down the broom stick, "and swollen like spots on skin," I sat down next to the radio, "you can cure it by spraying the trees with a white liquid you can get from cooperatives. Our agriculture engineers will help you."

I ran to Daffash and shook him until he woke up. "Daffash, I've heard something on the radio. Can you get some from your master, Samir. Daffash, the oranges."

"You wake me up to tell me about your filthy oranges."

"No, listen." After three repetitions of the same explanation, Daffash understood what I was saying.

"He will subtract the price from my wages," he said.

"By the soul of our mother Maliha, please bring some of the medicine."

"All right, I will," he smiled.

Three weeks later, a Land Rover stood in front of our gate. I had built a small fence around the henna and radish bed to stop the pasha from running over my plants. One of Samir Pasha's servants jumped out of the Land Rover and handed me two barrels full of stinking white liquid. I covered my nose with the end of my scarf and waved my hand.

He was tall and black. He said, as if giving orders to the kitchen boy, "For your sick trees. You wear these rubber gloves."

I gaped, I had never seen rubber gloves in my life. They looked like hands cut off from a body. He pushed my hesitant hand into one of them and smiled.

"Fill the ewer carefully with this liquid. I have already mixed it for you. Make sure that you don't spill any on the ground. Spray the trees from top to bottom. Do you understand?"

I shut my eyes and opened them in agreement.

"Good-day." He jumped into the Land Rover and drove off, raising a cloud of dust behind.

I put on the gloves and carried the barrels to the farm. It was hard to spray the tall trees, but I found the two wooden boxes which Daffash had brought from his boss's farm. I placed them on top of each other and sprayed the top of the trees, singing, "Your bath is cold, sheikh, cold and cooling, sheikh." Soon I would be washing the tender limbs of my son. "Cold but cooling, my son." My trees were swaying silently. It was for their own good and they knew it.

The stink of the medicine rose high, high up to the sky. My hair, robe, arms, and feet were all stained with the white liquid. I took off my scarf and headband, then threw the gloves in the barrel. Sometimes I felt a deep distrust for city people's help. What if the remedy the pasha had brought was just some plaster which Arabs used to paint their houses. The pestle inside me started grinding. I could not bear losing the oranges. Stupid me, wait and see.

I went back to our house, boiled some water, then washed my aching muscles. My belly was big and ripe. The kicking had increased lately. My mother's embroidered velvet robe was the only clean garment I could find. My hands were as cold as ice when I hung the washing on the line. The chilly breeze came from the mountaintops carrying the smell of snow with it. I lit the kindling in the brazier and let the wind fan them to smoldering embers; I then carried it inside and placed it in front of my father who was listening to the radio. "By Allah, I can understand some of their ornamented talk," he said excitedly.

A knock on the door, then Tamam entered the room. "Welcome, my aunt," I said, and kissed the back of her hand.

She puffed some smoke in the already smoky room and said, "How are you, my child?"

"I am fine, my aunt, just some back pain."

"You will give birth soon. And how is Sheikh Nimer?"

"I am fine. Nashmi is getting old."

She puffed some smoke through the long pipe and said, "Stop listening to that machine. Our tales are better."

"Please, tell us a story."

"All right. Switch this machine off first.

"There was, or maybe not, in the oldest of times a mother and her son. The mother was baking bread and her son was playing next to her. While she was flinging the dough on the baking tin, her son shat on the ground. The mother could not find anything to wipe him with, so she asked Allah to help her. He sent her a piece of silk. Overtaken by greed, she refused to use the silk and wiped her son with a hot loaf of bread. Instantly, thick hair started springing out of his skin. His bottom was scalded by the bread and became glowing red. Her son turned from one of the sons of Adam into a monkey. May Allah protect us from greed and deformation."

"The only monkey I ever saw was with a stranger who stayed in our village," I said.

"Oh, that driveling liar!"

"May Allah grant you a son with hair like gold, a mouth like a ruby, and eyes like emeralds. Amen."

"Some coffee, aunt?"

"Bless your hands, Maha."

I looked at the tiny eyes and smiled. The soul of Harb was stamping its feet around the house. Why couldn't I let him in? Help him come back from the land of the missing. He was with us. His child was kicking inside me.

"You will give birth soon, Maha."

I smiled and showed my aunt the carpet. "Look, aunt, I wove some more."

"Why don't you dye the wool like the other women of the tribe."

"I like cream and brown."

"Maha, you think you are different from the women of the tribe," Tamam said.

"Brown? My hands are getting darker every passing day," murmured my father.

"No sound in the house and no news."

"Tomorrow, your grandson will dance around you."

"Praise be to Allah."

The next morning, I stuck the end of my robe into my trousers and tied the headband tightly. I must have a look at the sick oranges to see if they were improving. I took the pick and jumped across the canal, heading towards the orchard. The sick leaves were all on the ground and some of the orange trees were stark naked. I hoped that the medicine was the right one for the illness. I leaned down and rooted out some weeds and threw them near the canal. A slow dull pain slapped me on the back. I plunged my hands into the water and washed my face. It was only a back pain that comes and goes like hesitant waves. I collected some stones and piled them near a tree bed. I would use them to block the water out of the beds. A higher wave of pain hit my back. I tried to ignore it while tilling the soil. I must let the plants breathe properly.

I put my pick on the ground and sat next to the canal. With both hands I held my waist tightly. When I placed my head on the freshly turned soil the smell of wet fertile fields filled my nostrils. I lay on my back to get rid of the uncomfortable tides of pain. The twittering of sparrows and the sound of running water mingled in my head. It was cool and damp under the lemon tree. I dug my fingers in the ground and smiled. Two strong hands gripped my waist and started squeezing and twisting. An earthworm slid near my hand, winding its body then straightening it. Curling and straightening. I was brownish-pink. The sound of Nashmi's lazy barking urged me to stand up and go to the house. I raised my head, but another wave of pain attacked my body like sharp blades. The sun was a sparkling ring under my eyelids. I placed my cheek on the cold soil and closed my eyes. The warm water of the Dead Sea massaged my body. Flap, flap, flap. Cushions of ease. Harb's hands caressed my shoulders and the back of my neck. When I opened my eyes, beads of sweat and tears were clinging to my eyelashes. I sighed and waited for the second wave. The nightingale came flapping over the water. The plain of the Dead Sea opened up under the moonlight like mother of pearl. The water glittered underneath my eyelids. Oh, Maliha, my mother, save me. I sank into the sea again.

The pain increased and I placed my hand over my mouth to stop myself from screaming. My father might not survive hearing the sound of a cry. I stretched my body and opened my legs wide. The pain grew more ferocious. I could hear the drumbeats of gypsies who did not worship Allah. A short intake of breath, then probing pain. I bent my knees and gasped for air. I bent my knees again, pushing my thighs upwards to fight the tearing and pulling. Distant barking and pipe tunes. A skin bag snapped open and water and blood gushed out of my body. I threw off my headband and scarf and yanked the wet plaits. Tides of pain followed by swimming in the sea with Harb. My father's flaky fingers stroked my hair and said, "You will be fine." I was no longer in control of my body. My muscles started contracting. I tightened my grip on a handful of soil, took a deep breath, and pushed with all my might to throw the pain out. A rounded piece of red flesh swathed in blood and muck slipped out to the ground.

My son? I touched his slippery body and started laughing and crying. My son fell on his grandfather's land. A carpet of happiness and ease. He was blind and worm-like but my heart flew out of my chest to embrace him. When I stretched out my hands, picked him up then hugged him, he started crying. He was objecting to the human touch after months in warm water. He was tiny and as red as a nectarine. His fingers and toes were connected to each other with thin skin. While I rubbed his body with my scarf a strange warm feeling seeped through me. I fell in love with the worm-like creature lying in my lap and crying loudly. My father kneeled down and said, "Courageous, Maliha. Praise be to Allah." Sheikh Nimer kissed the soil covered with blood and with a sharp bamboo knife cut the umbilical cord. With a ribbon slashed from his headdress, he tied the navel of my son tightly. "Let us go to the house." I held my baby and walked back to the house leaving a trail of blood behind.

Tamam, Hulala, Hamda, and Nasra all rushed into the room ululating. "Maha and Harb's son. Allah took and Allah gave." They lit a fire in the brazier and brought a container full of warm water and herbs. "Praise be to Allah, Protector of souls and Giver and Taker." Tamam rubbed her grandson's body with olive oil and salt, rubbed his hands and feet with warm flour, put kohl in his eyes, then wrapped him with a big piece of cloth. They helped me undress and washed my body. The scent of the basil and lemon leaves they had added to the water filled the room. When I finally sat down on the mattress I felt dizzy but happy. They tied the body of my son with a cloth, then fixed it with bands. He looked so small and helpless. I started weeping silently. My suckling was a tied orphan with no father and no backbone. Nobody to lean on. Who would teach him how to ride? Who would... Tamam smacked her lips and said, "A breastfeeder must not cry. Your milk will dry up."

137

Nasra said, "So beautiful, your son."

Hamda cleaned up the room, added some incense to the embers and put a small mattress in the rocking bed. Tamam's present to her grandson. My son started crying. My heart fluttered in my chest. I held him and kissed the kohled eyes and the big triangular amulet pinned to his chest. I pulled out one of my breasts and placed the nipple in his tiny mouth. Instantly, he stopped crying and started sucking the milk out of my full breast. He opened his eyes and two big amber pools stared absently at me. My body glowed with pleasure and I forgot about the pain of labor under the lemon tree. His round head leaned on my chest and I felt that I would do anything to protect it. Stroking his thick, black hair, I asked, "What shall we call him?"

"We shall call him Mubarak. Your mother wanted another son. Allah took his deposit," said my father.

"Mubarak, listen to your grandfather," I said, and my sisters started laughing.

The Storyteller

In the name of Allah the Beneficent, the Merciful. Peace be upon the soul of Jesus, son of Mary, the day he was born, the day he died, and the day he shall be raised alive. Mary had withdrawn from her people to live in a chamber overlooking the east where darkness gives birth to light. Allah's spirit did not leave her in her solitude. Assuming the likeness of a perfect man, the spirit visited her and told her that Allah would bestow her with a faultless son.

He is not the son of Allah who was not born and never gave birth. Allah said to the spirit, "Be" — and it is. Mary was chaste and pure, but Maha of Qasim was foul and evil. Her husband was dead and had not mounted her for months. How had she conceived and who was the unfortunate father? People say that when she spent a night in the mountains looking for the remnants of her husband Harb, a creature with human legs and horse's head rode her near the mouth of the well. Her belly was getting bigger and bigger and the deformed creature inside her was growing. It became heavier at night and its kicks

139

were so painful that she used to spend nights moaning and cursing.

She left the house of her husband the minute they told her his spirit had gone to its maker. Tamam cried and cried and begged her to stay to ward off the loneliness and help her in her old age. "No," the young widow cried.

When she arrived at her father's farm, an evil spirit possessed the whole area. With the help of two jinn soldiers of our Master Solomon, she turned everything upside down and spun her nest over the property of her virtuous brother Daffash. She scrubbed, she swept, she ploughed and weeded, she bowed to her master the jinn and stretched out her hands. People say she was pregnant with a creature who in his previous life was a woodcutter. A jinn who with one stroke of his hand cut the heads off trees and left leveled trunks behind. The heavy fetus while growing was tearing her insides apart. She moaned and cried and kept springing up and kneeling down.

Her father knew what was ailing her, but refused to come near her. He used to spend long hours sitting on the barley sacks in the storeroom. He sat on a sack and cursed the eastern wind which was blowing mercilessly in the valley. He did not know whether he was seeing things or whether two giant hands were really tilting over the earth making the surface of the universe uneven. He held his stick firmly, shuffled his feet across the ground carefully, hoping not to fly away like a bunch of rags. Once, when he went to the shrine to pray, he asked one of the men about the mountains of Jerusalem. "They are gone. Disappeared, turned — puff — into thin air. Where are they, Salah? Where are they, Hakim?" he whimpered, then sat on the cold floor of the shrine and started weeping. The giant hand, he thought, which is tilting over the western part of the valley, will keep pressing until the whole village is devoured by the void.

Sheikh Nimer of Qasim, was run down by the storm his daughter created when she came back to his house. He started hallucinating and driveling, refused to eat any of the food she cooked because once he saw a lizard's leg floating in the milk. The centipede tried to poison her father to secure a spacious property for her son who had goat's legs. "Father, oh father, can you please move out of this room? I will clean it at dawn," she hissed. Sheikh Nimer moved to the second room. She knocked on his door with her clenched fist and hissed her

order, "Father, oh father, can you move out of this room?" She kept
knocking and ordering the old man to move from one spot to another until he ended up in the store-room. She shut the door firmly,
fixed a big lock on the handle, and left the old man to rot in his own
shit and urine.

Men say that when Sheikh Nimer of Qasim started building his
house he decorated the doors with white stones sliced from the sides
of the Mountains of Balqa, the mountains where nymphs live. The
bright rubiginous hue of pomegranate trees covered the mountains. In
spring, the color becomes warmer when mixed with the glossy crimson of the pomegranate flower. If you travel to Salt Valley and walk
on the river bank with your donkey and monkey you will eventually
have a flickering glimpse of the bright blonde hair of the nymphs
floating on the glittering water like melting gold.

The golden breath of the sun was filling the valley when Maha
dashed out of the door decorated with white stones. Her black hair
ran loose on her shoulders like the slimy tar with which Greek peasants used to stain the doorsteps of adultresses. The sun was in the
middle of the sky when the valley of sadness heard the savage shriek,
the cry which dived in the Dead Sea and woke up the pillars of salt
sleeping under water. Her cries, which were dry like the arid land
north of the village, gradually became wet. Tears of pain and frustration ran down her cheeks. She cursed Allah on His throne, His angels
and His prophets — I seek refuge from the fork-tongued woman —
for the pain they caused her, for the gift of the foul spirit with goat's
legs which slashed her flesh open. Evil gave birth to evil and will
outlast us all. Slap the tambourine across your thigh. Tring, tring, trang.

She hugged her blood-and-slime-covered baby to her chest and kissed
its hind legs. With her tongue she sucked and swallowed the blood,
snot, and water until her son was clean. When she spanked him on
his bottom he spat on his mother's face and started crying. Gradually
— praise be to Allah, the Lord of creatures — the hair on his goat's
legs started falling off and the hind legs retracted into the sides of his
chest. When he stopped crying, the sky was crimson and the wind
carried the fetid breath of Iblis, the disobedient angel. His body had
metamorphosed to become like ours with two legs, no horns, and a
normal chin. People say that when they went to see him, he did not

141

speak in his cradle like Jesus — peace be upon him — but his eyes seemed to talk. He was looking at the distant horizon, at invisible objects floating in the air. People swear that in his irises they saw the reflection of the palaces of Midyyan in Yemen. The son of only yesterday was dreaming of becoming the king of the Empty Quarter and Aden. A sad look, but full of greed and determination. The son of the witch of Qasim kept gazing at the distant riches and spitting on people's faces, gazing and spitting. She called him Mubarak, and the people of the village called him the son of the black widow.

Maha

Lying on the floor in the darkness, I was looking at the bright face of my son. "May Allah protect you from evil eyes and my eyes." The moon that night was like an old crooked bone. Its shimmer seeped through the small window into the quiet room. I wanted to hear the breathing of my son. I heard the cries of Raai and a distant barking of dogs. The cradle was painted blue and decorated with white crescents on the sides. Blue to ward off the evil eye and the white crescents of our master Muhammad. I tried to go to sleep but could not. I called the most pleasant thoughts to mind. I was young, fearless, and in Harb's warm arms. "Beautiful eyes, Maha," he said, and I moved closer to him. Mubarak started crying. I picked him up and began breastfeeding him. My Eyesight had no father. He would grow up to become the best horseman in the tribe and protector of our dwelling. The sucking brought a dull pain to my back and more bleeding. Suck the milk, suck the milk and grow up. I felt that the milk was sliding down to my stomach. "With happiness and good health, my son."

The next morning I switched on the radio and started sweeping the floor. Since the stinking medicine cured my trees I had been listening to the man talking about farming. "My brother, the peasant, the season of picking . . ." I put the dirty diapers in a container and was about to put in some washing powder. No, I thought, and used gentle Nabulsi soap. I rubbed and scrubbed, filling the room with steam and the smell of soap. After hanging out the washing, I pulled my old robe from the wooden trunk to use it as a holder. The smell of dust, dirt, and soot wafted out of the trunk into the room. I tied Mubarak to my back and headed towards the field. "There, there. You have a sack now." I went to the orchard and found my pick lying next to the canal. My father must have buried the umbilical cord. I untied the sack and placed Mubarak on the ground. "The soul of your mother. I want you close to the earth." I pushed the stones and mud to one side, letting the water run to the beds. One by one the thirsty trees drank from Allah's water.

I remembered what the radio had said that morning. The Jordan Valley is fit for planting vegetables, especially tomatoes, ladies' fingers, and cucumber. Why not plant some in the yard? Daffash sprang out in front of me. I couldn't believe my eyes. Daffash actually came to the farm. His thin moustache was well twisted but there were dark patches under his eyes.

"Welcome, my brother."

"Girl, you've made me an uncle."

"Yes."

"I want to hold my nephew. By Allah, you have given birth to a man. I want to hold him," he said with a voice full of excitement and joy.

Daffash, smiling? I did not know what he looked like when he was laughing. My chest tightened when Daffash held my suckling.

"Your uncle will teach you how to ride and shoot and drive. How is that?" He is smiling, by Allah.

I wished Daffash would leave me alone; leave my son alone; go to the city and drown himself in the fake lights of Amman. "Are you working today?"

"Smile to your uncle. Heh. Mubarak, I'm going now. I'll see you later."

He twisted his moustache with his thumb and forefinger and said, "Since you've given birth to a man you may stay in my house." He held my arms and kissed me on the forehead. The scent of washing powder filled my nostrils. His thin body stalked across the muddy ground. When the white cloud of his robe disappeared, I ran my fingers on my suckling's face, saying, "I seek refuge from the damned devil."

A week after, I started the preparations for the circumcision ceremony. I made sure that we had enough grain and rice. A sheep and a goat were bought from Sheikh Talib. Nasra insisted on slaughtering Nawmeh for Maha's son. I tried to talk her out of it because I knew how much she loved that goat. Nasra shook her single earring and said, "A son, I have. Your son, Maha." I hugged her. Nasra was thinner than usual and her face was caked with dirt and soil. My friend was growing old. No marriage for Nasra.

Nasra and I went to the mountains to collect bugloss and camomile for Mubarak. I left him with my aunt sucking sugar and water. It was a bright day with a striking blue sky and a glaring sun that gave no heat. The wind was cutting cold. Did I close the window before leaving the house? Would Tamam cover my son with one more sheepskin rug? When we reached the top of the mountain, the view of the valley was so clear that it hurt the eye. Humble mud houses huddled together and a large white house hovered over them. "By Allah, whose house is that?"

"It's the new house of Samir Pasha. Work there, your brother." I sat on a rock facing the western wind coming from Jerusalem. The Jordan was still trying to shake the Dead Sea back to life and the village looked bigger. There were some green patches on the west bank of the river. A strong peasant woman must be working in their fields day and night. Not a lot of greenery on our side, except the green oasis of the pasha's palace. I wondered what those people ate and how they greeted each other. The sun was sliding down the horizon to its hiding place. Nasra bolted off like an arrow to collect her herd. If the sun set on grazing sheep, Nasra thought the ghoul would slaughter them to feed her children. The women of Qasim were running around busily. Black spots which looked like active ants, no more, no less. All their lives, they sweat and dig the soil to build nests for their men and children and at the end they die and are forgotten. Ants without names, past or future. The sun stooped to its maker. I strolled back home hugging a bunch of bugloss and another of camomile.

The next day, I anointed my son, who was seven days old, with olive oil and salt and waited for Imam Rajab to come and call for prayer in Mubarak's ear. The house was full of women and the tent in the courtyard was full of men; Sheikh Talib, my father, Raai, Imam Rajab, Murjan, and Daffash who was pouring coffee and welcoming the guests. Early that morning, I had baked the bread and boiled the grains. Nasra cut the slaughtered sheep and Nawmeh into tiny pieces and threw them into the boiling water. I saw her wiping her tears while cooking the rice. I should not have let her kill Nawmeh. Hulala came with a collection of herbs and earth to put on the would afterwards. When she spread her bundle, I gasped. Alum, dung, woodworms, and fenugreek were mixed together. Hulala laughed, handed me a tiny sack, and said in her sharp voice, "Mix these for your baby." Tamam thanked her, opened the sack, then placed the sugar candy, some fenugreek seeds, camomile, and aniseed on a piece of gauze and tied the ends forming a tiny bundle. I soaked it in water then stuck it in Mubarak's mouth. My son, my Eyesight, started sucking the bundle as if it was my nipple. Hulala shook her head approvingly and said, "He will go to sleep. Go and finish your work."

Before the sun stood in the middle of the sky, Imam Rajab coughed and entered the room. Hulala was grinding the dry dung patiently with two flat stones. Without saying anything, he rolled up his sleeves, fixed his turban, and started calling for prayer in my son's ears. "Allah-u-Akbar. Allah-u-Akbar."

"He will get used to the sound of Islam. He will grow up to become a good Muslim," Hulala explained.

"Allah is great," shouted the imam loudly. I was afraid that my son would be deafened by the loud noise. The imam put Mubarak on the mattress, placed a rounded dung under his glans, and took a sharp dagger out of a worn leather bag. My heart sank to my trembling knees and the pestle inside me started grinding. "In the name of Allah." He held the end of Mubarak's penis in one hand and the dagger with the other. "We will get rid of infidelity and dirt," he said and slashed the dangling skin. The women cooking outside were singing,

> "Circumcise, hey Shalabi,
> His precious tears run down."

Blood ran on his tender thighs. Hulala put the mixture of ground dung and alum on the wound. "Carry him, Maha, and go round." I carried my son who was bleeding profusely and paced around the house seven times to ease his pain and ward off the evil eye.

> "Circumcise, hey Shalabi.
> Sharpen your knife,
> Lighten your hand."

My suckling kept crying until his tears dripped down to his ears. While running, I tried to put the fenugreek bundle in his mouth. He rejected it. I went to the store-room, pulled out my breast, put the nipple in his mouth. He kept yelling and refused to suck. After several attempts, he held the stretched nipple with his tongue then started sucking. While drying his tears with my sleeves I too cried. The Eyesight of his mother was in pain. He would let go of my nipple then take it again. He was in pain. The wound, full of blackish powder, was still bleeding. Oh, where was his father? Where was Harb?

> "If you hurt the beautiful
> I will curse you, Shalabi."

I returned to the main room. The women were eating the leftovers of the *mansaf* and the men were sipping coffee in the tent. I wanted to wrap up my son, but the old hags refused and said that the wound must stay uncovered to heal quickly. With her sharp voice Hulala added, "His urine will heal it." I placed Mubarak in the rocking bed and offered some raisins and boiled grains to my guests. Voices of departing men reached the ears of the women. "Congratulations." "Praise be to Allah." "May you see him a bridegroom." My father entered the room and stuck five gold dinars under Mubarak's pillow. I kissed his hand and said, "May your blessings stay hovering over our heads."

He must have seen the traces of tears on my face because he shook his stick and said, "Do not be sad because you are the highest." I nodded and followed my father to the door. The men wrapped their cloaks around them and said goodbye, all except Sheikh Talib who was talking seriously to my brother. Since when did the head of the tribe have time for my brother? We live and see.

With every cry uttered from my son's lips my heart fluttered. The wound was still bleeding lazily. I did not understand the meaning of that cut. Imam Rajab ordered me to bury the foreskin in order to prevent cats or dogs from eating it. Under a citrus tree, I lay a part of my son. Mubarak kept waking up and crying that night so I carried him and paced around the house to ease his pain. The cold wind might fan the wound. Nashmi barked occasionally but the cries of Raai were more frequent. Raai was busily protecting the honor of the women of the tribe. How could he protect the women from their dreams? I held Mubarak more tightly to my chest and strolled around the house. The palm trees extended to touch the dark sky. In the moonless night, they looked like burnt sticks. Two lovers. I was seeing things. Harb's soul was imprisoned in the sky. He wanted to be with me and his son. I could hear the sound of his footsteps. Set him free. "Harb, you are the twin of my soul, my husband, my love, my life." The light of the morning spread across the sky, transforming it into dim blue. The moment of dawn lifted my heart up, up to the Latroun Mountain where the monks were reciting morning prayers. When the cry came from the minaret, "Allah-u-Akbar," Mubarak closed his big eyes and succumbed to tired sleep. I put him in his bed and covered him with a light white cloth.

Um Saad

"Maha, sister?"

The moon tonight is like an old crooked bone. I am rotting in that white hospital and will perish soon. I pulled the white sheet over my chest and said, "Yes, Um Saad."

"I've heard the sound of clicking doors. Dr. Edwards, Salam, and Kukash must have gone to sleep. Eh, eh, days have come and days have gone and I was still peeping at the world through the vine leaves surrounding the veranda at the Castle Mountain. Because of the numerous births, the midwife Um Gharib became my friend. She used to come in the morning and help me roll the vine leaves and stuff the eggplants and zucchini. She even taught me how to stuff turnips and potatoes. The flood of guts, intestines, and stomachs kept coming and the cleaning kept me on my toes. I stopped doing the cleaning in the kitchen, though. Peddlers began selling plastic utensils. I bought a big washbowl and a box with a tight cover. First, I squeezed the dung and food out of the guts into the box, then I placed them in the bowl

149

and scrubbed them with lemon and flour. I used to cover the box tightly to get rid of the stink of blood and excrement. That stopped the flies buzzing over our house. Abu Saad stopped getting his hands dirty. My two eldest sons and three bedouins from the Jordan Valley worked in the shop. My husband, sister, started wearing white shirts, white headdress, and black trousers. My back was broken from washing and ironing. In those days, we used to put the iron on the kerosene stove until it got hot, wipe it with a clean cloth then slide it over hems and ends. Keeping Abu Saad happy and shining was hard work. He once said that he would buy me the daughter of Abu Hassan who was working in his shop. Have a servant in my house? I just could not accept it, so I went on singing and working.

> 'The dark man made me mad,
> He stole my brain from me,
> I will not fall for anyone but him.'

"The days of Saideh and her master have ended. The songs became shorter and lighter. When I was young, we used to sing about spring, crops, meadows, and life. By your life, all the songs nowadays are about love. For the younger generation, nothing is important except love and lust. When you cannot get something, you keep thinking of it all the time. Fifteen years after Muhammad's proposal, I bumped into him in the city center. He did not recognize me, but I knew him at once. His beautiful blonde hair was ash gray and his blue eyes had lost their brilliance. 'Muhammad,' I called.

"He stopped, eyed my face and said, 'Haniyyeh? You are still in Amman! I thought your father had sent you to Syria to get married.' His voice was low and tired. When I caught sight of the minaret of the Grand Mosque behind him, I felt lonely and sad.

"'No, I got married here and I have eight sons.' He smiled, giving a glimpse of the Muhammad I fell in love with twenty five years ago. 'What about you?'

"'I work in Aqaba. They are building a port there.'

"'Did you . . .?'

"'No, I did not get married,' he said, and hid his aging fingers in the pockets of his old jacket.

150

"For just a second, I felt like hugging him, kissing his puffy eyes and gray hair. 'I wish you all the best,' I said in a dry voice. Maha, my voice is never dry.

"He thrust his hands even deeper into his pockets and said, 'Goodbye.'

"My sister, my heart was chopped into pieces when I saw Muhammad. Oh, he was old and lonely. We grow old. That is the way it goes. I walked back home struggling with a basket full of vegetables. I threw the vegetables into the wash-basin, rushed to the bedroom, took off all my clothes, and stood in front of the mirror. My belly was big, my breasts almost touched my waist line, my black hair was gray, and my face was wrinkled. I realized then that my youth had passed silently. I had never had a day of real happiness. Just my sons and their beaming faces. For Abu Saad, I had been and always would be a container into which he could get rid of his frustration. For Abu Saad, I had been and always would be a slave girl like the one he wanted to buy from his employee. I sat on the bedside and cried. At that very minute, Abu Saad entered the bedroom and was shocked to see me naked. 'What happened to your brain, woman?'

"I put on my brown kaftan and went to the kitchen. You see, the kitchen was my domain, my space. I could shut the door and nobody would disturb me there. I wanted to talk. We never ever talked, Abu Saad and I. He gave orders and I listened. While chopping the radishes, I started humming the song of the Father of Light. He missed his homeland. By your life, my days were just a series of jokes. Very funny and trivial. My heart fidgeted in my chest and yearned to roll out of my body, roll into another beautiful body and another identity. I went out on to the veranda and peeped at the hiccupping cars which filled the streets of Amman with soot and steam. As if that absent-minded city needed soot and smoke to make it black. It was black already. Amman has a black heart."

Um Saad was pulling down her pink scarf when I turned my head on the pillow. I wish, I wish . . . Her smooth voice flew to my ears,

> "Don't say we were and there was.
> I wish all of this had not happened.
> I wish I never set my eyes on you."

Maha

I tried to fold my legs underneath me, but they refused to respond. I placed my head on the pillow and tried to go to sleep. A piece of wet velvet. Shining daggers. Harb's stallion galloped and raised its hind feet. Metal eagles. Harb's chest was stained with fresh blood. The smell of blood, sweat, and the sound of heavy breathing. Courageous. My son, covered with butter and soot, was tied to a string Daffash was holding. Tight around his neck. Tighter. He shrieked with laughter. I sprang up, searching for the face of my baby. He was breathing heavily and his eyes were rolling under his eyelids. When he was about to cry I remembered what my father once told me. When angels tell a child his mother is dead, he starts crying in his sleep, and when the angels tell him his mother is alive, he smiles in his sleep. Mubarak's mother was alive and strong and would protect him even if she had to fight the angel of death himself.

Samir Pasha came to our house one morning and asked me to come to his farm on Friday to give his cook a hand. I was washing Mubarak's diapers. His guests, he said, wanted to have a taste of a true bedouin *mansaf*, but his cook was Sudanese. I smiled. He told me the cook knew nothing about goats, rice, and yogurt. He said both my father and brother had given me permission to go to his mansion on Friday.

"Yes, pasha, I will come on one condition: that I can bring my own dry yogurt cakes with me."

"Agreed, my lady," he said, and smiled. His gleaming white teeth and the long rubber boots which prevented his bare feet from touching the ground spoke of his foreignness. His khaki trousers and the shirt covering his tall figure made the pasha look like an army deserter. I went on scrubbing the diapers of my suckling, then soaked them in soap and water. I tipped away the dirty water and poured some more from the barrel. The pasha jumped into his Land Rover and drove off in a cloud of dust. My father shuffled his feet across the ground. He sat down on the doorstep and placed Mubarak on his lap. "If you go, take care."

That night I dreamt of spacious rooms and see-through curtains flapping in the wind. The floors were well covered with Chinese rugs and mattresses in silk cases. Brocaded cushions and pots and trays made of bright brass. The men would be wearing trousers without robes and the women would be semi-naked with lots of feathers in their hair. Thin-lined eyebrows and thin-lined lips. Hulala said that city women open their legs for any man. Would they do it in front of everybody? No, no. I felt a strange emptiness growing inside me. I rocked Mubarak's cradle then closed my eyes. Colorful rings of lights floated underneath my eyelids. The palace would look like that on Friday evening. Harb should have been there, touching me, caressing me, kissing my ears. The crow of Sahi told me that I must catch some sleep. Forget about the world and shut your eyes firmly. You might, you just might go to sleep.

On Friday afternoon Samir Pasha and Daffash came to pick me up. "Father, I've made you several tiny bundles of fenugreek and sugar candy. I won't be long," I called, and pulled the end of my robe to get into the Land Rover. When he shut the door and started the engine, I realized that I was being carried away in a machine. Metal doors, windows, wheels, and a purring engine. I felt dizzy because my feet were not on the merciful soil. I gripped the chair and held my breath. Daffash saw the look on my face and started laughing. The pasha said, "Don't be afraid. It's like a horse really." As we sped past the Mountains of Hamia, I saw a black stallion galloping down the mountain edge. Lately, I had not lined my eyes with the sight of horsemen. Mountains folded mountains and fields folded fields. Suddenly, birds filled the cold blue sky. Flying out of the valley? I did not blame them. The dry low shrubs disappeared gradually. The northern hills of the valley were covered with yellow saffron and pink and black iris. The further they went, the greener the surroundings. The bright plants and meadows were painful to look at. I wiped my eyes with the end of my scarf and leaned on the windshield.

We turned into a narrow side-road lined with huge willow trees. A black man holding the big gate waved us in. He was wearing a long thick coat and a rifle hung from his shoulder. I smiled to him, then caught sight of the field. I could not believe the thickness and the greenery of the trees around me. I was proud of my forty trees. In the pasha's orchard, there must have been hundreds of them. Boughs were caught together blocking out the sun and leaving the place cool and damp. A smell of citrus leaves and dung filled the air. Light green groves spread from the small road to the skyline. We passed through another iron gate and turned round to face a sparkling white mansion. From the top of the hill, it had looked like a big white spot at the end of the horizon.

The pasha stopped the engine and parked the car on the asphalt yard. In the middle of the courtyard there was a circular flowerbed full of jasmine trees, white fuchsias, and coral oleander trees. The jasmine flowers gave off a lovely scent and drenched the whole palace in a cloud of perfume. I sniffed some of the white flowers. The pasha turned his head and smiled, "Do you like jasmine?"

"Yes."

He looked at my face for the first time. Really looked at my face and saw me, saw that I was a woman who loved jasmine flowers. Before, I was sure, I was for him one of the black tents roaming the valley. "I will send you a shrub."

The back garden was teaming with olive, palm, and banana trees. The windows were big oval sheets of glittering glass.

Each door was as big as a whole room in Hamia. Urban people

were eager to get in and out of houses very quickly. With such windows and doors they could not beat the cutting cold. A house made of glass overlooked a rectangular lake. "The swimming pool," the pasha explained.

"Why? Can't you go to the Dead Sea?"

"I prefer to swim in fresh water," he said, and ushered me through a back door leading to the kitchen. It was spacious and full of tools I'd never seen before. The Sudanese cook stood protectively near the cooking machines. His red cap tilted forwards. His big rounded eyes told me that he disliked me and objected to my presence in his spotless kitchen. "Please feel at home," the pasha said, and left the kitchen.

"Hello, uncle," I ventured.

"No hello and no greeting. Start working, girl."

"Listen. The pasha asked me to come here and give you a hand."

"And you answer back too?" he said.

I went to the sitting room to complain to the pasha. The curtains were thick and yellow, the chairs dusty green, and the rugs on the floor were like the ones my sisters and I wove. He was talking in a foreign tongue to a black handle with a rounded ear. He continued talking while looking at me. "Yes, Maha," he said when he put the handle down.

"I want to give your cook a hand. I did not leave my suckling with my old father and come here to be humiliated. I am under your roof and protection."

"Al-Hadi! I am sorry. I'll have a word with him." He stopped and added, "Bedouin women are like Arab mares." Harb used to call me his beautiful mare. I would cook for them and go back home. I tightened my headband and stuck the end of my robe in my trousers. If they want original bedouin food, they would have to listen to me.

I was sitting on the stone steps watching the swaying colors of the oleander trees when the pasha called my name. I went to the kitchen and asked the cook for three big sacks of rice, as many slaughtered sheep as they had, and a big clay bowl. I decided not to cook in the spacious clean room and asked al-Hadi to light a fire outside in the back garden. The pasha smiled and asked the cook to listen to me. Daffash and al-Hadi went to the barn to slaughter the sheep. A thin old man was carrying logs and piling them in a clearing in the back garden. I poured some water on the cakes of dry yogurt and started rubbing them in the clay bowl.

"What is your name?" asked the old man.

"Maha, daughter of Nimer."

"I am Esrur, the gardener."

"You have green fingers, uncle."

"Since they bought me I haven't stopped working in this garden."

"You are not free?"

"No, my daughter."

The flames were blazing when I finished crushing and rubbing the yogurt cakes. I placed the big pot full of yogurt on the fire. It was getting dark and cold. I wondered what Mubarak was doing. My nipples stood up when I started thinking of him. The scent of the jasmine tree grew stronger; it was the flowers that were greeting us mortals before they went to sleep. I sat next to the fire, waiting for the meat to arrive. The windows were just panes of dark glass. I had a glimpse of a figure standing near the window on the second floor. Somebody was keeping an eye on the servants and cooks.

Um Saad

"Maha, my sister."

"Yes, Um Saad."

"What shall I tell you? Everything in Amman changed suddenly. The maize carts driven by coachmen and pulled by mules were replaced by noisy machines which filled the air with black smoke and steam. The coughing and tooting of the cars mingled with the clinking of liquorice juice peddlers' crymbals. I missed the cooing of pigeons and the silence of the nights. The radishes and cabbage fields along the banks of the stream dried up because of the poison the cars puffed out in the air. Even people changed. They took off their veils and capes and walked half-naked in the streets. A devil resided in Amman. The government built schools for boys and girls. The price of pale blue cloth went up because of uniforms. Children flocked to their school in the morning with wet flattened hair and bulging bags.

"I made some coffee then woke up Abu Saad. Mornings were the hardest because I could not usually tell my head from my feet. Washing faces, feeding mouths, boiling tea, and liquefying powdered milk usually consumed the whole morning. When they'd all left, the preparation of lunch would start. Abu Saad bought me a transistor radio which I used to put in the kitchen cupboard to protect it from splashes of water. I used to love listening to Listeners' Requests.

> 'Your eyes can wound and heal.
> If you want to leave me . . .
> I'll follow you, always.
> Behind you, always.'

"On Fridays, I used to invite all the family for lunch, including mother and father, Allah bless their souls. My father would smoke the hookah with my husband and my mother would snap the leaves of coriander to add to the ladies' fingers and tomato sauce. After I'd served the afternoon tea, I would collapse on the armchair. The municipality's bulldozer would not have been able to pull me up. My children cracked jokes about this habit. 'The hajjeh has sat down and only Allah will make her get up.' My legs got swollen like melons and my fingers became very stiff. I had soggy hands anyway. They are dry and smooth now."

"Mine are smooth too."

"We've become soft." Um Saad fixed the pink scarf over her head and started laughing, but there was sadness in that dreary hospital room.

Fingering the sheath and the plaits under my pillow, I asked Um Saad if she'd ever felt happy with Abu Saad.

"I loved the scent of the honeysuckle, but I tried hard to get used to the smell of black iris. The stink of guts used to turn my stomach upside down. I tamed my stomach, trained my stomach even to like the stink. When Abu Saad slept with me, I kept my mouth shut. I had a husband, children, and grandchildren. I got used to the lack of conversation between us. We just coexisted. Do you like this word? My son Walid liked it. He would say things like, 'I exist in this house. Actually, I coexist with you.'

"I existed. Mind you, I stopped dreaming about having firmer breasts, longer legs, and round hips. I just wanted a cream which might stop

158

the net of days spreading over my face. Um Gharib used to boil almonds and cucumber and leave the mixture to get cold. When I put some on my face, my skin become taut and I felt that it was going to crack up if I smiled. What was the use? When I washed it, back to normal."

"Why do you want to change your looks?"

"Bedouin women are different. Aren't they? They never use creams and rubbish. Do they?"

"No, they don't."

"They are wiser than us. We wax our legs, cut our hair, line our eyes, paint our lips. The problem is men never notice the change. Um Gharib, may Allah reward her, used to say that we are just vessels. That is how men see us. That is what men care about. So, sister, I got used to the house at the top of the Castle Mountain, to the noise of traffic in the city center, to the dusty stones of the Roman theater, to stuffing stomachs and ironing white shirts. I forgot completely about al-Shater Hasan and his Cap. I used to sit in the sun, read the Qur'an, and count the beads of my rosary."

Maha

The guests of the pasha started arriving in funny shaped cars which puffed out smoke like Tamam's pipe. The rice and mutton were well cooked, the yogurt was thick and rich, the bread was baked, and the almonds were peeled and fried. The breeze fanned the embers over which the big pots were boiling. I wiped my forehead, then collapsed in laughter when I saw al-Hadi. His white robe was smeared with soot and stained with blood. I laughed and thanked my mother for my black dress. The stars glittered in a clear, dark blue sky. It would be a magnificent evening. I washed my face and hands, shook the dust and soot off my dress, and dipped the wooden spoon in the yogurt.

I tasted the hot yogurt, scalding my tongue. Blonde hair and grand uniforms flocked to the well-lit front garden. I had a glimpse of gold eagles decorating chests. My hands started shaking. I threw the hot spoon into the fire and rubbed my forehead. The mountains. Harb's body was sliced into two halves like the mutton I was cooking. Nothing was left of his right leg. Flies licked frenziedly at his bright brown eyes. I pressed my hands on my head and asked Esrur, "Who are these people?"

He made a gesture with his thin black hand, as if snipping a rose, and said, "Our masters, the English."

"Uncle, have I been cooking the *mansaf* for them?"

"Yes."

I saw Daffash shaking hands with one of the English officers. I walked towards him. When he saw me, in my black robe and black head-band, walking towards him, he flinched. I said to his astonished face, "I want to have a word."

"Not now," he hissed, and continued smiling at the Englishman.

"I must talk to you now," I said.

He walked away from the guests and followed me to the back garden where the two big pots of yogurt were bubling. His voice was full of cold anger when he said, "What do you want, black widow?"

My chin was quivering as I asked, "Is it true what Esrur has told me. Are they English."

"Yes, leaders of the best English tribes."

"But the English killed Harb," I said, and tried to compose myself.

"Rubbish. These people are not capable of killing a fly," he said, then spread his cloak and went back to the congregation of foreign guests.

I sat down and began stirring the rice. I tried to control myself. Esrur was watching me with sad eyes. I sighed, but when I saw Daffash, standing by the gate and waving his hands in the air, making some of the guests laugh loudly, I stood up shouting, "Bedim the moon. Dark upon your heads." I began spinning round and round in circles like a newly slain goat. Shame on you, Maha. "Shame on you." Daffash, the son of a dog. I did not know I was cooking for the English. I kicked the hot metal pot with my foot and went to the front garden where clean, fragrant guests clad in white were conversing with each other. I held my head high and asked the pasha in a loud voice, "Why didn't you tell me I was cooking for foreigners?"

"They are not foreign," he said, sucking his cigar.

"Who is she?" asked an old army officer in funny Arabic.

"I am Maha, the daughter of Maliha, the daughter of Sabha."

161

Daffash rushed towards me, but was held by the pasha and al-Hadi. The guests found what I had said amusing and started laughing.

"She is one of the domestics," the pasha explained.

I saw the stars which guide travelers sparkling in a dark blue sky. I rubbed my forehead and tensed up my back. My chin was quivering when I said, "You killed my husband Harb." With metal eagles. The hum subsided and all the eyes were staring at me. Tears running on cheeks, head held high, I stepped forward, wrenched the eagle off the chest of an elderly man, threw it on the ground and stamped on it. I collected as much saliva as I could and spat on the surprised face of the English officer. Total silence except for the plaintive tunes of Nasra's reed-pipe and the cackling of burning kindling. The hoarse sound urged me to leave the mansion, to leave the den of foxes who had eaten my husband's flesh.

Daffash barked, "I will kill you, Maha."

"Foreign killers, all of you," I cried, then marched past the parked cars, past the flashing lights of lamps, past the mud hut of the guard, and out of the wide gate. If I kept walking by the river towards the left I would end up in our village. Hakim had told Nasra that the English had killed Harb. He never lied. I could not bury all the dead horsemen, so I had just sprinkled sand over their gaping corpses to protect them from birds of prey. The pasha must have drunk from their milk. He just shrugged his shoulders when I burst into tears. Feeding the people who had chewed on my husband's flesh. Shame on you, Maha. Curse Daffash and his shameful deeds.

It was pitch dark and cold. The trees looked like human beings in the dim light of the tiny moon. I continued marching, guided by the sound of running water. As long as the Jordan was beside me I would be fine. I realized at that pitch-dark moment that I was just a simple peasant woman. Yes, I did not understand many things really. I did not understand the language the pasha used when he was talking to the black handle; I did not know how to operate the machine which cooks meals in the kitchen, I did not understand why Esrur kept talking to the water in the pool. All the same, I knew who was responsible for murdering my husband. The English. The English killed Harb, the twin of my soul, and made my son Mubarak an orphan. Forgive me, Harb. The ice-cold wind hit my face and froze my tears. Bitter cold tears, eager to escape their bulgy bottle. Daffash the dog.

Out of the darkness, a wide cloak appeared. In the name of Allah! Was it Daffash? "Daffash?" The figure moved closer.

"Who is it?"

"Me, Sheikh Talib. What are you doing here at this hour of the night?"

"I am going back home."

"Why alone?"

"Because . . ."

He held my hand and said, "Poor widow." I did not want to be touched. I stepped back. "My wife is ill and blind. I always think of you. Strong Maha." He tried to pull me closer to him. Damn that hour. I pushed him with all my might. He fell down in the shrubs. His mumblings flew to my ears. Run, run. My feet barely touched the ground. Damn the English, Daffash, and the dirty old fool. Why didn't they leave me alone? I hadn't harmed anybody in my life. I even carried the beetle to safety on my broom.

Mubarak's cries filled the dark alleyways of the village. I started running faster to reach him and hold him to my chest and comfort him. The nipples of my breasts stood up ready to feed my suckling. Oh, why did I agree to go to the big mansion? When I entered the dim room I made out the figure of my father holding Mubarak and trying to lull him to sleep. He was sobbing. His eyes were red and swollen. I hugged him, pulled out my breast, and put it in his open mouth. He could not suck at the beginning, then gradually held my nipple. I wiped his face and asked my father, "When did he begin crying?"

"A while ago."

"Thank you, father."

"Where is your brother Daffash?"

"I left him there." My father held his stick, stood up, then shuffled his feet across the concrete. He was perishing under his robe. One day he would disappear.

My heart got rid of the mad beat. The cries of Raai could be heard. Where was the mighty watchman when Sheikh Talib tried to attack me? The village was blind. I lulled my baby to sleep singing one of my grandmother's old songs,

163

"Close your eyes and go to sleep.
May the eyes of your enemies never sleep.
Your moon has appeared in the sky.
May the night of your enemies never die."

I placed Mubarak gently in his rocking bed. Morning with his light feet was rushing towards us. I put my head on the pillow and tried to get some sleep. The right side was more comfortable than the left. All that kneading and stirring. All that running. Curse the English and their metal eagles.

Morning light slapped me on the face. I opened my eyes reluctantly. My muscles were as stiff as tent poles. Allah protect us from the evils of that day. My son smiled in his sleep. His mother was alive. Suddenly, Daffash pushed the door open and entered the room. His chin was bristling and his eyes were cold with rage. With his master's boot he kicked me in the face, "You bitch, you daughter-of-the-dog. What did you do last night? You humiliated me in front of my friends."

I stood up and attacked his face with my fingernails. He threw me on the rug and started slapping my face. My father entered the room and when he saw Daffash on top of me he raised his stick. Daffash snapped the stick and started beating me all over my body. I spat blood and saliva over his face. "Curse your religion. I will kill you now." Mubarak's screams urged me to stand up. I could not. Two of my teeth were lying on the floor. I collapsed and started crying and shouting, "Cursed. Slave to the English."

"She still can speak. If you don't shut up, I will break your bones one by one."

My father's headdress was on the floor. "Your father."

"I will break both of your arms." With his ammunition belt Daffash started beating me. The cold metal of bullets flayed my skin. I must protect my breasts to be able to feed Mubarak. I sat on the floor, folded my legs underneath me, wrapped my hands around my breasts, and bent my back. I did not know when the beating stopped. No. Just the hands of Nasra and Hamda trying to unfold my body. I resisted the frail hands of the women. They poured cold water over my head. I drew a long breath and sank into darkness.

164

When I woke up, Hulala was trying to force a piece of bandage into my mouth. The pain of injured flesh started hammering my head. My son. I wanted my son. All the women were gazing at me and weeping. Tamam's tiny eyes slid in front of me. "No bones were broken. Bruises everywhere." "We must do something about her gums." "Salt and warm water. Gargle. Gargle and spit." I spat into the can and shivered. I was spitting blood. Tamam threw down her pipe and started giving orders, "Nasra, boil some water, Hamda, heat some olive oil and mix it with basil. Jawaher, close the door. Hulala, do not open your mouth."

"I will open my mouth and spit on Maha's face. She is a disobedient girl and deserves to be beaten up."

"I said shut up."

They held me like a feather and helped me to sit in a rounded wash-basin. They folded my robe and placed it between me and the cold metal of the basin. Tamam said, "In the name of Allah the Beneficent, the Merciful," then poured hot water over my head and rubbed my hair. With warm water and soap, she massaged my body bit by bit. She creamed the bruised hands with egg and olive oil and tended my flayed back. She covered the bruises with bandages and cotton. "We must keep her warm." The warm milk scalded my open gum, I shook my head in refusal. Nasra held Mubarak and tried to feed him. She dipped a clean piece of muslin into the milk then put it in his mouth. He was so hungry that he sucked the milk from the muslin, leaving it stiff and dry.

I lay on the mattress open-eyed. Tamam covered me with a thick blanket and held Mubarak. Nasra was blowing her reed-pipe outside, not far from the tiny window. The tunes complained and complained. The sky had ears, but one made of mud and the other made of dough. Deaf. I wanted to die, I prayed to die and get rid of the piercing pain. A crazy shepherd was flailing my flesh with a sharp dagger. Our enemies. My brother. Why couldn't I defend myself? Why couldn't I hit back? Why couldn't I pluck out his eyes? I choked because my throat was full of blood and tears. Why couldn't I punch him on the nose? Anger and humiliation were bubbling inside me. The yell I uttered whirled in the village, rattling closed windows, waking babies and shaking bolted doors.

165

The Storyteller

In the name of Allah the Beneficent, the Merciful, "Or as darkness on a vast, abysmal sea. There covereth him a wave, above which is a wave, above which is a cloud. Layer upon layer of darkness. When he holdeth out his hand he scarce can see it. And he for whom Allah hath not appointed light, for him there is no light."

One dim morning, the mist soared over the village of miseries like a turban and the shrill twittering of birds pierced the ear. When the muezzin announced the hour of morning prayer, the black widow fidgeted in her bed. Raai put down his gun and unlocked the tin door of his store; Salih carried out the furnace and the bellows and placed them on the platform of his shop and Nasra steered her herd of sheep to the mountains. Maha's blood was boiling, her heart was drumming, and a drop of blood rose to the whiteness of her eye. She threw off the quilt and ran barefoot to her brother. When he saw the loose long hair and the wild eyes, he mentioned Allah. She smiled sweetly and kissed her brother's hand. Daffash couldn't believe that Maha had turned into a well-behaved sister.

166

"Good morning, my brother, lion of the prairies and protector of the dwelling of Qasim." He rubbed his eyes and looked at the bright smile. "What do you want?"

"Do you want me to help you put on your boots?"

"Yes."

She smiled, knelt down, kissed his toes, pushed the boot up, and tied the laces.

Allah warned His loyal worshippers in His wise book against the cunning of women, especially widows and spinsters. When there is no man to hold the rein, to mount them and drown them in the sea of cooking and children, women start laying snares. They whisper their songs in men's ears; they smile; they hiss their spells until they snatch men's souls. Maha, the black widow, helped her brother wash, cut his hair, dressed him up, and fed him honey and butter. She kissed his forehead, the back of his hand, and his toes. "Daffash, my beloved brother, please find me a job in the pasha's palace? I will buy more orange trees with the money I earn. By the soul of our mother, Maliha, find me a job."

Daffash was riding with the pasha to Um Qais when the question of Maha was raised. The pasha was searching for old clay jars and coins to sell to English travelers for handsome sums of money. The bedouins, who helped him dig out the old rubbish, believed that the ancestors had made the jars and pots so their descendants would have no difficulty in creating the same utensils. Local wealth made of local soil, they thought, and can be reproduced when necessary. They excavated the land and handed the old bowls, pots, and jars to the pasha, grinning.

The pasha, while examining the rusty coins with his magnifying glass, said to Daffash that since he had hired the new cook he hadn't had a decent meal. Daffash remembered Maha's pleas and asked the pasha if he would hire his sister to cook his meals. The more orange trees he had on his farm the more money the strangers would pay for it.

"Is she strong?"

"As strong as three she-asses tied together."

"Fine." When they'd finished wrapping the clay jars, the rusty coins, and the bits of rubbish, they rode back to Hamia. Daffash told his sister Maha that the pasha had agreed to hire her as a cook. She started jumping up and down on the mattress.

"Steady."

"Oh, my brother, the son of my father and mother, I cannot thank you enough."

Maha, the bitter colocynth, could neither calm down nor go to sleep. She spent the night memorizing recipes and reciting the hymns of witchcraft.

> "My father Gog and Magog,
> My uncles Harut and Marut,
> Help your daughter grow your fruit."

She had a bath, weaved her hair into two plaits, splashed some rose water on her breasts, rubbed her lips with cock's-crow petals, and lined her wild eyes with kohl. She left her son with her old father. She tied her things in a bundle and walked to the palace humming softly. When she got there she kissed the palm of the pasha, who smiled and withdrew his hand. She swept and wiped the floors, washed the bed linen, watered the plants in their pots, shook off the dust from the rugs, and cooked the best *mansaf* an Arab had ever tasted. She even started picking green olives and pickling them in big jars. The wide-shouldered pasha sucked his fat cigar happily. For the first time in months he did not get stomach-ache after dinner. That woman, he thought, was valuable and worth the one dinar he handed her at the end of the month. He did not know what was happening under his roof at night when the wolves started howling and owls started hooting.

When the moon gathered its light and retreated, when darkness descended, Maha's ankles started itching, her blood bubbling, and her heart beating. "Not tonight," she begged her masters the magicians. The itching continued, then her ankles started twisting and twisting until her left foot was facing east and her right facing west. Her fingernails grew harder and her mouth extended. The pasha took off his boots, riding breeches, and shirt. He blew out the candle and went to bed. Under the wings of darkness, the black widow entered the pasha's bedroom stealthily. He heard the light footsteps of the twisted feet.

"Who is it?"

"It is me, Maha. I want to close the curtains." She looked through the window at the dark garden and the gleaming water of the pool. "Grand," she said, and sighed. The pasha was watching the silhouette of the slim figure and the sparkling loose hair. He continued watching when, humming softly, she began taking off her clothes. She walked to the bed and fell on her knees. "My beautiful master," she said, kissing his toes lightly. It felt like the brushes of fluttering butterfly wings. The pasha had never been kissed on the toes before, so a string inside him snapped. She continued kissing and sucking his toes until he threw the thin covers on the floor, stooped, and took hold of the moaning lips. Like two tempests lost in the sea of desire, their bodies met. The hyena launched an attack on him armed with her tongue and teeth. The wide-shouldered pasha was transformed into a baby crying for milk and attention. She chewed and blew at him, chewed and blew until he became foam in her hands, a sponge, easily wrung dry.

Morning light found the sinners in their bed, the pasha's head reclining in the black widow's lap. She was stroking his hair and humming softly. From that morning on, the pasha became like a ring on Maha's finger. She would rub the ring and he would bow, listen to her orders, and obey. Men say that she started asking him for money, trees, sacks of rice, sugar, and gold bracelets. In a blink of an eye, the mighty pasha started selling pieces of land, unripe crops, and silver cutlery. The stream of gifts running from the palace to the farm became wider and wider. Like a file of laborious ants, the pasha's servants carried presents to Maha's orchard. Sacks of rice and grain were at the beginning of the column, utensils at the middle, and furniture at the end. Raai swore that he saw a convoy of mules bearing sofas, beds, armchairs, and even stoves heading towards Sheikh Nimer's farm. Arabs say that the black widow took possession of all the pasha's riches, even the clothes he was wearing.

One day, the sun stopped emitting bright light and started shedding crimson light on the valley of misery. Old hags, imams, and sheikhs held a meeting to find out the reason behind the glowing shame of the sun. What kind of sin was being committed in their valley. Who was breaching the creeds of Allah? The old hag living in the dolmen smoothed out her cloth and sprinkled it with sand; she drew lines and poked holes; she bulged her eyes then uttered the dreadful truth. "Maha, daughter of Maliha." Daffash stood up, fixed his head-dress, and galloped to the palace. The guard, the cook, the gardener, and the two servants were lying dead with yellow rings around their mouths. The curtains were fluttering and the rooms of the palace were empty, no rugs, no tables, no chairs. Nothing. Daffash unsheathed his sword and ran up the stairs to the pasha's bedroom.

Oh! What an ugly scene! Oh, creatures of Allah. His sister and the pasha were lying in bed and sucking each other's blood from opened veins. The pasha was no more than a skeleton covered with a thin layer of skin. His face was pale, his eyes were dull, and his teeth were red. Maha, the black spider, the destroyer of high houses, was well rounded and radiant with pleasure. "Allah is great," Daffash the lion of the prairies shouted, and hit the disobedient neck of his sister. She sprang to her feet, opened her big mouth baring two sharp fangs. Her fingernails grew longer and sharper until they became like needle points. She ran towards her brother to stick the needles in his flesh. He pushed her and swung his sword. She bent her back and changed her hands into hind feet. She jumped on Daffash's back and began wrenching his shoulder muscles. He looked pleadingly at the pasha who was en-grossed in sucking an invisible vein. Daffash threw himself on the floor, her cat head hit the concrete, she squeaked and started growing wings. The falcon hovered, then dived to snatch Daffash's flesh. Daffash threw himself on the floor and did not budge when he felt the grip of the claws on his back. The falcon did not feel any life in the corpse, so she turned into a trail of smoke.

Maha

The days sealed the cut in my gums, but did not heal the gaping wound in my heart. Humiliation, anger, and sheer helplessness. The women of Qasim restored the body to its former shape; stubborn and dignified, the heart refused to be mended and continued weeping silently. Save me from that village with its narrow alleyways and tiny-eyed mud houses. A leech sucking the mountainside. Unlike earthworms which are blind but sensitive, the village was blind and thick-skinned. Must breastfeed my suckling. The soft tissues around his fingers would disappear, his eyes would dry up, and the gap in his skull would close. Mubarak would grow up, would become a strong man. Would he protect me from his uncle? Would he break the hand which killed his father Harb and slapped his mother? I wiped my face with my hands and sighed.

I left part of my veil loose to cover the bare gums whenever necessary. Not all the time. Only when the men of the village greeted me and started laughing at me. My father, Sheikh Nimer of Qasim, the

171

tiger feared by the hawkish Hufour tribe, had been refusing to eat or drink since Daffash broke his crooked stick upon my back. He insisted on sleeping in the store-room among hay sacks and barley. He driveled all day. "It is full of hay," he kept repeating. He would hug Nashmi our dog and cry, "Take us, oh Maliha." I was worried about my father's health. Shrinking and murmuring all the time. I prepared his breakfast, placed it on a straw tray, and went to say good morning to him. He was leaning on one of the sacks, stroking Nashmi's neck. His trousers were yellowish-brown with urine, the white lines of his shirt had turned dark gray, and the cracks in his feet were full of dirt. The flies covered the blisters at the corners of his mouth. "Good morning, father."

"Maliha, you came back."

"I am Maha, father. Please drink some tea," I said, and placed a glass of steaming tea on the filthy floor. I wished he would let me bathe him and wash his clothes.

"Maha is dead. I gave her the land. Mubarak can have the farm now." I did not know what to say. I held his head and placed the rim of the glass between his dry lips. He sipped some tea then turned his head. "Enough. Leave me, now. All of you, leave me alone."

I wiped my eyes and carried the tray back to my room. Mubarak was gurgling and spitting. I wiped his face and head with a cloth soaked in warm rose water, changed his diaper, and tied him to my back. I must see how the orange trees were getting on. The old stones lining the canal were covered with green moss, the water was murky and smelt of rotting parsley. The henna and radish bed was as dry as the Empty Quarter.

I untied Mubarak and placed him on the shawl under a young tree to shelter him from the heat, birds, and insects. I filled the ewer with water and poured it in the invisible mouths of the plants. While tilling the soil with the mattock, I felt as if I were being punched. Daffash was beating me. Anger had reduced me to bare bones. Must try to go on living for Mubarak's sake, the son of Harb Ibn Qasim. You keep on living, starting, waiting for the sun to rise even if scarred, even if you feel like digging your heart out and burying it under the baby orange tree. My father loved Mubarak, loved me, and always stroked my hair with his flaky fingers and said, "My daughter, you are better than that scoundrel brother of yours. I wish you were a man because the land must go to its ploughman."

Nasra announced her arrival in the orchard by playing a short tune that sounded like, Mu-ba-rak. I smiled. Nasra dashed towards my son and held him tightly to her chest, "Missed you, Mubarak cuckoo," she kissed him noisily on the cheek. She put him in her lap and started blowing into her reed-pipe. The tune was intermittent and bouncy. My son started crying. "He does not like music. He is a tough horseman." Nasra pointed at my gums and circled her hand in the air.

"Fine and bare," I answered.

"Come back home, Daffash?"

"No. He took all his belongings. He is sleeping in the lap of the English and their servants."

"Must go. The sheep," she said, and bolted like an arrow between the trees.

The orchard was healed by Samir Pasha's medicine. The boughs grew together, forming a tent of leaves and fruit. I would not see the sun turning its back on me. Mubarak was teething. I had lost my two front teeth. The season of engagement would start soon. Wide-eyed girls would spend long expectant nights waiting for the season and its hidden promises. I would never place my head on any arm but Harb's. I was glad Sheikh Talib did not show his face after he'd fallen down in the shrubs. I kept out of everybody's way. I even stopped visiting Tamam. Daffash on that ill-omened night had filled the village with his loud barking, "Bitch, the daughter of an old dog, curse your parents. You are only a woman. Lick my boots, lick the general's boots. Obey your masters . . ." Sheikh Talib must have been laughing. He kicked my father and threw him on the floor. Murjan, Allah bless his hands, together with Nasra saved me from being killed. Daffash had been tightening his grip on my neck. I saw the colorful lights of Jerusalem, the lamplight in my wedding procession, and the faint lights of the shrine. A strong quern was grinding my ribs one by one. The pain of the flesh was nothing compared to the pain of the bones. Bone-deep ache. A cold eastern wind which penetrated flesh, arteries, spines, and even cut through iron nails.

I squeezed a slice of orange over Mubarak's mouth. Daffash had squashed my body and tried to push my soul out. I survived and he left the house, taking the magic powders — the radio, his rifle, and some of the sheepskin rugs. My father begged him to stay under his roof. "Maha will never repeat what she did again. Maha has repented. You are the master of the house. No one will disobey you." I could not hear most of what my father was saying, but his voice was weak and yielding. I shut my ears with my hands and went to sleep. The next morning, Samir Pasha's Land Rover was parked near the gate. Daffash threw his things in the back, got in next to the pasha, and slammed the car door. The humming of the engine drowned the whines and whimpers of my father, Sheikh Nimer, the tiger of Qasim.

My father refused to sleep on his mattress next to Daffash's metal bed. He would not stay in the room of the disobedient son who had never listened to his father. Was it true that he gave birth to a poisonous spider? Not his seed, surely. From that day on, my father slept on the filthy floor of the store-room. A dark green water gathered underneath soggy sacks. The air reeked of decay and urine as if I stored dung not clean hay. I shuddered whenever I entered my father's hiding place. Moss, decay, and weeds reigned over the store-room, paving the way for the departure of life.

I even took Mubarak to my father to drag him out of his corner with the force of young life. I placed Mubarak in his lap and asked him to say good morning to his grandfather. "Good morning, my little Maha. Did Maliha feed you properly?" Mubarak started crying and fidgeting. I shushed him and asked him to smile at his grandfather. When the blue flies landed on my son's face and licked his eyelashes, I could not leave him in there any longer. My old man was rotting in his shit and urine. The flies were sucking his blisters and the filth was chewing at his clothes. He was a heap of rotting bones. I marched out, placed Mubarak in his bed and marched back to drag my father out of his misery.

I boiled some water in a barrel and carried it to my father's hiding corner. "I will give you a bath."

He smiled and said, "Maliha, you are back."

"Yes, sheikh, I am back." I undressed him carefully and threw his clothes outside, then swept the floor and asked him to sit down on the rug. He obeyed me like a child and kept mumbling Maliha's name. I rubbed his hands with the loofah, then washed his back, his thin legs, and his head. Soap suds ran over his body and dripped down to the floor. Damn the barley and the hay. They were getting wet. My father's loose skin was shivering. I felt I was fighting Azrael, the angel of death. My father's eyes failed to look at me and instead they looked through me. Nothing could attract them back to earth. Nothing could stop them wandering. I rubbed and rubbed until my right hand ached with pain.

For the first time in my life, I searched for clothes in Daffash's room. He had never allowed me into his territory. There was a big picture of a smiling blonde woman in the trunk. She was licking her lower lip. Foreigners and their deeds. Shameless. In a pile of old clothes I managed to find a clean white robe, trousers, and a headdress. I dressed my father slowly. His hair had grown long and his chin was covered with short bristly hair. His hands were too shaky to hold the razor. I wrapped his head with the headdress and tied the ends at the back of his neck. "Come with me, sheikh."

"Yes, Maliha." I held his shaking hand and helped him step outside.

"Praise be to Allah. It is a bright night. Remember our moon, Maliha. Summer, I can smell summer. Yes." I helped him lie on the mattress and covered him with a light rug. "Remember our wedding, Maliha. We slaughtered a hundred camels, thirty goats, and twenty chickens. Remember the lights of . . ." His gritty voice dwindled into murmuring. A raven squawked into the extended darkness. No departures, raven of parting. Do you hear me? No parting.

175

Um Saad

"Maha, sister."

I rubbed my forehead and turned my head. The moon was growing old and tired. His gray light shrouded everything in the hospital room, including Um Saad's face. "Yes, Um Saad."

"Days had given birth to days and to disasters. As I told you before, I had really got used to my half-existence behind the brick walls of Abu Saad's house at the top of Castle Mountain. A few yards away from our house, they built a museum to display Roman bones, coins, and rusty bowls. I used to hear the restless bones rattling at night, eager to be buried under the ground. No Jordanian — they called the country the Hashemite kingdom of Jordan — no Jordanian would pay ten piasters to see rotting bones and mossy stones. We hated looking backward, seeing the past, learning. Rotting bones reminded us of death, transient pleasures, and the wrath of Allah. You know who used to come to the museum? Old English women wearing glasses and leather sandals. We used to laugh at them."

176

"The English killed my husband, Harb."

"May his unlived years be yours, sister. This is the way of the world. Don't worry, they left our country."

"I know. May they never return."

"At last, the English left our country after building clubs which no one could enter and strange-shaped toilets which no Muslim could use. Abu Subhi, the guard of the something Jack Club, told my sons many stories about the English. How strong men would chase a brainless tiny ball for hours. How they didn't wash themselves with water after going to the toilet. By your life, they just wipe themselves with paper. They loved dogs like their children and never worried about their hair and impure saliva. The kids used to give Abu Subhi the guard a hard time. They kept climbing the high chicken-wire wall and stealing cans of beans and sweets. But they left, sister, let your heart have a rest. When the government turned the clubs into schools then the locals, who were not allowed to enter the clubs before, flooded in and smashed the infidels' toilets and siphons."

"Siphons!"

"Yes. You pull a string and water flushes down all the dirt."

"We need one in Hamia, my village."

"They left our country and I saw the celebrations and procession from the veranda. Independence Day Festival. Cavalry, tanks, camel regiments in colorful uniforms, and music. Brass. 'Long live the King.' The Jordanian flag fluttered on our roof. Black for the Arabs' fearful anger, white for the Arabs' generosity and kind-heartedness, red for the blood of martyrs, and green for our fertile meadows. Colorful dreams we had because most of our plains were just arid desert. The lights of the Ammon Hotel did not go out until the morning. The country was happy and free, my sister, but it was the beginning of my slavery. The country danced light-heartedly till the dawn. The realization of dreams makes me cry; splits my heart in two. The country had realized its dream and was giddy with happiness. I slept that night with tears on my cheeks. They asked the blue dove why she was crying and she answered, because of her strong eyesight. I said, 'My eyesight is piercing; I see the future and cry over the days to come.'

"One afternoon, I was wiping the floor of the sitting room. My hair, eyebrows, lashes, and kaftan were all covered with dust and water.

177

Wet. The floor was wet and the chairs were piled on top of each other. It was summer time and I felt hot and sweaty. It was laundry day and my back throbbed with a dull pain after washing a heap of dirty clothes and linen. I could hear the faint sound of the transistor radio singing in English in the boys' bedroom. I raised my head and saw them. They were holding hands and laughing."

"Who?"

"Him and her. The man I had been calling my husband for the past twenty years and the woman in green who licked the side of her mouth like a snake. She laughed when she saw me squatting on the floor and wringing the dirty mat. 'Is that thing your wife?' she asked. Abu Saad held her wrist and said, 'Yes.' She said, 'I don't blame you.' I stood up, smoothed my kaftan, and asked, 'Who is she?' He said in his pathetic voice, 'Yusra, my new wife.' He said she was his new wife, my sister. I, Um Saad, mother of happiness, Haniyyeh, happy, tipped the murky water out of the bucket on the shining floor. Stupid thing to do because I had to dry it myself later on. She was a young, artificially blonde woman in high heels. The silk green dress clung to her body like smooth skin. I saw hundreds of blue flies hovering in the sitting room and fluttering their glittering blue-green wings. Disgusting. I said to the man I had been calling my husband, 'How dare you bring another woman to my house?' I said, 'How dare you do this to me.' He ignored me. He had no eyes for me. He ignored me and asked his young bride, 'Shall I show you the bedroom.' Maha, my sister, may Allah widen your chest for you and prevent your ribs from closing in. Abu Saad took her to my bedroom and closed the door. I saw red and green. I saw blood. Gripping the sharp kitchen knife, I stood close to the bedroom door. When I heard their suppressed sighs, the laughter, and the husky pleading, I could not open the door; I could not bear to see what they were doing on my bed. My hands were shaking and the knife was on the floor. I went to my son Walid and cried on his shoulder. He said, 'I am glad you know. The whole of Amman knows.' Amman the absent-minded city knew about Abu Saad and his new wife and was still smiling.

"That night, I slept with my kids on the floor. Did I say slept? By your life, I could not shut my eyes. The minaret of the Big Mosque was crying 'Allah-u-Akbar' when I found my belongings flung on the floor of the sitting room. My dresses, my two nightgowns, my capes and veils, my underwear, my kaftan, my Ramaj perfume, my two Max Factor lipsticks, and my comb were lying on the floor. I emptied one of the cupboards in the kitchen, folded my clothes carefully, then placed them in it. I decided to start sleeping on the kitchen floor. The fresh breeze coming from the top of the Crown Mountain might lull me to sleep.

"Abu Saad came in to the kitchen and asked, 'What's for breakfast?' When he asked me about breakfast, an invisible cord in my head snapped and I started slapping my face, wailing, and kicking his fat legs. 'Stop it, stop it.' I refused to stop. I could not stop, even if I'd wanted to. He smashed one of the chairs, picked up the legs, then broke them one after the other on my sides. I remembeed Abu Saad the butcher, the stink of blood, and the early days of my marriage when he used to beat me before sleeping with me. Yusra was standing in the doorway in her see-through red night-gown. Red is the color of Arabs' anger. Red is the color of my heart. Red is the color of blood. My angry heart shed red blood all over the Castle Mountain. I shouted, Haniyyeh shouted, Um Saad shouted, 'Beating me. Have you no respect for my gray hair?' He said that he got married to a second wife because of my gray hair. My gray hair was responsible. What can I do, sister? Can you check the flow of days and the spread of gray hair. They are unstoppable. Aren't they?" she asked, and fixed the pink scarf over her straight gray hair.

"Yes, they are unstoppable, Um Saad." I stretched my arm across the gap between the two beds and grasped Um Saad's hand. "No, you cannot stop the days," I said, then squeezed the freezing, trembling fingers.

Maha

Under the feeble moonlight, the face of my father looked younger, more relaxed. He opened his eyes, looked at me breastfeeding Mubarak, and smiled. "Maha, my lovely child. Is Mubarak all right?"

"Yes, father, just a bit hungry."

"I always wanted to be strong and protect you, but Allah wrote something else. The land must go to its ploughman. No, ploughwoman. The land is yours, Maha. This is my will. I have said it in front of the imam and Raai. Daffash does not deserve one span of it. It belongs to your son after you. They have witnessed my will."

I smelt departure. The smell of sweat, tears, and long untrodden paths. "Long life to you, my father."

"You've suffered a lot in your life. Allah's will," he said, and turned his face towards the lamp. My hands were shaking, were useless. "The heart does not want to leave you. I will miss you. I want to kiss Mubarak." I took Mubarak to my father and held him close to the dry lips. He kissed his forehead and praised Allah. "I testify that there is no god but Allah and no prophet but Muhammad." His gritty voice ebbed away. The moon disappeared behind the dark clouds. I could make out the head of my father lying on the pillow. I kissed his forehead, he must have sensed the warmth of my lips and smiled.

Clean as a baby, my father departed the earth people live on. I sobbed silently over his corpse. Loud noise would not bring him back. If tears brought back the dead, Harb would have been living among us. I was still wearing the black headband; I was still mourning my husband. I swayed and swayed to ease the pain in my chest. I massaged my ribs to urge my heart to continue beating. Shake your head to let the air enter your lungs. A devil up there was sucking the air out of the valley, leaving us floating in a void. Silence was the emperor, was higher than the king of noise. Silence, moss, and decay triumphed over the forces of life. Mubarak started crying loudly. "Shut up, you orphan, you son of an orphan."

I marched silently in the funeral procession through the narrow alleyways of the village. My father's body was washed, shrouded, and put in a coffin made of olive wood. The smell of incense burning reminded me of faraway places, souls leaving bodies and the scent of Harb. Tamam trudged beside me in the procession. It was a hot day. Hulala and Tamam started beating their chests and yanking their hair. I did not have any strength to lift my arms up. I masked my face, hiding the sweat, tears, and bare gums. My grief was deep, deeper than the valley of Abu Saleet. When you were standing at the edge, you could not see the animals and the trees at the bottom. So hollow and deep. No ashes, no rending of garments, no face slapping for me. Just a deep solitary mourning like the awesome silence of Abu Saleet.

Daffash, the son of my mother, attended the funeral and carried the coffin. Imam Rajab, Raai, Murjan, Sheikh Talib, and Salih, all participated in lowering the coffin into the grave dug in the ever-expanding cemetery near the shrine of Abu Aubayydah. They prayed the prayer of funeral for my father's soul. "Ease his grave torture, lift his loneliness, and forgive him his sins." The women were not allowed to enter the big hall of the shrine. They prayed in the sun outside. The men stood in files and raised their hands towards the sky. I did not know how to pray so I aped Tamam who kept hissing incomprehensible words, bowing, kneeling, then prostrating. Worship,

181

honor, and obey the designer of departures. Obey silently your Lord. Prostrate. Seal your lips, seal your soul, and hiss with the crowd. "May Allah accommodate Sheikh Nimer in his spacious paradise." Amen. The people who participated in the funeral walked back through the narrow alleyways to Sheikh Nimer's house to have lunch. Raai was crying from the platform of his small store, "A piaster each," while pointing at the glass jars full of sweetmeats, candy, Turkish delight, and roasted chick peas. "We have Marie biscuits," he told the approaching procession. Nasra, who was walking beside me like my shadow, said, "Raai stinks."

The clink of coffee cups, pestles, and brass ewers filled the two funeral tents erected in the courtyard. Nasra held the big tray and I piled the rice in the middle. My stomach turned upside down when I saw the men stuffing their mouths with mutton and rice. Butter was dripping down their beards and their faces were stained with yogurt. They wanted more rice, more meat, more butter to fill their bellies. I placed my head between my knees, ignoring the dough on the baking tin. The smell of toasted bread brought Daffash running. "Stupid woman. Can't you bake a piece of bread?"

I kept my head firmly pressed between my knees.

He yanked my plaits and barked, "I am talking to you."

With a blank expression, I looked at Daffash's mouth, his thin moustache, and the inquisitive eyes of the men of the tribe. Birds of prey were plucking the fighters' eyes out of their sockets. The pigeons of the Jordan Valley hovered over the citrus orchard then landed on top of trees like snow-flakes. My plaits would turn ash gray. I picked out the burnt bread and placed another loaf on the tin. I loved the smell of burning ashes. My nose searched for it in bread, meat, and even roasted coffee. Mubarak was crying. I gathered my dignity, covered my mouth, and marched back to the house. Did I see Sheikh Talib grinning smugly? Nasra and Hamda took over and managed to feed all the men. The women and children waited patiently for the leftovers. Mubarak was hungry and took hold of my nipple as soon as it touched his lips. He was starving. Yasmineh, Hamda's youngest daughter, was running after the trays of food like a tiny puppy; scurrying and scurrying from hunger. Hamda shouted, "Yasmineh, sit down. Enough of this running."

Sheikh Nimer of Qasim, the tiger feared by the hawkish Hufour tribe, had left this earth to be reunited with Maliha. I wished my soul would seep out of my body to meet its twin Harb. When I took out the unfinished carpet from the trunk, the women of Qasim were puzzled. Tamam smacked her lips and said, "You are not supposed to be working the second day. You will make the angels angry." I wanted to keep my hands occupied or else I would smack somebody or something. Ignoring what Aunt Tamam had said, I hit the bars of the loom. The faces my heart craved to create were numerous. Click and bang. Sabha's tattooed chin, Maliha's warm smile, Harb's brown eyes, or the crooked figure of my father. Click, bang. I inserted thread into thread and hit the loom. Click, bang.

That night, I saw two tiny moons. That night, while changing my son's diaper, I saw two teeth in the small mouth. He bit me when I was breastfeeding him. My missing front teeth flowered in Mubarak's mouth. I ran my tongue along the cavity between my teeth and smiled. I had not lost my teeth after all. My son, the apple of my eye, was growing. His legs had become stronger and would support his body soon. I held his head close to my chest and whispered in his ear, "Grow up, grow up, son. May you only see happiness. Your father used to be the best horseman in the tribe, your grandfather used to be feared by all our enemies, and your mother . . . I don't know what to say about your mother. She is like an earthworm which crawls under the sand in order not to be seen." I fondled his tummy and he started babbling and spitting. The sound of his playful gurgling filled the room. I kissed his cheeks noisily then rubbed my face on his belly. He started laughing. He started laughing. A clear innocent sound like the sound of running water. A sound bubbling out of a newly born heart. I fed him some rice and yogurt, washed his face, then rocked his bed until he went to sleep. While pressing the cradle with my foot, I saw a flock of white doves fluttering their wings over my suckling's head.

Silence reigned again in the valley. My ears were searching for the cries of Raai, the chirps of cicada, and Nashmi's barking. Where was Nashmi's barking? "Nashmi," I cried, opening the latch of the door. I looked for him in the courtyard, the store-room, Daffash's room. No trace, I went out of the yard to look outside. There he was lying under the palm tree. When I stroked his head, I realized that he was

183

dead. His hair was cold and his eyes were shut. No breathing whatso-ever. In the dark, he looked like an old man squatting under the tree. I carried him, crossed the canal, and dug his grave under the best orange tree. As I lowered his body in the hole, tears that had been suppressed began to flow.

Um Saad

"Maha, sister."

"Yes, Um Saad."

"Maha, my companion in this empty hospital room. Days have gone and days have come and I lived long enough to see another woman occupying my own house. She would play cards with my sons, listen to English songs with them, dance and crack jokes. The way they used to dance was strange. They would shake all of their body and jump up and down like monkeys. Very different from our smooth swinging and swaying. She would imitate the way Abu Saad spoke and my sons would shriek with laughter. I would hear the echoes of laughter while cooking in the kitchen. I still cooked stomachs and guts, rolled vine leaves and stuffed eggplant. I also dried mint, parsley, and coriander. I did the sweeping, wiping, dusting. I did not clean the bedroom though. Abu Saad forbade me to enter that room, my room. Now her room.

"I used to lie on the mat spread on the kitchen floor and utter a long sigh of relief because the day had ended at last. For a few hours

185

at least, I didn't have to bend that stiff back of mine. Although the breeze traveling from the top of the Brown Mountain was cool and refreshing, I could not shut my eyes and go to sleep. The illness, my son Farid told me, is called 'insomnia' or something. You just cannot go to sleep. I used to place my head on the pillow and listen to the sounds of the city. The wailing of police cars, the swish of traffic skidding by, the barking dogs, the thudding of the mill, and the airplanes' dull whirring. I even heard the sound of splintered glass rising up from the Ammon Hotel. I would know that it was nearly dawn and that the big guys were so drunk that they could not hold their wine glasses. Any sound was welcome. Any sound was better than the ahs and ohs of the woman in my bedroom. 'Please, here,' and 'Please more,' and the grunts of Abu Saad, the man I had been calling my husband for the past twenty years. Because he was my husband, I knew what the grunts meant. I would stuff my ears with cotton wool and hope that sleep would visit my eyes.

"When Um Gharib my friend noticed the swollen eyes and the shaking hands, she took me to a holy sheikh living in a cave at the back of Castle Mountain, towards the city center. 'Sheikh Salim has got the key for your door. Your misery will give birth to happiness.' I followed Um Gharib up the steep mountain ridge until we reached a plateau. The cave, which was closed with a wooden door made of empty vegetable boxes, overlooked the even plateau. We sat on the ground waiting for our turn. Other people, mainly women, were waiting patiently for the wooden door of the cave to be opened. All the faces looked tired, sweaty, and dusty. An old woman with sparkling eyes addressed the waiting crowd saying, 'I have no problems other than dandruff. My husband adores me.' The women nodded their heads in unison. We all claimed that we were physically ill and that we had loving husbands. Of course, for all the women the illness was in the heart. Suddenly she asked, 'Do you see my sparkling eyes?' Her eyes were really sharp and shining. 'Whenever I make a salad, I squeeze some fresh lemon juice into them.' I looked at Um Gharib and smiled. 'Do sparkling eyes save you? No, they don't. What are you doing here. All of you. Don't you know that Sheikh Saleem is a crook? Curse your religion.' When the old woman got tired her voice became a murmur in the background noise of the busy traffic flowing to the city center.

"When my turn came, my armpits were wet and smelly. As I walked into the cave, I kept my head down, afraid to be seen by one of our neighbors. If Um Jamil was there, only Allah could save me from her tongue. The cave was cold, damp, and empty. My body welcomed the cool shade after sitting for hours under the glaring sun. A bald man with a white cap was sitting on the thin rug. He waved his hand, ordering me to sit down. 'Yes, our master.' He rolled his eyes and asked me what was wrong with me. 'My husband has married another woman,' I said in shaky voice.

"'Uh, a second wifer,' he said to an invisible servant. 'Put some money in this box.' I took off one of my gold bracelets arid threw it in the box. He rolled his eyes and handed me three dark sticks. 'Burn them at sunset and slide the ashes under her door. Wear this amulet all the time. Never take it off. Next time, bring me a single thread of his hair and his dirty underwear.'

"'Yes, our master.' His body started jerking as if hit by an electric current. He said in a deep lazy voice, 'Whenever-he-touches-her-she-will-turn-into-a-rattling-snake. Whenever-he-kisses-her-he-will-see-a-black-slave-with-cracked-lips.' His voice echoed in my blazing head as I walked back home. I expected to see a leopard snake sitting on my bed. No black slave girl, no leopard snake, no shit. After the heartache, several sweaty climbs to the cave, and the loss of five gold bracelets, Yusra remained a young woman with dyed hair. I would burn the sticks and the thread of hair and wait patiently in the kitchen for Abu Saad to come running to my arms. I hugged myself and thought about the following proverb, 'Donkeys cannot climb up the minaret's steps and call for prayer.' It is impossible.

"The cries of the night grew louder. I started leaving the kitchen and pacing around the house just to get some fresh air. The pacing became marching and the marching turned into running. One night, the breeze had a velvety, playful quality. I remembered the urgent kiss of Muhammad and the rubbing of chins. I fingered my lips and cheeks and found them rough and dry. Run, Haniyyeh. Run. My feet were barely touching the ground when it happened. Like birds, I fluttered my arms in the air. I slipped out of my skin and rolled into another identity. I was Hind Roustom in a film dancing to Farid al-Attrash's tunes. I was young, a well-rounded woman with dyed hair. I held the

187

tin gate of Muhammad's store firmly and began seeing rice. Grains of rice everywhere, floating in the air, rising and rising until they formed a cloud of rice around the minaret. I felt light, happy, and free. Later on, my husband and two strange men found me in the Big Mosque's yard, pushed my hands into a long-sleeved jacket, then tied the sleeves behind my back. Do you know what I was doing in the yard? By your life, I was sleeping. I was having my first deep sleep in months. They woke me up, threw me in a car, and brought me to this paradise."

"Um Saad, this is no paradise. It is a madhouse. You must not forget that."

"Yes, Maha. It is a madhouse. Must not forget, must I? Tera-lam-tera-lam.

> To the madhouse, he sent me
> He never visited me, me.

Beat the drum!"

"There is no drum here."

"Beat anything." I started banging the cupboard with both hands.

Um Saad's voice was flawless. I joined in, "To the madhouse, where mind sparrows twitter and bees fly away, he sent me, meee, meeee." We shrieked with laughter. The English doctor entered the room and started shouting at us in a different tongue, then said in Arabic, "Shut up."

I eyed his steel-blue eyes, his thin fingers, and wide white robe, then shouted, "No, you, shut your foreign mouth."

Maha

When I opened my eyes, the room was flooded with dazzling sunlight. Birdsong and the cooing of pigeons filled the orchard, filled the valley. What a blessed, bright morning. I rubbed my eyes and opened the door and the window. Mubarak was breathing evenly in his sleep. Air bubbles swam to the surface of the cold water of the barrel when I plunged the ewer into it. I poured the freshening water on my face, on my head, on my hands. A rabbit bolted towards the field. White and soft. I opened all the doors and windows of the house, even the door of Daffash's room. Before I went to the well to fetch morning water, I made a big fire in the yard. I must burn the motheaten clothes and the mossy sacks of barley and hay. Why should I keep the barley with no horses, camels, or cows to feed? I heaved the sacks one by one on to my back and threw them into the yard, then added the sweepings to the pile. I placed my father's and Daffash's mattresses in the sun, then threw Daffash's old headdress and boots on the fire. After pulling my plaits in front of the tribe's men, he came back to apologize. "Sorry, sister. I lost my temper." I added the picture of the blonde woman. Every rotten piece of wood, every mossy shred of cloth, even my father's broken stick found its way to the yard's fire. I scrubbed and cleaned until the whole house of Nimer smelt of washing powder. I left the doors and windows open for the air to dry up all the moss and damp.

With a black piece of cloth, I tied Mubarak to my back and headed towards the field. Mubarak was getting heavier every day, I thought, as I placed him under the young tree. I rooted out the weeds and watered half of the trees. Nasra had brought me goats' droppings to fertilize the orchard. When the box of droppings was empty and every tree was drinking the nourishing water of the fertilizer, sweat was trickling down my spine. I tied Mubarak once more to my back, jumped over the canal, and marched back to the house.

Nasra came running towards me carrying two roasted quails. "Caught and cooked them, me."

We spread a mattress in the yard and carried Mubarak's rocking bed outside. He was asleep, so I covered his face with the piece of tulle Tamam had given me. We ate the crisp roasted meat and drank some yogurt. The frail limbs of the quail always made me feel sorry for the poor bird. Nasra's green eyes were sinking in their sockets and her bare gums chewed and chewed at the meat. My son drew a long breath and turned his head on the pillow. The buzzing of bees looking for flowers filled the valley. Mubarak opened his eyes and smiled. I said, "What a lovely day!"

"Yes. Sends his regards, the wise Hakim. You strong, he said."

Strong, wise old man! Maybe if he sent me some good medicine, a mixture of rare herbs, then my heart would be cured. "Nasra, will you keep an eye on Mubarak. I want to gather some herbs and kindling."

"Go, sister."

I tied the loose end of the veil around my face to cover the bare gums, tightened the headband, and marched towards the mountains. I collected dry sticks and boughs, chopped them into similar shape and length, then tied the bundle to my head. I looked for bugloss, sage, camomile, and thyme. I made a bunch of each and tied them to my waist. From the top of the mountain overlooking the valley, the village looked small and withered. The two shops, Salih's and Raai's, stuck out like two bulging eyes. The shrine dominated the east side and the mansion the west. Samir Pasha on one side and Imam Rajab on the other. The village was besieged by sounds from the minaret and the noise from the mansion. Allah-u-Akbar. The husky music of the English. I followed the sinking sun with my eyes. The Dead Sea looked like a thread of silver spread out to the end of the horizon. The air tasted of bitter salt. The sun knew that she would sink behind the sea, she would die at the end of the day, but she never repented. She would pull herself together and rise again. I preferred to take the short cuts home, stepping on thorns and weeds. The footpaths looked bleak, trodden, pale in the orange glow of the setting sun.

I put down the heavy bundle of dry kindling quickly, and greeted Tamam, Hamda, and Halimeh, who were sitting on the mattress in the yard. "Welcome, my aunt," I said, kissed Tamam's hands, then kissed Hamda and Halimeh on the cheek. "Welcome, guests of the Merciful." Nasra was pulling faces at Mubarak who responded with bursts of clear laughter. I lit a small fire and boiled some tea with sage. The aroma filled the yard, the orchard, and the village, soothing tired hearts.

"I wanted to see how my grandson is getting on. Is he all right? Soon, he will start walking. Praise be to Allah."

Hamda handed me a bundle of fresh dates. "For his teeth, rub his gums with dates."

Halimeh could not raise her head and look me in the eye. The cave and Daffash was a bad memory hanging in the air. I held her hand and said, "We are the daughters of today, Halimeh."

She laughed nervously and pulled a small sack out of her garment front. "I brought you some seeds and bushes to plant around this yard."

"What do you have?"

"Tomatoes, eggplants, zucchini, peppers, water melons, cucumbers, okra, and Arabian jasmine. Raai brought the seeds for Salih from the cooperative."

I laughed. "I've always wanted jasmine. I will have a proper garden."

"You eat from what you plant," Tamam said, puffed some smoke then asked, "Can I have some of your henna?"

191

"Aunt Tamam, you are too old for such things," said Hamda. With the end of the long pipe, Tamam spanked Hamda on the hand. "Hey, girl. I am not old." They all started laughing at Tamam's indignant face and her washed-out plaits. I looked at the flushed face, tiny eyes, twisted lips, and wrinkled skin. Aunt Tamam's heart was still green and youthful, was still waiting for the reaping season to come.

Nasra picked up the reed-pipe which was hanging around her neck and placed it between her lips. Sage tea boiled on the ashes, the gentle tunes of the pipe and the smell of burning tobacco. Coming back home after a long, sweaty day. I sighed. The glow of the sunset was dimmed by the creeping darkness. We drank tea and talked about our children, our husbands, and our plants and trees. We laughed at Raai's jumpy walk and his cowardly heart. We talked about our predictions for the engagement season. Tamam said, "I think that young man Murjan has an eye on Jawaher."

"My daughter? She's still young, aunt."

"Almost eleven. She's not young."

Nasra stiffened when Halimeh asked about Daffash. "When will your brother get married? Better than chasing foreign women." I shrugged my shoulders. I had nothing to do with Daffash. "Sheikh Talib is looking for a wife." An ear made of dough, another made of mud. I did not hear what Halimeh was saying.

"Can you do me a favor, sister?"

"Your support."

"I want a metal latch for the three doors and an iron gate for the yard with a lock . . ."

"Do not be afraid," interrupted Tamam.

"I am not. It is better to be cautious. There are a lot of strangers in the village. Will you take two boxes of oranges in return?"

"I will ask Saleh first."

Washing my face, I watched Mubarak strutting behind the chickens trying to imitate the cock Sahi. "Mmm, food," he babbled, and I did not know whether he was referring to himself or the hens. By the spirit of Sabha my grandmother, days succeeded days and my son was growing up quickly. His dark hair surrounded the rounded open face and framed his big brown eyes. His legs looked straight and strong in the trousers Halimeh sewed for him. I put some grains in a pot and handed it to Mubarak. "Feed them, go on." I scattered some grains in the yard to tempt the lazy birds. My son did the same and all the chickens followed his hand. I sang to him,

> "Cock, cock, cock and chickens.
> Chicks, chicks, chicks, chicks.
> Egg, egg, egg, egg, QUACK."

When I shouted, "Quack," my son laughed from the depth of his innocent heart. I joined in. "Heh-heh." That was his signal for me to start chasing him. I walked slowly towards him. He stuck his hands on his sides as if somebody was trying to tickle him and started giggling. On his face I saw a mixture of glee, excitement, and mischievousness. I jumped and he shouted, "Humm." I kissed him noisily on the cheek. He kissed me back. A faint, weak "Bbba." My heart wanted to fly out of my chest and wrap Mubarak with its wings, protect him from the assaults of time.

The plants I had been watering for the past two years grew and flourished. The Arab jasmine filled the yard with its refreshing perfume. I covered the vegetable bushes with the plastic sheet Nasra had brought me, and enjoyed picking two crops a year. Nasra told me that she had seen the plastic sheets in Samir Pasha's orchard. "Protect your plants from cold." The baby orange and lemon trees grew up, the sick old ones were cured by the pasha's medicine and the whole orchard started bearing fruit. I sold oranges and lemons to Raai, who had found an interested city merchant. A dinar a box. I bought a goat to feed Mubarak from its milk and a dog to protect the house. I called the dog Nashmiyyeh after Nashmi and the goat Nawmeh to please Nasra.

The women of the village considered my house their house and they came every afternoon, carrying their embroidery, spinning, weaving, and stories. They would sip sweet tea, weave colorful rugs, and unload the burdens of their hearts. I offered mint tea, sage tea, cinnamon tea, and tea with cardamom and fried paste with butter and honey. The sun enjoyed listening to the whispers and laughs of the women of Qasim; it lingered in the afternoon sky to give them light and warmth. When sniffing the jasmine, I felt the warmth of my mother's hand through my robe, my father stroked my hair, and Harb, the twin of my soul, kissed the back of my neck. Their eyes were protecting the house and the orchard. The firm white jasmine flowers emitted a strong perfume which left me breathless and content.

On one of the afternoon visits, I realized how old and weatherbeaten Nasra looked. Her green eyes had lost some of their brilliance and looked like olive leaves: dusty green. The warm brown hair was turning to ash gray. The fire of years was burning the hair of all my sisters, all except Hulala who still had pitch-black plaits. Time had punched Tamam's mouth, pulling it to the right. I taught Mubarak how to kiss the back of his grandmother's hand to put some happiness in her heart. The old pipe would laugh and smack her twisted lips. Hamda's husband got married to a second wife and left their dwelling. Hamda who used to be full of vigor and zeal looked like a broken stem. The women tried to console her, to bring her back to life, to remind her how useless her husband was. She would sit on the wool rug and watch the still palm trees. "He is the father of my children," she would say suddenly. Jawaher came to visit us and looked as bouncy and unfettered as a free bird. Since she had married Murjan — may Allah lengthen his life — she choked with happiness. Once upon a time, I was young, free, and in love with a tall horseman. Then, the hands of days were as smooth as silk and as bright as clear dawns.

Why couldn't I touch the passing days, smell them, or even sense them? I would have tried to prevent the days treading over the plains of my face. You look in the mirror and see the gray hair, the lines running down the face like permanent tears, and the dimming eyes. Once, I was young and attractive. Everything around me was getting loose: my skin, my clothes, my world. A creature inside me kept shrinking and shrinking, tired of life and its treasury, it sought peace and quiet. Even the palm and orange trees were becoming harder to see. I spun and spun like a silkworm; I dug and dug the soil like an earthworm; and at night I curled my spine like hedgehog and went to sleep under the solitary sky.

I heard Nasra's pipe singing, "Mu-ba-rak." Her robe was tatty, was fading black. I must ask Halimeh to make another robe for Nasra. "Need a new robe, Maha." I laughed and said that I thought that

Nasra was the one who needed a new garment. "Will leave our land, the English."

"What?"

"Told me, Hakim."

"No, it cannot be true."

"I swear by Nawmeh. Will leave our land, the English."

I ululated and ululated. My eyes were full of tears when I said, "A white day. A bright day, Mubarak." I ran and hugged my son tightly. "Mubarak, the apple of my eye, the English will leave our land." I kissed my son and wept silently. Where was Harb, the twin of my soul, Mubarak's father? Where were my teeth? My husband had no hands, no head, no legs when I saw him in the well-bed. Just a dagger, a chest, a boot, and shreds of burnt flesh and cloth. Dark upon dark. I held my head high and cried, "We must celebrate. We must celebrate."

"No. First. Want to get married, me."

I hugged Nasra and said, "Your turn will come." She blew a long plaintive "Oh" into her pipe then bolted to the mountains.

I spent the morning stuffing dates with almonds and frying paste. We must sing, we must dance. A blessed day. The English tried to change our lives and our land, but failed. Occupation was like a thin cloud, which was blown away by the wind. The orchards never stopped bearing fruit, the sky remained clear and blue and Hakim, the wise old man, the spirit of Arab resistance, was still alive. I had lost my husband, the twin of my soul, and the rider of the best stallion. Although my hands were shaking while kneading, I felt strong and content. I must prepare the best tea, the best sweets, the best coffee for my sisters. I would add sugar and cardamom to the roasted coffee grains. No bitter coffee, that day. I made a necklace of jasmine and put it around Mubarak's neck. The English had left. Too late. The heart had forgotten how to flutter in the chest, how to spread its wings and fly, how to soar and hover over our valley.

The Storyteller

In the name of Allah the Beneficent, the Merciful, "Lo! it is those who disbelieve in the Hereafter who name the angels with the names of females."

One gloomy morning, in a flash, Daffash remembered Hulala the Diviner in the dolmen. He rode to Hulala and explained to her his ailment. Maha was not his sister, she said, she was not a daughter of human beings, she was not an Inns like them. "A semi-demon, your sister is," she said. She smoothed out a red cloth and sprinkled it with sand, then drew lines and poked holes. She frowned and shook out the cloth then said, "Your problem is an entangled net. The pasha will be cured if you feed him for seven days royal jelly made by the black bees residing at the top of the dark mountains. The beehive is guarded by a black-sworded man, the toughest horseman of the Hufour tribe." He put on his cloak and was about to leave the dolmen when Hulala warned, "Beware, my son, of the big black queen. Her sting is deadly."

Daffash chose three of the best-trained young horsemen of the tribe to accompany him in his pursuit. The horses flew like wind, crossing plains and climbing mountains. The horsemen's eyes only saw the glare of the sun, their ears only heard the cries of eagles, and their mouths only drank the salty waters of the Dead Sea which quench no thirst. The hooves of their Arab horses cut distances like sharp daggers. While swaying on horseback, Daffash — yes, Allah — saw a huge black cloud. Black what? Black cloud. Could it be the hive or could it be a mirage created by exhaustion and thirst. Who am I? Who am I?

I am the storyteller.
My box is full of hives.
I am the yarn-spinner.
I spin and spin many lives.

When the band of horsemen saw the tall well-built Hufour guard, they knew they were in the right place. The hive was hidden under a sharp rock sticking out of the mountain overlooking the deep hollow of the Dead Sea. The bees formed a pitch-black cloud hovering around the hive near the spring. The water dripped from the tip of the rock but never reached the bees. Praise be to Allah, a goatskin full of pure honey, hidden behind a curtain made of water-drops. The Qasimi men dug their knees in their stallions' sides. Unsheathed their swords and charged. The clink of swords could be heard in Hamia and their twinkle could be seen in Jerusalem. Clash, clink, and STRIKE. Clink, STRIKE, and clash. The guard was strong and quick with his sword. Wahdan, the best fencer of Qasim, attacked like thunder, threw the guard of the hive on the ground, and put the end of his sword on his throat. "By Allah, don't kill me," the guard pleaded.

"Wear your headband around your neck for the rest of your life. Tribes must know that you are only a woman in battle." Quickly and with shaking hands the guard slid his headband down his head. At that instant, the queen bee left the hive, flew to Wahdan's neck, and stung the vein of life. He fell off his horse, a corpse. The queen bee flew away and all the other bees fluttered their wings and followed her dutifully. A black cloud of buzzing bees soared in the pale sky, then

197

disappeared like a trail of smoke. The band placed the hive carefully in one of the saddlebags, tied Wahdan to the back of his horse, and trotted back to the village.

When Daffash got to the palace, past midnight, the pasha was having one of his fits. The sound of crying and banging filled the empty rooms of the deserted palace. Daffash tucked the pasha into bed, tied the saddle belts around him, filled a spoon with royal jelly, and stuck it in the pasha's mouth. The jelly dripped down his throat. The cutting taste of the jelly made him cough. Loyal Daffash kept feeding, and filling his mouth with jelly until he huddled himself and went to sleep for the first time since he had met the she-devil who had deprived his eyes of sleep. Daffash laid his exhausted head upon his headdress folded like a pillow and went to sleep too.

The sound of wailing woke Daffash up. The pasha was crying and calling her name, "Maha. I want Maha," he repeated.

"My master," Daffash said, "she will damage your health."

"You don't understand. All my flesh is itching for her. I want her even if it means my death." Every night, the pasha would plead with Daffash to let him go to Maha, would beg him to release him, would cry in a broken voice, "Please, let me die." Daffash ignored his pleas and kept him tied up to the bed. He continued feeding him jelly, honey, and milk until he got stronger and his protruding cheekbones were covered with flesh. Gradually, he started walking around and talking about the farm. All the same, Daffash locked the doors and kept an eye on him.

One night, Daffash woke up and did not find the pasha in his bed. He ran to the stables, jumped on his stallion, and rode to the orchard. He found the pasha running towards the big gate of Sheikh Nimer's orchard. Daffash threw himself on the ground and grabbed the pasha's ankles. The pasha fell flat on his face. While resisting Daffash's grip, he pleaded, "No. Please, no. I just want to see her, that's all. I beg you." His tears were rolling down his face like water from a spring.

"No, my friend." Daffash had a glimpse of a shadow lurking near the doorway and heard suppressed laughter. "Criminal! Dream peddler! Destroyer of souls!" he cried, and helped the pasha, who had already lost all his strength and become as light as a child, on to the horse.

Maha, the black widow, suppressed her laughter when she saw the skeleton of the pasha clinging to her gate. She turned round, shut the door, blew out the lamp, and went to nightmareless sleep.

Maha

My forehead was damp when I offered glasses of tea to my sisters. Jawaher was beating the drum, Nasra playing the pipe, and Halimeh and Hamda were dancing on the unfinished rug. Tamam was smoking heavily and Hulala sat quietly leaning on the wall. Mubarak and Hamda's son Khalif were chasing the cock. The jasmine blossoms blown by the afternoon breeze landed on our heads. The perfume of flowers and the aroma of cardamom tea and fried paste filled the house, the orchard, and the valley. Rise up, up to the noses of the departing English, may they never come back. I placed the tray on the floor and said, "By the soul of my husband Harb, I will dance." I stood erect, stretched my arms towards the sky, swayed my hips, jumped then landed gently on the bare rug. My captive body was set free by the drumbeats and the excited voices of women. The gentle water of the Dead Sea stroked and stroked my shoulders, my waist. A perfect moon sent forth pearly light over the sea plain. "My lovely mare." Flap, flap, flap. Sway your hips and sway your hips. When the women uttered a long-drawn trilling sound, the sky turned warm orange.

> Qasimi women of Hamia,
> Be happy, be happy.
> Your enemy has departed.
> Be happy, be happy.
> Days of fig and olive,
> are coming, are coming.

When we finally sat down and started weaving, Nasra looked me in the eye and said in sharp voice, "By the soul of Nawmeh" — I shuddered. I did not like the memory of that goat — "want the farm, your brother."

"Which farm?"

"This farm."

"Nasra, are you truthful?"

"Told me, Murjan."

I rubbed my forehead, pushed up the headband, and asked my sisters, "What shall I do?"

Hulala said, "He is a man and has priority."

Tamam puffed some smoke and said, "The imam and the guard witnessed your father's will."

Hamda said, "Your father, Allah bless his soul, gave you a share of the land in his will."

Halimeh's voice was low and composed when she said, "You are the ploughwoman of this land. You must fight. We will support you."

"Yes," shrieked Nasra.

When the moon had disappeared behind the dark clouds, I heard a knock on the door. "Who is it?"

"Daffash. Open the door."

I put on my robe and slid the latch open. "What do you want?" I said to his dark face.

"Just a visit."

"At this hour of the night?"

He barged in and stood in the middle of the room. "Mmm. You have a decent house."

"It took a lot of cleaning."

He kneeled next to Mubarak's bed, grabbed his arm, and shook him until he woke up. "Welcome, my little nephew. I am your uncle. Shhhh. Don't cry."

I sought refuge from the evil devil. "What do you want?"

"I just came to inspect my property."

"Your property? Since when?"

"Little sister. It is my property."

He took a piece of yellowish paper out of his pocket and said, "Sign this."

When I placed the paper under the faint light of the lamp I made out some writing and two rounded seals. The letters were like dry tea leaves scattered over grains of rice. Meaningless. "What does it say?"

"It is a deed of cession. You will give me your share of the land." I shook my head and said a simple no.

"What do you mean 'No'?"

"I will keep what my father gave me."

Daffash barked, "No. You will stamp this piece of paper with your precious thumb."

"I will do no such thing. By the soul of my grandmother Sabha, I will keep my share."

He blinked several times. Mubarak cried and cried. He pulled out a black pistol. It looked like a cockroach. He put the cold mouth of the barrel on my temple and said, "Now. Stamp the paper."

The dim light of the lamp was dwindling. My son's tears ran down his temples, dripped down his ears. I swallowed my saliva and shut my eyes. Shut your eyes firmly and let your soul roll out of your body and tumble down to the Jordan. It would bounce to Harb's palms and after all these gray years you would hold his lean fingers again. In a thin voice I said, "I would rather you killed me." He placed his finger on the trigger. "But not in front of my son," I pleaded. My nipples shrank. Please, let a soft-hearted woman take care of my son, change his clothes, bathe him, wipe his nose, and offer him a glass of milk. Please.

Daffash dug the barrel into my temple. My eye was pulled to the left. Shut your eyes firmly. A blink and it would all be finished. My son's voice was husky. The barking of Nashmiyyeh. Piercing pain in my side. Daffash had kicked me. I fell on the ground, winded. He stuck his pistol in his belt and said, "I will not dirty my hands with your blood. Sheikh Talib has proposed. He wants to get married to you, owl face. I gave him my word." He left the room, slamming the door behind him. I was writhing on the floor. His soiled boot had left its mark on my belly. I would never marry another man. Pain twisted its sharp teeth. I staggered to my feet and straightened my back. Why hadn't he pulled the trigger? Why hadn't he?

I hugged my son and licked his bitter, salty tears away. I repeated in his ear, "It's over. I am here. It's all right." He gulped some water. I placed him on my legs and rocked him to sleep. His eyes were red and swollen, his sighs were long. I carried him to his bed and covered his tiny body with a blanket. The sky was moonless. What should I do? No father, mother, uncle, or husband to lean on. I was all alone in this world but I had to fight Daffash. I continued folding and unfolding my hands, continued pacing the yard. The cold light wind did not put out the fire inside me. What should I do? Oh, how I needed Harb, the twin of my soul and the horseman of the best stallion. "I will never place my head on another man's arm." No other man would ever see or sniff or touch my body. That was it.

I shut the door of the room, tied the end of my scarf around my face, and marched through the blind alleyways of the village. Silence was broken occasionally by a baby crying or a cough. The barking of dogs had subsided and was replaced by the shrill screeching of cicadas. I was sweaty and panting when I arrived. I knocked on the door. No answer. Knocked again. Murmuring then, "Who is it at this hour of the night?"

"It is me, Maha. Open the door, aunt."

"In the name of Allah, what has brought you here at this hour?" Tamam screwed up her tiny eyes.

"I don't know what to do? Daffash . . ."

"Continue, woman."

"Daffash wants to marry me off to Sheikh Talib."

"And what is wrong with that?"

"I vowed never to get married again. My soul is still married to Harb."

Tamam hugged me and rubbed my back. "Allah protect us from what is to come. My daughter, go back to your house. I will come to

203

see you tomorrow. Rely on Allah. Go now. Go to your son."

As I walked carefully in one of the alleyways I heard the light foot-steps of Raai. If he saw me alone at that time of the night he would start a scandal. The daughter of Sheikh Nimer roams the valley after midnight. I found an opening in the stone wall I was passing. Slowly, I slid through and squatted quietly in the dark. I made out a figure with a rifle hanging across its shoulder; another figure, a donkey with a monkey on its back. A monkey riding a donkey! I must be seeing things. When the clinking sound subsided, I left my hiding place and ran to my house. I hoped that Mubarak was still asleep. He was. I lit the lamp and sat waiting for the familiar sounds of galloping hooves.

I was floating in a sea suspended between wakefulness and sleep. My first kiss was on the right side of the mouth. I fingered my with-ering lips and remembered the missing front teeth. Maybe Uqla, the gypsy peddler, would replace them with golden ones. He covered exist-ing teeth with a thin layer of gold, but could not make new ones. I placed my hands on my hips and thought how thin I was. Just bones and skin. Tomorrow would bring relief and ease. My sorrow would be dispelled, tomorrow. The twittering of sparrows and cooing of doves announced the arrival of daylight. I lay face down and the warmth of the mattress seeped through my thin robe.

Gentle tapping on the door woke me up. "It's me, Tamam." I opened the door and asked Tamam and Hulala to come in. "I have discussed your problem with Hulala." Hulala shook her head. "And as far as we're concerned nobody can marry you without your consent."

"Aunt, remember what he did to me. He will shoot me this time."

"We have made a plan. You refuse politely and quietly when Imam Rajab asks you if you will accept Sheikh Talib. If you see evil in the men's eyes, say that your throat is dry and that you need to get a glass of water. Mubarak will be in my house and I will take care of him until Allah executes his command. Nasra will be waiting for you at the farm. You will both run away."

I rubbed my forehead and said, "But I don't want to run away."

"Just go for a while. Until the men's anger subsides. Nasra will show you the way. In the meantime, Hulala will try to reason with the men. Stay away until I send you some green mint with Murjan."

I held Tamam's hands and said, "I am so afraid."

"Do not be, my daughter. What is written on the forehead, the eye must see."

I chopped the okra into small pieces, chopped the tomatoes and cooked them in olive oil. Mubarak was running after one of the hens. He had started eating ordinary food. "Mubarak, come here. Your lunch is ready." I looked at the sky while dipping bread in the sauce and feeding Mubarak. It was still spread above our heads like a tent. No air. No breathing. "Mubarak?"

His mouth was full when he answered, "Mmm."

"You will stay with your grandmother Tamam for some time. Do not give her any trouble. She's old and tired."

"Sahi?"

"No. She does not have a cage for him. He might get lost." I chewed at the morsel of food then swallowed with difficulty. My throat was shut.

"Why?"

I smiled because it was the first "why" coming from my son's lips. "I have to go to the mountains." His eyes were watering, were full of fear. I hugged him tightly, kissed him, and said, "My love, I won't be long. Just a day or two. Your grandmother will take care of you; will let you play outside; will sing for you,

> 'Cock, cock, cock and chickens.
> Chicks, chicks, chicks, chicks.
> Egg, egg, egg, egg, QUACK.'"

My son burst out laughing. I looked at his smooth black hair which covered his ears; his few teeth gleamed in his small mouth, his big eyes glistened with happiness. His laugh vibrated through my bones. A clear, pure sound bubbling out of his young heart.

"Now eat your lunch. We want you to grow up quickly."

205

Um Saad

"Maha, sister."

"Yes, Um Saad?"

"Maha, sister, in an old German car, they brought me to this place. Without my hands, I am not even worth a piaster. When they tied the sleeves, I could neither talk nor walk. I could not do anything. I was like a hooded falcon: blind, unable to fly. I was used to having free active hands. 'I'll cook for you, sweep for you, feed your new bride honey and almonds. Please, please don't send me there. I will kiss the toes of your second wife, wash her underwear, even prostrate myself before her. By Allah, let me stay. May Allah keep your women chaste.' No change, sister. His heart was made of flint, of cold metal. Without my hands, I could not keep my balance so I stumbled into the back seat of the car. Inside the car, Um Kulthoum was chanting a song of my youth,

'To whom shall I go?
To whom shall I turn?

PILLARS OF SALT

You are my joy.
You are my wound.'

The driver was humming along with the song. From outside I could hear also the tinkling cymbals of liquorice-juice peddlers. Set fire to the parents of this city. 'Shut up,' I shouted at the driver. The man who had picked me up sat comfortably in the front seat next to Abu Saad. I kicked and kicked the back of the seat of the decaying car. Through the thick circular layers of his glasses, the man gazed at me. 'It is all right, she is mad.' My husband nodded. The muscles of my legs ached. I looked at my thin thighs and realized that I was still wearing the brown kaftan Abu Saad had bought me in the days of gladness. Um Kulthoum continued wailing,

'To whom shall I go?
To whom shall I turn?
Who will give me justice?'

When I arrived here and saw the white building hidden behind vine trellises, I became angry. I started rolling on the floor kicking, biting, spitting at the thick glasses of the porter. He was joined by the two nurses. A hand hit me on the mouth. They stuck a needle into my arm. I entered this room and saw you curled on the bed like a big black bug. I lost control of my body. I abused them, and cursed them and called them names. Warm blood ran down my chin and dripped on to my chest."

Dr. Edwards entered the room quietly, interrupting Um Saad's story. "You never stop talking." The almost blind porter, Kukash of the disheveled hair, and Salam were right behind the English doctor. He snatched the pink scarf off Um Saad's head and Um Saad objected, "There are men in the room. I shouldn't show my hair to strange men." Um Saad's straight gray hair touched her shoulders. Out of nowhere, the doctor produced a pair of scissors, and gave them to Salam. Um Saad understood and started shouting, "Not my hair." She held her head protectively with both hands.

In a sad voice, used to the miseries of life, the doctor called, "Kukash." Instantly, he handcuffed Um Saad and held her neck down with both hands. She looked like the goat Raai and Jarbwa slaughtered for my wedding. The English doctor, who came from the land of churches and clubs, started clipping her hair. Her head was almost in Kukash's indifferent lap. Instead of blood, gray tufts of hair dripped to the concrete floor. She moaned and moaned. He produced a silver tool with two wings which when pressed together made a metal mouth which ate the hair, leaving the skull bare. This is what they do to control us. I turned my head to face the wall. In the uneven white paint I saw a black poisonous spider, a wide-open mouth. When the whirr whirr of the tool stopped, when the door was shut, when Um Saad finally uttered a long sigh, I turned my head and opened my eyes. She ran her hands on her bald head. I leapt out of bed, pushed her hands away, picked up the pink scarf then tied it around her head, making sure I covered the bald skull completely. Her black eyes were dull, were turning white. She opened her mouth, shut it, then started crying like Mubarak when he was one week old and had just been circumcised by the imam. I put her head on my chest and the heat of her tears seeped through my white jacket, my black robe. My nipples shrank. I wanted to breastfeed my son.

Maha

A herd of men flocked to our courtyard making it like a beehive. Buzzing, waving their hands, stroking their beards and praising the Merciful. I slipped one shirt over the head of my son, then another shirt, then helped him put on the thick jacket Halimeh had made for him out of old rugs. That should keep him warm. In the triangular shawl I used to wrap him with when he was still a tender baby, I put a bottle of rose water, his comb, two pairs of trousers, one shirt, and some sugar candy. I placed his feet in the sandals Tamam had brought him. When I tied the leather thongs around his ankles, he complained; he did not like the strain. My son had a free spirit and preferred to chase the hens barefoot. "You will stay with your grandmother."

"No grandmother."

"Yes, love."

He turned his small hand forming a circle.

"No, I won't be long. Just a day or two."

I hugged him, kissed him, then sniffed his neck. He bore the scent of Harb, his father. Tamam held his hand, carried his bundle, and walked out of the room. I listened to the dwindling tap tap of his light footsteps as he walked away with his grandmother. If You are up there, watching with eyes full of boredom, please protect my son.

The men sat on the ground outside, forming a dark crescent. Sheikh Talib, Imam Rajab, and Daffash sat in the middle. I saw flickering light at the end of the horizon, a running deer? A dove flying away? Or a diving eagle? I washed my face with cold water and tied the veil around my head to cover the bare gums. My heart started beating loudly.

"Maha," barked Daffash.

I took a deep breath, glanced round the room, then rubbed my forehead. My grandmother's mirror, the almost finished carpet spread on the floor, the blue rocking bed, and the three mattresses stared silently at me. The clay jar was covered with dew, a mist which ran down to the floor like tears. I stuck the sheath of Harb's dagger and Mubarak's amulet in my robe and marched out of the room. The sun was bowing down towards the west, eager to disappear behind the bright skyline.

"Imam Rajab will ask you some questions. You answer yes," Daffash said as he twisted his moustache between thumb and forefinger.

I looked at the solemn faces of the men of the tribe.

Imam Rajab stood up with difficulty and said loudly, "Maha, daughter of Nimer, will you accept Sheikh Talib as a husband?"

My body grew lighter and lighter and began rising up, up towards the sky. I saw my mother's smiling face, my father's stick, and Harb's arm. I would only place my head on Harb's strong arm. Daffash was rubbing his clenched fists. My voice was weak and thin when I said, "I want a sip of water."

Imam Rajab smiled, showing uneven brown teeth. Dark words could grind your teeth and tint them. "Daffash, she is shy. Let her have some water." I turned my back on them and went to the house, found a cup, marched out of the house, threw the cup on the soil, stuck the end of my robe in my trousers, and ran, ran to the orchard.

Nasra was leaning on one of the orange trees talking to Murjan. She grabbed my hand and said in her shrill voice, "Quick, the mountains." The soles of my feet were blazing hot, Mubarak's crying filled the valley, the men would shoot me between the eyes if they caught me. Then, I could only hear the noise of my lungs rasping for air. Thorn shrubs, grass, dry soil, and bugloss sped under my feet. Sweat trickled down my nose. We took one of the footpaths leading to the top of the mountain. Nasra was pulling me forwards. I felt very hot although the air was getting cooler. Murjan was right behind us. When we reached the top, I stopped and shouted to the wind, to the sick light of dusk, "No." I would not accept Sheikh Talib as a husband.

The jaws of Abu Auqab's cave were wide open. A lion ready to devour his prey. We entered the cave and threw ourselves on the rug-covered ground. My lungs felt as if they had been slashed by a dagger. Murjan and Jawaher had prepared the cave for us. A clay jar, a lamp, bread, and some butter and dates. "Enough for a few days," Murjan said. "Close the entrance with the rock outside. I will keep an eye on the path leading to the cave. If you hear any noise, run south towards the Dead Sea. Do not stay here. If you hear voices, sneak quietly out of the cave."

"May Allah lengthen your life, my son," I gasped. Nasra brought a cup of water and told me to drink.

The foxes' barking and the howling of dogs besieged us in our cave. Nasra's face twitched under the dwindling light of the lamp. Sleep was far away from me. My heart quivered beneath my ribs. Mubarak. Would Tamam feed him, undress him, wipe his tears? I rocked and swayed my body to try to go to sleep. The rounded rock they pushed to lock the mouth of the cave seemed to crouch upon my chest. From now on, fear and exhaustion would be my sisters, my companions in the land of my tribe. No arrivals at all. The cave was dark, the rug I covered my body with was cold, my luck was scattered flour.

I was floating lightly between hazy clouds when Nasra shook my shoulder. "Wake up. Voices." We stood up and placed our ears on the ground. Faint sounds vibrated through soil and stone. "We must go." We pushed the rock slowly to one side and left the cave. A procession of torches climbed up the mountain like a glowing snake.

"Run."

Following the sounds of waves, we dashed to the south towards the hollow of the sea. Swishing waves crashed on the shore with all their might, then retreated. My muscles ached, my eyes watered, and the soles of my feet were bleeding. The running blood would leave a trace on the soil, would make it easy for the men of the tribe to find us. The salt covering the pebbles on the seashore rubbed into my cuts, inflaming them. Fire, fire, fire. The mother of Hulala was licking the soles of my bare feet. Nasra's back was stiff, my feet barely touched the ground, and the only sign of me being alive and running was the deep sound of drawn breath. The wings of darkness hid our figures, protected them, enveloped us like a kind mother.

The sky was a cloud of black smoke suspended over the open plain of the sea. Nasra guided me to a spring of fresh water flowing into the sea. "We will spend the night here." A warm breeze carrying the smell of carbon hit my damp face. Some faint lights were reflected in the water over on the other bank. Darkness and heat swathed the vast salt flats. I placed my head between my legs to let the blood stream down and push out the dizziness. When I closed my eyes I saw the smiling face of Harb, his warm hands pulling me closer and the water lapping my body gently. Had I — Maha the Indian fig, bitter like colocynth but patient — had I run away from my house? Was I really sitting on the salty stones, looking at the awesome hollow of the Dead Sea without the twin of my soul, without Harb, my beloved and the father of my son? Why did I leave my son with Tamam? Why did I . . .?

The darkness of the clouds descended and enveloped Nasra and me. The landlocked water held its breath and nothing moved on that vast coast except water from the mineral springs which gurgled out then glided down the cliffs to the black mirror. Mist lined the water, the rocks, the springs, making breathing impossible. The stink of acids and minerals rose up to the sky. I placed my head on a flat stone and tried to listen to the sound of fresh water streaming down to meet its death. A drop of fresh water in the vast salty sea. The sapless cloak of death shrouded the low land, the tops of mountains and even Jerusalem with its high minarets. I would try to go to sleep, I would try to shut my eyes like Nasra; I would try to forget about the pillars of salt under the water and the vipers lurking in the dark.

The sun rose, lighting up the white sky, scattering flickering beams on the surface of the calm water. The dawn transformed every grain of salt into a sparkling jewel, a precious stone. The sound of water swishing and hissing in the wind ebbed and swirled. Nasra was still asleep on top of the flat rock. In her black robe, she looked like a thin black lining of the rock. I filled my cupped hands with water and splashed my face. The bitter taste of minerals stuck to my tongue, to the rims of my eyes. A contraction in my chest told me that my son was crying. Whenever I thought about him, I felt it in my breasts. I stroked my nipples. He must be hungry. He must be crying. His tiny feet must be searching for a crack in the cliffs to fit into. Curse my heart which caught fire as easily as dry palm leaves.

Nasra woke up, stretched her hands, and looked at the sky. Dangling her legs, she started blowing into her reed-pipe. She played sharp, bouncy tunes as a greeting to the morning.

"Nasra, sister, I want you to go to the village and bring me some news."

"Bring food?"

I looked at the dusty shrubs bravely sprouting on the banks of mineral springs. "Yes." Nasra leapt off the rock and washed her face. She stuck the end of her robe into her trousers and walked away. I watched her negotiate her way between the shrubs. When she had become just a crawling ant in the distance, I sighed and sat down. The heat started rising under the rude glare of the sun. My black robe absorbed the heat, stored the heat, baking my body inside. The swishing and hissing of the cool water filled my ears.

The transculent hands of the water waved to me, pulled me, held my wrists. The call of the sea was deep, husky, sad. My past. I untied my headband, flung the veil on a stone, then undid my plaits. I took off my tatty black robe, my trousers, and my petticoat, then stretched my naked body. My feet when plunged into the water welcomed the pleasant coolness. Whenever I dived in the Dead Sea my eyes hurt. The acids and minerals seemed to attack the tender tissues of my body. Must endure it till pleasure overtook the pain and I could see again. Fresh tears would wash out the salt. The lapping water, the wet hair, and the bitter taste of minerals brought Harb back. First he kissed the right corner of my mouth, then the left corner, then the center of my lips. I grabbed his shoulders and moved closer to him. When I enveloped him, curled around him with my being, he started crying like a baby. His expression was tender, was full of response. Receiving him was like coming home after a long sweaty day. My body turned into a light pestle swiftly grinding coffee and cardamom in a mortar. Whispers and swishes. "Mistress of my soul, deer-eyes." I hugged myself tightly. Tears, emptiness, and love. I dived to hold him, then floated. Murky green puddles followed by fresh air and dazzling light.

I thought I saw the crooked figure of Hakim. I wiped the water from my face. Yes, by the gray hair of my grandmother. He stopped, put his goat on the ground, then waved to me. His step when he continued walking was light as if he were only twenty years old. Holding his goat, he disappeared behind one of the high cliffs. I cried at the top of my voice, "Hakim." Nothing except the echo of my voice and the swishing of the waves. Maybe he could, with his rare herbs, cure my tired heart. "Hakim." Nothing except the echo of my voice breaking on top of the mountains.

The sun unchained its scalding flames and turned them loose in the plain of the Dead Sea. Sweat trickled down my face and my back. Two blurred crawling ants. Murjan and Nasra. Bearers of good news, I prayed.

"Peace be upon you," said Murjan.

"And upon you, my son," I said.

"Fine, Mubarak," said Nasra.

"Maha, my mother, your brother Daffash had taken possession of the orchard, the house, and your son."

"Rooted out your vegetables, Daffash."

Grains of Dead Sea bitter salt lined my throat, stuck to my tongue, rimmed my eyes. "I am thirsty." Murjan handed me the waterskin. I gulped some water. Nasra offered me dates. I shook my head.

My orchard, the gem hanging on the valley's forehead. The golden dawn gently fingered the citrus tress and lifted them up, up to the sky, and suspended them there. The icy water running in the old canal split the orchard in two and filtered into the soil, blunting the edges of the dry grains, making the whole area cool and damp. The scent of the blossoms carried me smoothly to another world. The cloud of perfume filled the valley. The clear water ran to the depth of my heart, wiped my tired soul clean, and left me fragile, transparent.

Shielding my eyes, I looked at the sun. What was I, Maha, daugh-

ter of Maliha, daughter of Sabha, doing there? How could I leave my
son and house? I must fight Daffash. Slowly, slowly, I turned round
and said in a determined voice, "I am going back to the village."

Nasra started slapping her cheeks and crying, "Crazy, Maha?"

Murjan gazed at the sea and said as if talking to the waves, "Do
whatever you feel is right."

Straight-backed, head held high, chin quivering, I marched across
the vast plain. The few palm trees were like drops of fresh water in a
salty sea. They could not change the plain to kind green. The forces
of the pale desert triumphed over the bright green spots. A camel and
a calf chewed and chewed the cud. Bringing the food back from the
stomach and chewing it was useless for me. The banana plantation
was the shortest cut to the village. A thorn pricked the sole of my
foot. Nasra and Murjan tried to catch up with me. Daffash, my brother,
the son of my mother, Maliha, my father Sheikh Nimer, and the grandson
of my grandmother Sabha, swallowed the farm and the house. I should
have killed Daffash in the cave as he mounted Salih's wife. I should
have pulled the trigger and shot him in the heart. I should have killed
him before Nasra's tunes had lost their warmth. I should have shot
Daffash before Nasra had lost her earring and the brilliance of her
green eyes.

I pushed the headband up, wiped my sweat, and continued marching
towards the forgotten village which clung to the mountainside like a
leech. Only two days and the village seemed older. Gloomy brown.
Mud domes, mud walls, mud ears and eyes. I left the Dead Sea behind, roaring in its low land. The land belonged to me. Mubarak was
my son, a piece of my heart. I planted the lemon and orange shoots,
waited for three years, watered them until they threw their first crop.
My fingernails were lined with soil, with dung and mud. I had dug,
cleaned, uprooted. My brother's hands were clean, were never plunged
into mud. The land was mine. It was better to be shot between the
eyes than see the orchard withering away. I would prefer to lie in
peace under the ground, entangled with the roots of my orange trees.

When I reached the main alleyway, Raai, who was standing on his
platform, greeted me, saying, "You should have accepted Sheikh Talib's
offer." I looked at his trimmed beard, his shifty eyes, and the colorful
jars of roasted chick peas in front of him, and shook my head. Salih

215

jumped off his platform when he saw me walk off and said, "Peace be upon you, daughter of Nimer. Why have you come back?" Salih did not work with metal only, he was made of metal. He thought he could bend anything, even mothers' hearts. Imam Rajab shuffled towards me and said, "May Allah damn the sinner. You are all infidels." I looked at his long, larded beard and his bulging belly and smiled. The women of the village did not dare leave their houses to welcome me back. They stood behind doors and windows and peeped at the woman who had spent a night on her own in the mountains.

Suddenly I heard the imam crying, "Stone the sinner." The young children started picking up small pebbles and throwing them at me. I straightened my back and continued walking. The sizes of stones began to grow bigger and bigger. The tingling became nipping, the nipping became smarting. I would not look back. I would not turn my head. I reached our orchard and turned through the gate. A herd of young boys were kneeling, bowing, stretching their hands ready to throw stones. Grinning faces, bare bottoms, and snotty noses. I uncovered my face and stared at them. They retreated, got rid of their stones, turned round, then ran down the steep alleyway.

At that very moment, when I was about to enter my house, when I was about to embrace my son, the dark green Land Rover crawled towards me like a giant bug. Samir Pasha, my brother, and two men in white coats jumped out of the car. Daffash barked, "Here she is. Look at her. She is mad. The bee of her brain has flown away." I saw the end of Mubarak's white shirt dangling out of his trousers. My son. I wanted to see my son. When Nasra dashed towards them, Daffash shrieked with laughter and panted, "Look at the company she keeps! The mad shepherdess."

Nasra was not mad. Nasra was the princess of sane people. Nasra was the herb which had healed most of my wounds. How dare he? I raised my head towards the forgetful sky, rubbed my forehead and said loudly, "Nasra, Daffash Pasha, is more sane than you are." Children had started gathering again. Tamam, Hulala, Hamda, and Halimeh appeared from nowhere and stood beside me. Under the palm trees, a group of men were crowding like cockroaches. Sheikh Talib with his thin old body, Salih, Raai, Imam Rajab, and Uqla, the gypsy peddler. Murjan crossed the wide dusty space and joined the row of the women.

"First of all," Daffash barked at the top of his voice, "I don't talk to women. No brain and no faith." The imam nodded his head approvingly. "Second, what is the use of talking to crazy women?" The men laughed in unison. Like the cracked voice of the raven of parting, their laughter soared in the blind valley. "Third, lower your head or I will shoot you between your eyes."

The warmth of Nasra's hand seeped through my back. I cleared my throat and said in a low voice, "First, I don't talk to rapists." A hushed silence landed over the valley. "Second, I don't talk to disobedient sons. Third, I don't talk to servants of the English." The echo of the word "English" traveled far, bouncing off the walls of houses, scaling the mountains until it broke upon their tops in a horrible echo.

Hulala limped to the middle of the gathering and said in her sharp voice, "This is ridiculous. All of you gathered here, men with bushy moustaches, to fight a group of helpless women. The women of this village were and will always be obedient mothers, wives, daughters, and sisters. If you send these two strange men in white away, I promise you Maha will become your slave girl. She will sweep your floor, cook your food, and wash your clothes. Just send them away."

I rubbed my forehead. "I will get married to nobody, I will not sign any deeds, and will never cook for the English."

Like a tied bull Daffash started stamping his feet. "This spider is not praying for the soul of Muhammad."

Imam Rajab winked at Daffash and reminded him, "Allah said in his Wise Book, 'Beat them up.'"

Daffash crossed the space between the men of Qasim and the women, stretched out his arms and held my neck. He started pressing. I kicked him on the thigh. He lost his temper. "Daughter of the dog." He threw me on the ground and sat on top of me. I kicked, punched, and even tried to bite him. He tightened his grip on my throat until I saw floating lights, no longer his thin face, and sweaty forehead and angry eyes. The women tried to drag him away from me. Tamam hit him with her pipe on the head. "She is the mother of Harb's son." Hulala stood with the men watching. Nasra jumped on his shoulder and tried to free my neck. Halimeh called her husband Salih, "He will kill her. Do something." The men stood under the palm trees watching, scratching their heads, stroking their beards, twisting their moustaches. I could hear the barking of Nashmiyyeh, the sounds of galloping hooves, and the panting of Daffash. I could see Hamda's inflated face and her hands on my brother's neck. "Let her go, face of disasters." He loosened his grip on my neck and was about to hit Hamda with his elbow. I leapt up determined to kill him. I held his hands by the wrists. As he lay on the ground, I could see the pain on Daffash's face and the anger on Hamda's face as she tried to strangle him. Tighter, tighter, I prayed. I would gladly share the responsibility for his spilt blood with Hamda.

A closing-in noise. Hamda's body being flung on the ground. Nasra standing there without hands. Halimeh struggling, a hand blocking my voice. Tears, piercing pain stinging my shoulders. Banging on empty butter tins. Children, the same age as Mubarak, walking in a procession.

> "Wizz, wizz — wizz, wizz.
> The bee has flown away.
> Wizz, wizz — wizz, wizz."

The broken pipe of Tamam grew feet and skitted away. Samir Pasha was waving the hand holding the pipe. Men in white pulled, punched, handcuffed me. Jawaher cried, cried, cried on Murjan's shoulder. I was flung across a strong shoulder. The world went upside down. "Aunt, Harb, Nimer, save me. Save me." I kicked and kicked with my free feet. Tamam slept on the ground, head down, a lifeless corpse? I heard the tapping of tender feet on a concrete floor. "Mubarak, my son," I wailed, "my son, O people." Tap, tap, tap. No air in the valley whatsoever. I could not breathe. "You have orphaned my son," I wheezed. The house and the orchard fell prostrate, praying for a force under the ground.

> "Wizz, wizz — wizz, wizz.
> The bee of Maha's mind flew away.
> Wizz, wizz — wizz, wizz."

The banging of young hands on empty tins. "Mad — Maha. Mad — woman," tender voices chimed. A prick. Sliding, slipping down a brightly lit tunnel. Harb? It was always Harb, my husband, the twin of my soul . . .

Um Saad

U m Saad was missing that morning. No "Maha, sister" or "star-shaped holes." I felt so lonely, so tiny, in the almost empty hospital room. Everything was white. White was the color of sheets, of cupboards, bed-pans, dustbins, and foggy heads. The barred window overlooked a deep valley laden with vine trellises and pine trees. Bars. I was a prisoner in that castle. I smoothed the ruffled sheets which smelt of Um Saad's breath. Under her pillow, I found two fading yellowish-brown photos. One was of a smiling blonde man with open flat face and big jaws: Muhammad. The other face was fat with huge drooling lips: her dirty old husband. I put them back and sat on the edge of my bed. They always combed my hair with a fine comb soaked in kerosene. I had no lice. After the pulling and yanking they found none. The sharp edge of the smell of kerosene. The smell of thyme wafting to my nostrils through the window told me that it was springtime. Not one single word from my village, Hamia, which stuck to the mountainside like a leech. My son's light footsteps walking away with his grandmother echoed in my ears. "Mother," he used to cry, and roll closer to me whenever he had a bad dream. Everywhere I looked I saw his face: grinning at the cock, frowning at the dog, sliding across the walls, the table, the floor, the bed, the misty window. I placed my chin on the cold iron bedposts and wished that my heart was made of iron too. He used to roll his tender body seeking warmth and safety. Roll into another identity, said Um Saad. Just get rid of your skin, of your head, of your past.

When I heard the damned clink of the key in the lock, I jumped into bed and covered myself with the sheets. Kukash wheeled into the room a long trolley on which Um Saad's body was convulsing. Dr. Edwards followed the trolley as if it was a funeral procession. They held her ankles and wrists, lifted her up, then flung her on the cold bed. The foreign doctor turned round and walked out of the room. Kukash followed him silently. I could hear the heavy breathing of my sister. I thank you, whoever you are up there. She was still alive and kicking. When the sound of their footsteps disappeared in the long corridor, I got out of bed and crossed the cold concrete gap between my bed and hers. Her face was as pale as lemon. She had two bruises on her temples covered with a thin layer of foul-smelling paste. Her lips were dark blue and her eyes rolled under her closed eyelids. They had straightjacked my sister, but the sleeves were loose, not tied behind her back. The convulsions were subsiding, regressing like waves. Her body was as cold as the morning water of the Long Well. My hands were useless. What shall I do to bring back the heat of her spirit? In a cracked voice, I started chanting songs of hot summer days,

> "Our golden crop.
> Hay hay hay hay.
> Cut, put on top.
> Hay hay hay hay."

My voice lacked the excitement of reaping a new crop, lacked the expectation and fell flat. I rubbed her outstretched arms, her wide open legs, her limp belly. How many children did she say she had had? Was it ten? I massaged her neck, her bald head, making sure not to press on the bruises; I massaged her shoulders. I felt that if I could bring the head back to life, Um Saad would be fine. I went on rubbing, stroking, squeezing until it was almost dusk. I covered her body with my quilt and wrapped the tied limbs with sheets.

When Sura, the lumpish cook, put some food on my plate, I did not utter a single word. I got used to the mashed potato and the cat food which looked like dog shit. I remembered Um Saad and asked for one more cup of tea. Sura's oozy voice reminded me of melting fat, oil, and sauce. "Under the command of your highness, Princess Maha of Qasim." I did not say anything. I had not only had to get used to Sura's cooking but also to Sura's sarcastic tongue. She poured another cup of tea, placed it on my tray and pushed her trolley out of the room. Spoonful after spoonful the food slid down my throat. I drank the tea quickly, scalding my tongue, then placed the tray on the small table. I wiped my mouth, rolled up my sleeves, and was ready to fight for the soul of my sister.

I soaked a piece of bandage in rose water then placed it between Um Saad's open lips. "Um Saad, my sister, you must wake up. You must, Haniyyeh."

She opened her eyes slowly and murmured, "Please stop."

I squeezed her arm and said, "It is over. I am your friend and sister, your companion in this snakepit. I am Maha." I supported her neck with one hand and helped her sip the cold sweet tea. She sucked the tea. Mubarak, my soul, my son, used to suck bundles of sugar candy. She turned her head and tried to focus her straying gaze on my face. "Um Gharib. They didn't tell me you were coming." A faint smile, then she shut her eyes again and went to tired sleep.

That night, I did not have a taste of sleep. I just watched the weak face of Um Saad under the blue moonlight. It was cold, but I did not have the heart to take my quilt back. When the moon retreated to its world, leaving the blind world fumbling around in the darkness, Um Saad, my sister, started speaking. At first, it was a weak dwindling sound, then it grew stronger and stronger. She was talking to al-Shater Hasan. "At last, you came. What took you so long to visit feeble human beings. Wahid sang love songs in the bathroom, but on the screen I saw the face of Farid al-Attrash. He had thin lips, thin lips lined with lipstick. Crimson. My mother in high-heeled shoes went down the stairs, stumbled, ended up dead on the sidewalk." Um Saad shook with laughter until tears ran down her cheeks. "They told me they were going to squash me like almonds. Me, Haniyyeh, Um Saad, Broken-Neck, Gray Hair, dark-haired beauty and all." I tossed my head on the pillow as I listened to the driveling of Um Saad. Laughter, sighs, silence, crying, wailing followed by anger. She shouted at al-Shater Hasan, saying, "You illegitimate son of the devil, you flower of my youth, you dung of animals lining their guts. Bring your Vanishing Cap and come. Help me, Um Saad, Haniyyeh, Broken-Neck disappear. Come and hold me, come and hug me."

At last, the sun started stirring in her world, ready to rise above our heads again. The strong scent of thyme and mint drew me to the barred window. At the bottom of the steep misty valley of Fuhais, I saw a herd of black stallions with gleaming bodies galloping towards the morning sun. I wished my soul could gallop to its creator, I wished that after all these gray years I could hold the twin of my soul. I wished the heart could fly away to Hamia to embrace the apple of my eye, my son Mubarak. A millipede scurried down the white wall towards me. Mother of Forty-Four had forty-four legs. I had only two. I took off my slippers and was about to kill her. At that moment, when the millipede was a slipper-span away from her death, the English doctor pushed the door open.

"Good morning," he trilled. "How are we today? It is a beautiful day. Don't you think?" He flashed his waxy smile and said in his foreign Arabic, "Right. Your turn," pointing the sharp ends of the scissors at my head.

"You cut my hair when I arrived in this place."

"We must make it shorter."

The millipede scurries away through the metal bars to freedom. I am too tired to lift my hand up, to open my mouth, to screw my lips and shout, "Nooo." Not one single word from my village; my son is being brought up by his uncle Daffash, and Harb is dead. Mubarak will soon start twisting his fluffy moustache with his thumb and forefinger. My father is dead. My mother's carpet is still unfinished. Not one single word from my lips. Kukash, the porter of convulsing bodies, is sucking a cigarette butt as usual. I lower my head into the eager hands of the foreign doctor, who rules over us like a king. When the coldness of the chattering winged tool eating up my hair has seeped through my skull, I realize that I am being besieged by mirages flickering in the distance. Life is a long dream of arrivals and departures. Must stop thinking, remembering, chasing. Electric shock? Blank. No illusions of arrivals. People are fed dreams, stuffed with dreams the way I used to stuff the hens with grain. Suddenly you discover that what you have been eating all these years is dust and what you have been drinking is just thin air. Um Saad shrieks with mad laughter. Locks of gray hair tumble down to the concrete floor. My luck is like scattered flour. On a windy day, they ask barefooted men to collect the flour. The wind is howling and whirling in the deserted thornfield. My luck is like scattered flour.

The Storyteller

In the name of Allah the Beneficent, the Merciful, "How many a township have We destroyed that was sinful, so that it lieth to this day in ruins, and how many a deserted well and lofty tower."

Oh most illustrious master, my friends and companions, one day I took my she-ass Aziza and my monkey Maymoon and set off for the dwellings of the tribe of Bani-Qasim. We arrived in the valley of misery but could find neither the river nor the plantation. I continued riding in the empty river-bed over stones and pebbles hoping eventually to reach the orange orchard of Sheikh Nimer. The farm and the house were just a piece of flat land covered with belladonna, henbane, and colocynth. A stinging, bitter smell of sadness filled the air. The poisonous plants had conquered the sweet fruit, outlived the edible vegetation, and inherited the land. Life had retreated under the ground, leaving heaps of rubble and sand behind.

Men say that one day the Qasimi sun stood stubbornly in the middle of the sky and refused either to descend west or regress east. One hot

224

day followed another while the Arabs lay on the ground under the immobile sun. The sun was objecting to the sins committed in that village. Swarms of locusts hovered over the valley of shame, then landed in the blink of an eye and devoured the green and the dry. The locusts gnawed at the grain, barley, reed, citrus trees, shrubs, and the big flat leaves of banana. The jaws of the young locusts kept chewing and munching in the dark. Vast pieces of land completely covered with locusts fluttering their wings and moving their jaws. The worst famine ever encountered by the Arabs.

Men threw themselves on the ground to eat the leftovers of the locusts. Then they ate their goats and sheep, their camels, cows, cats, horses, chickens, dogs, even tortoises and cockroaches. Old thin women trapped the locusts and boiled their legs to make soup. Women dug out gold from their teeth to buy grain and milk from Syrian peddlers. The famine and the darkness continued until the Qasimis started biting the dust hoping to find an earthworm or a root in the morsels of soil. If you had blown on these mothlike human beings, you would have scattered them like carded wool. When the starvation cries of Allah's worshippers pierced the ears of the sky, Allah Almighty struck the earth with His right hand.

When the Wise and Mighty struck the land, the earth started shaking as if in labor. My most honorable masters, the earth was in pain, was eager to throw off its burdens. Graves longed to pour out their contents and birds of prey squawked loudly in the sky. All you could hear was the howling of the wind carrying the dark, fetid smoke and the ticking of burning hail. The sea felt that the land was being drawn from under its feet and swayed and raged to save itself from sinking. The waves rose up and embraced the smoke clouds and the dark sky. Melting iron and debris bubbled up into the crater, filling the valley with a glowing orange liquid which burned its way down to the belly of the earth again. Like a blister which keeps growing and festering, growing and festering, then bursts open, gushing pus and sickness over the face of the universe. When the blister dried up and the wrath of Allah subsided, the cut on the face began healing slowly. The vomiting stopped, the smoke and the fire lost their zeal when they could not find a single bough, stick, or broom on the ground to burn. The sea shrank back to its hollow and stopped roaring, stopped ranting.

Allah of the Muslims had destroyed the disobedient village, burnt it to dust then scattered its ashes over the Dead Sea. No messenger or news-bearer survived the earthquake. The Arabs of Hamia just had been.

Before setting off to another dwelling, I had a last look at the rubble and the sand-dunes. Oh, what I found! Oh, what I saw! I saw, my noble masters, footprints on the sand. I saw footprints of a woman and a three-year-old child. The truth is Maha, the black widow, the bitter colocynth, supported by the soldiers of our master Solomon, survived the series of catastrophes. The jinn carried her and Mubarak on their wings away from the lava and the fire. When the crater shut its mouth and stopped throwing up fire and destruction, they flew her back to safety.

In front of the flat stones of the dolmen of Hulala, Maha met the man of her life. Like her grandmother Sabha, she fell in love with a stranger, an occupier, an invader. The majestic crusader was surrounded by an entourage of two hundred black slaves and one hundred slave girls arrayed in dresses woven of gold and studded with emerald. The strong white king fell a victim to the arrows of the eyelashes of the black widow when he saw her weaving in the glowing light of sunset. Another casualty of the pagan, bedouin eyes. On his knees, with a tray full of precious stones dug from the depth of the earth and fished out of the bottom of the sea, he proposed to Maha, the daughter of Maliha. She laughed, took the tray and said, "It does not befit kings to fall on their knees." The king of faraway lands stood up, fixed the diamond crown on his head, then kissed the extended thin fingers.

Maha, my masters, is now living with her husband, the king, crosser of seas and conqueror of lands, in a big castle at the top of Sheikh Mountain. From the outside the castle looks ordinary, but oh if you set your eyes on the inside! The walls are lined with jasper, marble, lapis lazuli, and mosaics. The curtains are made of Chinese crimson silk embroidered with gold threads and the floor is covered with thick Persian carpets. All the pots, pans, and plates are made of heavy gold and the spoons are made of ivory and studded with diamonds. The window-sills are jade and the glass is held in place with gold frames. The castle is guarded by an army of strong Nubian slaves who fill the strongest hearts with awe. No human being with any sense in his head would dare go near the jade-green castle.

226

Men say, on clear summer nights, sitting on the stones of the black amphitheater of Um Qais, you can see the sheen of the castle's pinnacles and hear the humming of the she-devil, while she combs the hair of the mighty king. A faint shimmer and a dwindling sound of a song is carried by the warm breeze to your ears. The sound of Maha and the sight of the pinnacles are as frail as the spider's web. A puff of air or tiny drops of rain could kill the spider and destroy his thready shelter. The shimmer of pinnacles, the sad sound of a song, and the halo of clouds. Drops of rain can wash the spider out of his cobweb. The nostalgic humming, clouds and mist and the twinkling pinnacles. Frail, fine, fluttering shelter. Soon, we shall all perish . . .

Other titles in the series

From Chile:
The Secret Holy War of Santiago de Chile
by Marco Antonio de la Parra
trans. by Charles P. Thomas
ISBN 1–56656–123–X paperback $12.95

From Grenada:
Under the Silk Cotton Tree
by Jean Buffong
ISBN 1–56656–122–1 paperback $9.95

From India:
The End Play
by Indira Mahindra
ISBN 1–56656–166–3 paperback $11.95

From Israel:
The Silencer
by Simon Louvish
ISBN 1–56656–108–6 paperback $10.95

From Jordan:
Prairies of Fever
by Ibrahim Nasrallah
trans. by May Jayyusi and Jeremy Reed
ISBN 1–56656–106–X paperback $9.95

From Lebanon:
The Stone of Laughter
by Hoda Barakat
trans. by Sophie Bennett
ISBN 1–56656–190–6 paperback $12.95

Samarkand
by Amin Maalouf
trans. by Russell Harris
ISBN 1–56656–194–9 paperback $14.95

From Palestine:
A Balcony Over the Fakihani
by Liyana Badr
trans. by Peter Clark with Christopher Tingley
ISBN 1–56656–107–8 paperback $9.95

Wild Thorns
by Sahar Khalifeh
trans. by Trevor LeGassick and Elizabeth Fernea
ISBN 0–940793–25–3 paperback $9.95

From Serbia:
The Dawning
by Milka Bajić-Poderegin
trans. by Nadja Poderegin
ISBN 1–56656–188–4 paperback $14.95

From South Africa:
Living, Loving and Lying Awake at Night
by Sindiwe Magona
ISBN 1–56656–141–8 paperback $11.95

From Syria:
Sabriya: Damascus Bitter Sweet
by Ulfat Idilbi
trans. by Peter Clark
ISBN 1–56656–254–6 paperback $12.95

From Turkey:
Cages on Opposite Shores
by Janset Berkok Shami
ISBN 1–56656–157–4 paperback $11.95

From Yemen:
The Hostage
by Zayd Mutee' Dammaj
trans. by May Jayyusi and Christopher Tingley
ISBN 1–56656–140–X paperback $10.95

From Zimbabwe:
The Children Who Sleep by the River
by Debbie Taylor
ISBN 0–940793–96–2 paperback $9.95

Titles in the "Emerging Voices: New International Fiction" series are available at bookstores everywhere.

To order by phone call toll-free 1–800–238–LINK. Please have your Mastercard, Visa or American Express ready when you call.

To order by mail, please send your check or money order to the address listed below. For shipping and handling, add $3.00 for the first book and $1.00 for each additional book. Massachusetts residents add 5% sales tax.

Interlink Publishing Group, Inc.
46 Crosby Street
Northampton, MA 01060

Tel (413) 582–7054
Fax (413) 582–7057
e-mail: interpg@aol.com